FOOLS AND KINGS AND FIGHTING MEN

Dorothy Davies

FOOLS AND KINGS AND FIGHTING MEN

ZADKIEL

PUBLISHING

Dedication

He lost his kingdom, his crown – and his head.

Dedicated to the memory of Charles Stuart,
King Charles 1 of England,
1600-1649
Requiescat in Pace.

And to Ann-Jacqueline Davies for the help and guidance she freely gave during the troublesome time I had establishing a proper connection with King Charles. With her help and mediumship we came to an understanding with the King. It was far from easy and I owe her a massive debt of gratitude because of it. I needs must also mention her ongoing, loyal and loving friendship which has been of great help to me in many ways.

From 'Immortality'
Olton Pools by John Drinkwater
Sidgwick and Jackson Ltd.,1917

There in the midst of all these words shall be
Our names, our ghosts, our immortality.

Charles' dedication:

I wish to dedicate this book to the memory of Henrietta Maria, adored wife, consort and friend and to my beloved children;

To Sir John Oglander of Nunwell House on the Isle of Wight, friend and devoted servant. I had many friends, but few who showed the devotion of this man. He visited me throughout my time in Carisbrooke Castle, bringing news and comfort as best he could.

And to all who served me with loyalty and who fought and died for me during my reign. My sorrow goes out to all of you who gave your lives for my cause. I should never have let it get that far. Your deaths were a price too high to pay, in truth.

My grateful thanks go to;

Dorothy for her love, care and patience with me during the writing of this book. She never pushed, even when the work was going terribly slow, knowing I would get there in the end.

And to Dorothy's Inner Circle for their friendship and help throughout the writing of this book.

I also wish to give my thanks to Prince Ivan Grozny for his acceptance of me – to be honoured by one of the great Princes of history was and still is a very special moment.

Epilogue For A Masque

From Poems Of Love And Earth, John Drinkwater,
David Nutt, 1913

A little time they lived again, and lo!
Back to the quiet night the shadows go,
And the great folds of silence once again
Are over fools and kings and fighting-men.

A little while they went with stumbling feet,
With spears of hate, and love all flowery sweet,
With wondering hearts and bright adventurous
wills,
And now their dust is on a thousand hills.

We dream of them, as men unborn shall dream
Of us, who strive a little with the stream
Before we too go out beyond the day,
And are as much a memory as they.

And Death, so coming, shall not seem a thing
Of any fear, nor terrible his wing.
We too shall be a tale on earth and time
Our pilgrimage shall shape into a rhyme.

With coloured threads of laughter and of tears
They wove a pattern on the crowded years,
And wove aright, and we are weaving still
From dawn to dusk – God grant we weave not ill.

N.B: I had chosen the title and the poem before I discovered that Charles' father, James I, was responsible for bringing the masque to England.

History is the distillation of rumour.

Part 1 - Fools

Chapter One

The only sound in the room was the sighing of ash as it fell from the log into the embers. Such utter silence was unusual in a palace normally thronging with people: servants, courtiers, counsellors, physicians, clerics … an ever changing, ever demanding array of people. To be so silent, so alone, was strange and disconcerting to the man who lounged, clutching a goblet of wine, in a thickly upholstered chair before the hearth.

The flickering candle flame shone on his long dark hair, his pointed trimmed beard and his slender frame. It did not reach his shadowed sorrow-laden eyes and it did not even begin to lighten his thoughts.

I am a king with a Fool.

The transient image of tiny Jeffery Hudson flashed through Charles' mind, followed closely by his deep regret that the Fool was not with him this lonely night, when he might have been temporarily uplifted by the man's acute sense of humour, someone who had entertained him for so long, who was now entertaining or at least accompanying Charles' beloved wife in another country.

"What will happen to Jeffrey?" he asked aloud, more to break the silence than anything. "Loyal, devoted in a way few men are – he fought for me when others turned against me – I am wondering, worrying almost, what will happen to him when this time is done. Will Henrietta Maria keep him with her?" Even as he asked the question, he knew the answer. The little man was safe if he was with Henrietta Maria's entourage. She had a tremendous affection for Jeffrey Hudson, above the others who had entertained her over the years, the giant Welshman and the two other dwarves.

The silence wrapped itself around him again. He tried once more. "I would so like him to be here, but he had to go with Henrietta Maria. I would not beg him to return, that is not for a king to do and I am king to the moment of death, am I not? And, if I know this rightly and I think I do, my body even when no more than a skeleton, remains a king. I will always be King Charles I. Always. It is a thought to hold on to."

A stray tear escaped his left eye and began a slow journey down his face. He dashed it away with an impatient gesture of his free hand. What stupidity made him think he wanted any thoughts to hold on to, when the end was so close?

A surge of acid came up in his throat and he gagged on it. Bitter, bitter as my thoughts. "Am I blaming others for my downfall?" he asked aloud. The silence retreated to the hangings at the black-as-death windows and there hovered, waiting for him to stop speaking again. The wood in the hearth sighed and deposited more ash on the embers. He stirred, put the goblet down and sat up straight, grasping the carved arms of the chair, feeling the shape of the wood under his fingers.

"Do I lay blame and recriminations at my father's feet? Or Villiers, Cromwell and others? If so, I must release it, for I do not wish to go to my grave carrying cruelty, bitterness and resentment in my heart. I must go shriven and penitent to my God.

"Let me consider this:

"I am a king who has an extensive kingdom. I have great wealth and I am entitled by the grace of God to wear a crown. What and who will govern this land when this time is done is in God's hands but I fear for the country and my fellow countrymen. I fear they face a time of limited liberties, something they do not yet appreciate. I feel a sense of 'out with the old and in with the new' without regard of what the 'new' may bring them in the way of difficulties. Thanks be to God, it will be no concern of mine.

"I am a king with a court full of courtiers who even now bow to me and call me 'Your Majesty' whilst they await the final day and then – I know not will become of them. In truth, right now I find I do not have it within me to care. I know well each of them was there just to feather their own nest in any way they could.

"I am a king who had a court full of women who curtsied to me and called me Your Majesty. I saw them but never once gave way to their slyness and their flirtatiousness, no matter how hard they tried to capture my affections. I know not where they are gone, back to their homes and their masters, no doubt. In truth, right now I find I do not have it within me to care.

"I am a king who once had a populace which came to line the sides of the roads when I rode by, to remove their headgear and to stare at me in my rich clothes, at my pennants, my banners, my men at arms, my servants and my glory. Sometimes they even shouted greetings as I rode by. I thought they cared for me. What now are they thinking of me, those who know the result of the trial, those who know my life is about to end? Do they care? Am I anything now but an exhibit they will remember for the remainder of their benighted lives? Will they come to see my demise?

I am a king who once had a confidant and friend who held the title of the duke of Buckingham, who was struck down by an assassin in the prime of his life – and of mine.

"I am a king who had a loving but quarrelsome queen whom I adore beyond all reason, a queen who has been separated from me, along with my children, because of the circumstances in which we found ourselves. To what depths of sorrow and despair can one man be brought and still be living?

"There were many days and nights during my kingship when I repeated to myself; I am a king with a kingdom, the land is mine to rule and dictate and direct and govern. I repeated this to myself for one reason; I never thought it would ever be mine. If this seems strange to you, whoever I am directing these thoughts to this sad, lonely endless but inevitably ticking onward night, then follow my thoughts, for the path I walked seemed as inevitable to me as the ticking of the time which will bring the dawn and the end of life as I know it."

He stopped speaking, wondering why he was bothering, who was there to hear, or care, what he thought at this stage of his life?

He took a deep swallow of the wine and looked round for someone to refill the goblet, before remembering he was alone. For someone used to being attended every waking moment of his life and secure in the knowledge that there were guards at his door when he slept, this emptiness, this alone-ness, was as terrifying as the prospect of the morning to come.

But who sent everyone away? Who gave the orders that no one, not one living person, should enter his solitude this last night of his life?

"I would be alone this night," he told them, over their protests and their cries of despair. "I have many prayers to get through."

But he was not praying. This lonely heartbroken king was not communing with his God, as prayers had deserted him. It felt almost as if God had deserted him but this he knew was not so – God never deserted anyone, it was that person who shut God out. In his misery he had done just that.

Instead he had chosen to do something far more difficult … to go back over his life, stage by stage, from Then to Now, to see if he could find out just where his foot had slipped and he had lost the path he knew he should have walked. To work out how he was projected from innocent illness-ridden childhood through growing years and growing times, impatient times, sad times and mourning times, aware of indifference from his father and over attention from those who were commissioned to care for him and seek to influence him and make him what he now was and initiate, almost by default, what he had done. None of this was as easy as it seemed when he first proposed it in his mind, as a man will, that he go back and back and then forward and back until all memory is in place and in good order and in good light of the Lord God's great visage.

But then, truthfully, what else was there to do as he sat alone in the quiet of the room in St James' Palace, a room he knew well and which he much admired.

His thoughts rambled in all directions. He knew those around him sought to elevate themselves, sought riches and power. Ah, but who does not seek power in this age of enlightenment! He sought it still and yet he had it, but did he? Was he able to control all that he wished to control? Was he ever strong enough in mind and heart to take on the dissenters, the outsiders, the rebels, the independent minded ones who would not listen to what he considered to be his voice of reason or the churchmen with whom he could so easily dispute God's words?

It would seem that this time he was spending alone was to be lost in a torment of mixed thoughts, that nothing seemed as clear and right as it should be.

Was this not the loneliest position anyone could aspire to? Was there any person in England at this time who could understand how lonely it was to be king? It was well and it was good to tell himself he was the king, that he could do as he wished – to some degree - but he had to admit that beneath the trappings of kingship, the castles and the crown, there beat the single heart of a man who at times wished it could not be so.

It sounded easy when first said, but immediately the conditions arose in his mind, he would not, for fear of walking on the thorns of memory that prick so hard they can draw tears, look back into his childhood.

That condition, that stipulation, blocked the worst of the memories, he thought. What else could say about that time, other than he was cosseted and cared for, that despite the care he had poor health, limited physical ability, chronic lack of self-confidence and a stutter. That alone would be enough for any man to carry in the way of burdens, but add on the one thing which crippled most royalty, the fact he was a second son, and the burden became intolerable. A second son was a useless appendage created to ensure continuity in the event of God striking down the firstborn. If that did not happen, the second son remained a useless appendage and so he saw himself for many a long year.

It resulted in him repeating to himself, once the crown had been attained, 'I am a king with a kingdom, with wealth, with a crown.' And knew that all his life he had longed for the day when he believed in himself enough not to have the need to remind himself of who he was.

It was almost a shock to find himself totally alone on the last night of his life. He looked around the heavily shadowed room, wondering what shades lingered there and who would be waiting for him when he was no longer in this life. The thought sent violent shudders down his spine and he confessed to himself that he was mortally afraid of that moment, and all that went before it, too. What if he should lose his dignity, what if he lost control of his body, what if he broke down and gave way to his emotions?

"I DON'T WANT TO DIE!"

The words, almost a scream, rebounded from the panelled walls and came back to assault his senses.

"Fool!" he berated himself. "It matters not what I want, it is what they want, what they have schemed and planned and brought about. It is not my doing!"

The shadows retreated under the force of his voice and emotions, but then crept back as he subsided in his chair.

'I am alone this night, the last night of my life. Should any man be alone on such a night, left with no more than his thoughts, regrets and sorrows? Whoever ordained this, I say their cruelty is beyond belief. There are so many regrets, so many sorrows, so many heart-breaking moments to recall.

But recalling such sorrows – ah, forget not the happy times too! – is better than being in earnest endless prayer to the Lord God, who knows well what is to come, He is waiting for me.'

He reached out for the wine bottle and poured some for himself, noting how odd it felt and at the same time, how satisfying. Perhaps, he thought, I should have done more for myself before this time, not find out at this very late stage of my life that there is satisfaction in doing things with my own hands, rather than letting someone do it for me. How strange are the ways of life!

Tomorrow there would be the one thing he had to do for himself, walk with dignity and stoicism to his execution. This, he vowed, he would do carrying the full weight of majesty and pride that he had shown throughout his reign. He would not let the monarchy down by failing this last test. He would show them all what it meant to be king. In any event, he mused, the time will be small for it is a short journey to take and it will soon all be over.

The wine was good, it warmed him more than the dying log was doing. It released some of his inhibitions in walking the pathway of memory, helped him begin the task of reliving his past whether he truly wished it or not.

He brooded for some time on how the wine had loosened his thoughts as it would loosen the tongues of some men and the morals of some women. Then he wondered why he was thinking that way, as the last thing he wanted was the loose tongue of someone who was there because they felt they had to be, not because they wanted to be, or the companionship of some woman, for he would have found that distasteful. No one, no one measured up to Henrietta Maria in his eyes, mind and heart.

The Palace was virtually silent. The occasional, very occasional, clash of arms as guards were changed was the only sound he heard. And why, he asked himself, were there guards? Were they afraid he would try to escape again? As if he could go anywhere, at this point of his life, and be safe? Alternatively, who would want to rescue him, for the same reason? Guards. Well, palaces had to have guards, he supposed, but it seemed a foolish thing, thinking on it.

Charles I. The very first English king to carry that name. Of all the Henrys, Edwards, Richards, Williams, endless names, endless titles, he was the very first Charles. I may be small in stature, he mused, but my reputation will continue: I claim a permanent place in history for being what I am, King Charles I.

He never thought he would be king. Despite knowing his history, knowing how many times a second son became king, witness the great Henry VIII, second son, great king, he thought, he never believed it would happen to him. His brother Henry was strong, powerful, confident and much favoured by his parents. Charles had long since believed he would be Prince of Wales to Henry IX, there was no question of it. And then, the sudden devastating fever that none could control or cure, which had the sweat pouring from him and his skin turning bright red and hot to touch, striking fear into their hearts. His father stayed away, citing a fear of disease and waited in his chamber for news, his mother, knowing how bad it was, taking to her chamber and becoming consumed with grief, all of which meant no one was there to comfort and support Charles himself. He wandered the corridors of the palace, alone, lonely, grieving before the event because, young as he was, he knew that Death was inevitable. And indeed it was. The proud young handsome Henry was dead and that meant, inevitable as the sun rising the next day, one day he would be king.

The prospect was terrifying. Strange indeed were the ways of the Lord God, that He should strike the older son down with an illness none could cure and create a place for the younger, ill-equipped son to take his place, who right then was wearing the robes, the titles and the crown his brother had vacated to occupy his place in the tomb, the cold empty lonely tomb. It would not be before he too occupied his own place in a cold empty tomb. In a surge of emotion Charles thought, all this is in the hands of the same Lord God, to whom all praise be given for elevating me to the status of king.

He was acutely aware of the honour he had been given in his kingship. He was aware of it and before God was suitably humble and gave Him thanks for all he had. Only before God did he stand in humility, before all others, he was king.

It was as if he had waited a lifetime to put these thoughts together and yet, and yet, it was no more than a summer's afternoon in time. What was there to say of the time he spent with Villiers, of the time he spent learning to be more than that second son, of the time he spent learning – to be husband and to be king?

It was time to go back.

Testimony of Hannah Wybrand, nursemaid to the young Duke of York.

It is right grand, it be, that I get a chance to talk about my young man. Oh I did love him so! He was that small, that - what can I say? I thought on him being the runt of the litter. That do sound hard. But that was how it looked to me. There was the Prince of Wales, young Henry, right tall and good-looking and sure of himself, rode like, well, like someone born on the horse. And there was the little Duke of York with his poorly legs, his shallow breathing, and his stumbling over his words so that it were right hard sometimes to make out what he wanted. I got to know in the end what he were on about, but t'others found it right hard, so they did, and wanted him to say again and again and that made it worse for the poor lad. Oh I did love him so!

Well you see, there ain't much of life for us what slaves away for the rich ones, thems as has the money, thems as has the power, the power to throw us out in the mud if we don't please, so we doos our best to get it right first time. Poor little Charles, what the King did call Baby Charles all the time, didn't get much notice of anyone becos of his brother the Prince of Wales being the chosen one, him as had all the charm and all the talk and all the dancing and all the ways with the women and did every one of them fancy him when he walked by for all that he were a young lad. When I do say he might have been a young lad but he knew well what it was all about! And did he not use it and do it and thrill them that he did take his own. He never once looked at poor Hannah but I do say I did look at him... and right sorry and sad and tearful I was when he went and died.

But that were later, after the young Charles growed up a bit and got to walk a bit better cos we've worked with him, me and those who was around him, we got him to walk and we sat with him and we talked with him and we tried to talk posh, not the way we talks all the time and a'course he had the tutor what watched over him and got him to talk proper, not like us. Which was

20

like it should be. I do think the Duke would be happier were he like us, he weren't like the others, he didn't go looking at the girls, and now you gives me a problem. How much is it you wants me to say? How much doos you want me to give away? And doos it matter any more? He ain't here no more, he be in his grave, and don't you know I cried more over that than I did in my whole life. And me long since gone from the Palace too. Now how silly is that?

But you see, he were that soft with the pet rabbits, any kittens that was around, anything that was little and helpless that he could pick up and stroke and be nice with, that's what he did like. And I was only supposed to wash his small clothes and keep his bed fresh and clean his room but he would talk with me cos I was good to him, he said, cos I never pushed him when he stumbled over his words, I waited cos what else was I to do? I thought; if that were me, I would want someone to wait on me too. I only did what I would want. So the King didn't know and the Chamberlain didn't know and to the Queen didn't know and I do guess for one minute any of them would have cared a toss anyway that I was making a friend of the duke of York. What they knew, cos I heard it said, was that 'someone' was doing sommat to help him talk proper and they was right pleased. I could have said 'that were me' but I thought to keep quiet and let it be. It were my small pleasure and I wanted it that way for myself and for poor little Charles. Oh I did so love that boy and I never did get my own son and he was all I had for as long as I could be there with him.

We was going to talk about how honest I had to be, weresn't we? Well, like I said, he didn't do much around the girls but when he growed a bit and were big enough to use that which God give him, he did rather like the boys. I don't think he did anything with the boys, well I ... I am trying to be honest here, I don't think he did anything with the boys at that time. But I did hear tell that later when he was grown and could choose for his self that he did choose the young boys. I think it was cos he felt safer with them than with the girls. I can see that, girls can be nasty, they can be right bitches when they want, don't I know it? I and I know little Charles would not have stood that. He was easy crushed and so he went for safe.

Be that enough for you? You have my thoughts, you have my memories, I thank you again for letting me talk about my little boy, what I did love so much. I do wonder if he remembered me before they done took him and cut off his head. Oh I did cry so much when I heard the news. And there's me thinking I'd stopped loving him. All through that terrible war, when he set one man against another, one family against another, and I did think he was a terrible King, I did think I had stopped loving him. And now I see clear that I didn't.

There you have it. And right glad I am to have said it to you too.

Be kind to my king. You won't see the like of him again.

Chapter Two

The hour was late. The room was growing chill, despite the large log he had thrown onto the one which was crumbling away. He heard the guard change but other than that, he was listening to the sounds of his thoughts.

What had he started? Something, some devil, was forcing him to continue to take the pathway of memory to bring him from then to now, from duke to King, from second son to only son, from quiet life to public display, from safety to danger. For of a surety the trial he endured marked the end, day by day, hour by hour, of the time he had left in this life.

So, for all the determination not to walk through the thorn bush of his childhood, he had, of necessity to go back as far as the time his brother left the earth for the glory of God's heaven. What a loss to the country! What would they have done, how would history have changed, had he lived?

Charles was small, even considering the illnesses he suffered and his weakness as a child; he was small in stature. He lacked confidence. He spoke with difficulty. This person, this specimen of royalty, carrying titles of which the duke of York was the one of which he was most proud, was without warning facing the prospect of being heir to the throne of England. It seemed impossible; it was as if life had chosen to laugh at his expense. It felt as if the world had suddenly descended in the form of a robe of rock and landed about his shoulders. It was hard to stand, it was hard to walk and it was impossible to describe. It would have been difficult enough had his revered father remained solely king of Scotland, but the prospect of being king of the combined kingdom extended the boundaries of responsibilities beyond that which he could bring himself to visualise at that age.

He was just twelve years old when his brother, aged eighteen, died.

He recalled vividly the sense of loss and of emptiness, for Henry's had been a personality that overshadowed all who came near him. His ability to triumph over all adversities was something Charles had long admired and hoped one day to be strong enough to do himself. Had he the faintest inkling that his brother's life would be so abruptly snuffed out, would he have envied Henry so much? It was not a question he could answer, even in that most honest of times, the re-awakening and examining of past memories, when he was placing them before the Lord God and asking Him to make sense of them. If He would do so, of course. It may be that it is not His will to do that but for Charles himself, His humble servant, to make sense of them.

Most of all he recalled the sense of shock that swept the court and the family. He stopped to consider his thought. The court and the family. Not the family and the court. His parents were devastated with grief; they had lost a son who showed much promise of being a fine prince, a fine king, but they had a replacement, the second son. The court, on the other hand, had lost someone with whom they bargained, pleaded, befriended, cajoled into doing what they wanted, getting him to put their problems before the king, or the Chamberlain or someone, borrowing money, handing out favours, gaining favours and positions of power. This they lost, this they resented. Charles was not old enough or experienced enough to be a replacement. Even as they spoke of their grief and sadness he could see the truth behind the eyes. He shocked himself with the ability to see this for he was but a young man. Maybe that youth was what enabled him to see it all so clearly, for it was a fact that the ability had not been with him since that time. If it had, he would have seen others for what they were and would have seen all his problems

24

before they arose. He knew what was in men's hearts and he did not overly care for what he saw.

It was possible that time, that event, had coloured his thinking for the rest of his life. He harboured an element of distrust of virtually all people, the outstanding exception being the one he should have harboured the most distrust for, Villiers himself. But in truth Villiers bedazzled everyone, from the king to the lowest villain on the estates.

That is, apart from Charles' adored Henrietta Maria, the one who took Villiers' place in his affections and his trust. She distrusted Villiers from the moment she saw him. But for Charles, it was as if he changed one for the other, so smoothly did the transition occur. And whom did he blame for that happening? None but himself, who should have seen what was afoot and done something about it.

Henry's funeral was a grand affair, as befitted the ending of the life of the heir to the throne. Mortality was brought home to the young Prince in a rush, hitherto he had believed a person had to be either old or very young to die. Babies did not survive as a matter of course and of nature, the brothers and sisters who followed him had not survived; the old passed to Heaven as their rightful due for a long life lived in service to others. He knew, as an abstract piece of knowledge, that those who were between those two extremes had to live their lives until the day the Lord God called them to His kingdom for whatever reason and by whatever means. It had never occurred to him, though, despite all that he knew of the fragility of life, that his brother would be called home by God at such a young age. He did not live in circumstances which would have shown him this valuable lesson much earlier, he was surrounded by careful attendants and luxury, physicians to attend his every cough, sneeze or twinge of pain so that he would live a long life. The same consideration had been given

25

to his brother, but it had not helped. There was much to be dwelt on at that time.

Hold fast the thought! He had said clearly he would not walk the thorny path of childhood! But then, it had to be asked, when did he stop being a child and start being a man? In truth, it would seem that the occasion of his brother's funeral was that moment of time. What he recalled most clearly was his distress at the news of his brother's death, how he felt so hollow and abandoned and very, very young whilst the secretary who stood before him, wearing court mourning, informed him that he would be chief mourner at the funeral as the king and queen had 'declined' to attend. In that moment he threw off the constraints of childhood and took on the mantle of royal duties. It was not an easy step to take, but what else was there to do?

It seemed almost like a joke of some kind, this slender, almost inarticulate young man taking his place at the meetings to plan the funeral, who to invite, which order of precedence everyone took, where the burial was to be, who was to conduct the service – the detail was endless and necessary. He had to find time somehow to grieve but that time was limited. Tailors came to measure him for his mourning clothes, others were commissioned to provide the black velvet trappings for his horse. He chose the coffin for his brother, saw him gently laid in it and helped organise the lying in state and the guard of honour. At times he thought he would collapse under the weight of the responsibility put upon him but in other ways he learned a lot about being a royal son, as everyone deferred to him in all ways and took note of his requirements.

Fortunately the day of the funeral was dry and reasonably bright, no heavy rain or mud to contend with. Charles rode with his armed guards, all wearing the funereal black, noting the crowds who gathered on the streets to silently watch the procession pass by, doffing their caps, bowing their heads, whilst casting glances in his direction, he, the new Prince of Wales.

He sat motionless through the interminable service, feeling intensely alone, insignificant in the grandeur of the Abbey and the solemnity of the occasion, longing to cry as he observed the coffin containing the brightness and vivacity of his brother but the burning pain stopped him from even doing that.

Finally it was over, the coffin lowered into the ground, the congregation unashamedly weeping while he stood stone-faced and received the condolences of all who had been invited.

The funeral taught him another valuable lesson. Those of royal blood are watched at all times by those who are not. They were watched and commented on and criticised and praised - sometimes. The funeral taught him that he could not and should not allow any grief to show; he had to control his emotions, he had to be dignified and yet pleasant to all who spoke with him. He represented the family as he watched the burial of one of the family. He was more than aware of everyone observing his every movement, listening to his every word, ready to write their letters to whoever had commissioned them to be there.

He knew now, from the viewpoint of his more advanced years, that his parents should have been at the funeral. They should have led the procession, not allowed a mere boy to do so. Unfortunately his mother was incapable of being coherent, such was her grief at the loss of her beautiful son and his father harboured a morbid fear of disease and so stayed away. These were facts which were given to the world as their reasons for not being there. The truth was, neither could bear to face the public at such a time and the truth was, Charles was thrust into a role for which he was unsuited.

How easy it was for him to say these things now and how hard it was to carry them through at that time!

He was so young, so immature, so lacking in confidence that he felt himself to be a disaster, but there were those who said he did not lack the graces of a diplomat, so something must have made itself known to him during his formative years. From whom he did not know, for his mother was not a good teacher.

In truth, it had actually been good training for one so young, one with a distinct disability of speech, with a distinct weakness of limbs even then, for all too soon it seemed plans were being made for his marriage, all too soon he was engaged in the adventure of going to Spain with Villiers and coming home to great rejoicing from the populace that he had resisted the temptation to become Catholic, as if that were ever an action he would have taken!

Would that his thoughts could avoid Villiers at this time! But no, it follows as logically as day follows night. The young Prince had been elevated to heir to the throne. Standing between him and the throne was a dissolute father and an even more dissolute favourite for which he conceived a violent animosity which was hard to bear.

Am I then ashamed of that animosity, he asked himself? Should I answer true or false to this question? None can know of this king's thoughts, for they are secret. How foolish is this then that he should hold back from confronting thoughts which may hurt, even at this distance!

King or not, though, he lived within the body of a man. An ordinary man who needed to sleep, to eat, to drink, to walk and talk and obey the many commands of a body that needed to do certain things at certain times. This ordinary man also carried within him the ordinary emotions of love, hate, indifference, desire and ever onward, ever onward! How many are the emotions we carry, those of us who feel? And is not everyone different, every one of us, was he not different from the

Fool who used his miniature height to amuse, to entertain and continue to earn his living with the court? Was he not different from his wife, who he considered to be the true home-maker and fount of all wisdom? Was he not different from those who served him, those who worked with him, who advised him? Was he not different from those who were his enemies? Of course he was. And yet, binding all together as human beings are those self-same emotions, love, hate, indifference, desire and ever onward, ever onward! Forget not jealousy, Charles Stuart, he told himself, that most bitter of emotions, that most hurtful of emotions. He admitted, in the quiet of his own thoughts, when George Villiers arrived, he was jealous to the point of pain and determined that he would not like him. He knew his father admired and respected him and that in turn made Charles more determined not to. Why follow in his footsteps, he asked himself, why follow the swirl of his robes and bow to this newcomer?

George Villiers, 1st duke of Buckingham. The man who devoted a great many hours of each day to the grooming of his hair, his face and his body. Far more, in fact, than his wife ever did. His wardrobe was twice the size of anyone else's in the court, his servants had twice the work of the king's for his demanding ways ensured that they were kept busy cleaning and polishing and checking and washing and airing every last thing. His mind was a thousand times more devious than Charles' would ever be: sharp, precise, he could wound with a word where Charles would take a sentence to say the same thing. Charles had no idea, no real idea, why he felt so insecure in Villiers' presence, so useless, so tongue-tied. Why did he not have the courage of his own convictions when he was there? But listen to me, he thought, oh listen to me, listen to this fool of a king, was I not the same with Henrietta Maria when Villiers no longer walked this earth? Did I not defer to my wife as I deferred to my 'advisor'?

What could he say? It is the body, small as it is, the mind and the soul that resides within it that the Lord God saw fit to bestow upon him. Far be it from him to question His motives for doing so. Charles accepted His divine will. In everything. And that was the truth.

He thought suddenly, with a jolt that shook his entire body, I need to pray. I need to turn these thoughts to the Lord God Himself and ask for His blessing on that which I now explore within my heart. I need to be sure that these thoughts are not prompted by some evil imp of Satan, come to destroy such small peace of mind as I have managed to find during the last few tumultuous months. Can I be sure that these thoughts are sanctified in His sight?

For a long silent time he prayed and whilst there was no angelic visitation, no obvious answer being given, for the first time in an age he felt a sense of peace, of calm, of – rightness – and was eased. He could go on. He could go on going back. It seemed not to make sense and yet it did.

An unpleasing thought occurred to him then. He had inherited many things, the homes, the many servants who attended him, the crown, the position. All were inherited; none were his by choice. Even Villiers went to his father first. Only his wife, his beloved wife, was his by choice, if it could be called that. The marriage had to be approved before it could go ahead and some of that was taken out of his hands. All this made him feel second best. Because of that he felt he had to prove himself in the eyes of the populace, prove that that he was fit to be their king, to make laws, to have a part in the decision-making which affected their lives.

Memories of the family. His father, an ungainly man who held on to others to walk from chamber to chamber, who seemed overly large of body and slender of head, arms and legs, someone who had difficulty in eating and drinking and was not possessed of the best manners at the table. Fastidious Charles hated this part of his life, having to share the table with his father. It often put him off his food and so he gained very little weight throughout his life, as the tendency not to eat very much stayed with him. His father's ever rolling eyes worried him considerably as a child,

His mother was tall, elegant, given to strange histrionic fits at times, as if nothing in her life was right for her. On reflection, it wasn't, her husband was more interested in men, few of her children survived, court life was not entertaining enough for her and so she spent a good deal of her time arranging for expensive clothes to be made and attending plays and other entertainments. Charles tried to be the dutiful son but was aware his mother really only had time for her eldest boy.

Memories of his father's court. When he became Prince of Wales, Charles learned to play his part in day-to-day life; he spoke with emissaries, with courtiers and with secretaries. He took messages and entertained all visitors, as was his royal duty. He did his best to ignore the salacious goings-on, the open romancing of man with man, his father being the most prominent of all in this. He did his best to ignore it for was he not king and was he not Charles' father and did he not, deep in his heart, despise this aspect, this manifestation of the weakness of his father's character? Did he not wish, in the same deep place that only the Lord God saw, that his father was as most other men, moral, upright, devout? Did he not wish that his father would be devoted to his wife and family and no others? Did he not grieve that his father was not so? He did and the grieving hurt grievously, too. He made a vow during his morning devotions that when his turn came to take the crown, to draw on the mantle of kingship, to be the anointed, appointed one, that such happenings would cease immediately, that all would be decorous and devout. He carried that through. He banned all salacious goings-on and insisted that everyone should dress conservatively, worship God daily and keep their alliances behind closed doors. He cared not that they disliked it, He cared not that he gained a reputation for piety and propriety. He considered it then and still considered it a price worth paying. He would say to those who complained, 'am I not king, do I not have the right to say what happens in my own court?' The Lord God knows how much he wished he still had that right.

But to return to Villiers, that most charismatic, charming and enchanting of persons, the one he so disliked when the darts of jealousy shot through him at first.

George Villiers was tall, slim, languidly elegant, impeccably dressed, with a quiet almost seductive voice, an enchanting smile, beautiful manners and a cold calculating look that few people noticed, for they were too busy being overwhelmed by his beauty and his obvious flair and style. His wife was beautiful, rich and titled, everything he could ask for. She gave him two children which pleased him, and left him free to seek that which he really liked, other men.

He was created Duke of Buckingham, which immediately set him above many at court and caused a lot of ill-feeling, not that King James bothered about such things. For him change was everything and if change came about by promoting a favourite, all the better for him.

Villiers worked hard to conquer the feelings of all who were against him and somehow turned the people to him, seemingly with ease and with that smile everyone knew so well. Had everyone known then...

But life is full of 'had we known then-' he mused; it is impossible for any to turn back those days, peel them away as one would the skin of a fruit and discard it.

Would that we could peel back those days and drop them into the moat, allow the fish or wild life to consume them. Would that we could then relive those days and make different choices, but to do that we would have to return to those days with full knowledge of what had been so we could change it to what might have been. And so we are stopped from doing what we would most desire to do – change the past.

His father knew well his son was hostile to his new favourite. He did all he could to reconcile the two, ending with a banquet at which Villiers displayed his very best side and Charles was captivated, won over, all doubts cast aside. He should have seen … but in his heart he knew that at the time he was young, impressionable - and lonely.

He became even more lonely, if that were possible, when his mother died. During her last days, his father refused to go anywhere near her, for fear of disease, he said. At least, that was the story given out and one they all had to accept, for the king had spoken and who were they to argue with him?

His mother was not a good patient. As she had been throughout her life, she was demanding and impatient, tossing aside anything brought to tempt her to eat and asking for something that usually could not be obtained, for it was out of season or simply unavailable.

Charles did all he could to comfort her through her dying but he was no replacement for the beloved son and he knew it well. She did too but never mentioned it once, just called him her 'darling boy' and told him he would be a good king. Little did she know what would become of his reign, the depths it would descend to, the lives it would cost and the heartache and sorrow it would bring to the country she loved! Thank the Lord God she did not know and would not know. At least, Charles prayed she will not know what her 'darling boy' had done with the kingdom handed to him. She never once reproached her husband for not going near her before she died, either. Such fortitude, he thought, recalling those sad days. It is that I must show on the morrow. Ah, the morrow… no, think not on it yet.

Was he sorrowed by her passing? It was hard to recall. She was not – how could he think this without it sounding critical and possibly unfair? But then, who was he talking to? No one. He was completely alone. The log had burned half through, the flames had died back, the shadows had moved closer but they did not speak or even appear to listen. His mother did not oversee a family, she ruled a small empire which consisted of herself, her handmaidens, her servants and her friends. There, it is said. Father and he were appendages to that, Father ruled and therefore provided for her. Charles was her future, the heir who lived on.

Did his father grieve? This he do not know, he could not say. His father was ever closed of face when it came to family. Only when romancing another man did Charles see emotion and understand at times he felt the way a 'normal' person did. At times when involved in political argument with his counsellors and advisors, he would portray disgust, anger, impatience and, very occasionally, acceptance. But love, affection, caring – these were beyond his capabilities - with his family. Charles said this from his own heart, not from his own knowledge for it is a fact that he never spoke of his wife when with his son. So he knew not if his father had loved her or if he truly grieved. He may have been content that the dynastic marriage was over and at least he had one son to carry on. He may well have felt relief at being free to indulge his male lovers without the thought of her. Charles would never know. But in the night, at times, he thought about his relationship with his father and knew that, no matter what he might have tried to do, it would have remained the same for the king had his favourites, his lifestyle and his ambitions and none could gainsay any of it.

His thoughts were tangling themselves again. He knew he must desist and concentrate on what he wanted to do: think his way through from Then to Now, from second son to First King.

There was a melody threading its way through his mind, a lilting air the minstrels played one evening. It was light, fragile, quite charming and had no existence outside his mind at that moment, unless mayhap some other person that night has the same refrain running through their mind, too. What was he trying to say? Nothing is substantial; all is within the mind. Is kingship a state of mind, he asked himself? Is the reality of the crown, the oil and the consecration a visible thing that can be held in the hand and looked at, or is it really only in the mind?

Such questions he asked, such answers he could not find. Would that he had a wise person to consult, someone with the answers to these seemingly unanswerable questions. Would that he could find a philosopher among his attendants, one he could trust to ask these questions of and receive answers that would satisfy him. These were not new questions for this king to think on in the dark hours: they had been there for some time. They awaited answers and he thought many times he wished he could ask the Lord God to answer them in a way he could understand and accept. It was a constant theme in his prayers, but maybe He was too busy to answer, or was He too busy to find a way to answer him, or was He answering and Charles did not hear the answers?

So many questions! If he did not find solace in sleep this night, he would be unsure of his mood for the morning and the morning would bring many problems, many decisions to be made, many people to whom he had to be polite, if only for a very short time.

'Lord God, of Thy mercy, grant this humble servant the solace of sleep, I beg Thee!' and yet, even with the fervent prayer uttered, he did not leave his chair and find rest on the bed they had put in the room for him in the event of his desiring to sleep. It seemed sacrilege to sleep on the last night of his life. There was eternity in which to sleep, surely.

Testimony of George Villiers, duke of Buckingham

It is hard to know where to begin.

When I came to court, I had no ambition to become King James's favourite, but I thought it would be rather nice if I did. No, that is not being entirely honest. It was more a question of it would be extremely valuable if I did, rather than be rather nice if I did. I had a look around at all the other courtiers, decided that none were as handsome, as elegant, or as ambitious as I was. Of course this was just my opinion, but the fact I was able to dominate most conversations, to entice the King into my embrace with great ease, that I was able to withstand the scorn, the slander, and anything else that they chose to throw at me, proved that I was right in my assessment.

King James was malleable, but his son was not. Charles presented a challenge from the beginning. He obviously resented me in every possible way. I was everything that he disliked, I knew that well. But I did so like a challenge! There was this shy, slender, very good-looking young man, who I quickly discovered had no self-confidence whatsoever, waiting for me to conquer. His physical disabilities, the problems with his legs, combined with a stutter, did not help him at all. I knew as well that he was possessive about his father, believing that all should venerate him because he was King, and was openly scornful of those who would not do so. He did not seem able to comprehend that some people had

36

no intention of venerating this man, who quite openly preferred men to women.

I cannot ignore a challenge; I never have been able to. That is why, despite my inclinations, I was married and had children. It confused people, and that is something I liked very much. It kept them wondering about me, asking themselves whether or not this was the real me or whether it was something I did just to be flamboyant and contradictory. There is an element of truth in that, but it is not the entire truth. I did genuinely prefer men to women. I found women to be too flighty, too emotional, and extremely demanding. I agree, I concede in fact, that men can be flighty in their own way, but they tended to be more masculine about it, and very rarely gave way to the emotions. I did not have to face hysteria, tears, tantrums, and other such unworthy displays that no one should have to witness.

And so, even as I became an adviser to his Majesty King James, I was ultra-aware of his son. I knew that this was quiet seemingly unassuming boy, soon to be a man, would inherit the throne of England. That is of course provided nothing happened to him, as it had with his older brother. I do not have the gift of farseeing but somehow I knew that this boy, this Charles, would be King of England one day and it was in my interests to make sure that I had a heavy of influence with him. Otherwise I could see myself leaving court and that would never do. I had too much at stake, my future was there and my wealth was being added to by my position in court. I could not let it go. And to make sure of that future, I needed to have influence and power of the major players. There was major players were King James and his son.

I had to overcome Charles's jealousy. I began, for a while, to tone down the extravagance of my clothes, I wore less jewels, slightly less flamboyant clothes, desisted from openly romancing any man, walked around holding a large book which I consulted from time to time, to make myself look erudite and scholarly. I have the feeling that those two words mean the same, but let it go, it is what I want to say. I could sense a slight softening on Charles' part as I put this plan into effect, and I finished up by having a most splendid dinner one night, when I turned on all the Villiers charm that I could muster, and Charles was lost.

I knew then he was mine.

As I had made a policy of being honest, I have to say that I desired the young Charles to a degree that even I did not comprehend for a while. I also have to say, in all truth, I never touched him in that way once. This was because I held an idealised vision in my head of the love that we would share, whilst knowing that it would never happen. Because of that, it was better not to embark on anything that would destroy the vision. Nothing can kill a love better than having a desire, a fantasy, a dream shattered into a million pieces. I knew that Charles would not only reject me, but everything I stood for, everything I was, if I made any kind of advance to him. And so, with supreme effort, I held back from anything that could be construed in the wrong way. The good side of this was that everyone talked, and whilst they talk they are remembering who they are talking about and I did so like to be in the forefront of everyone's mind. The bad side of this was that no other man came up to the vision I held in my head of this pure love. It was extremely difficult until I learned to live with it.

Well there you have it. The unvarnished truth about any feelings between Villiers and Charles Stuart. I wonder if you are shocked, disappointed, feeling totally let down, because you were looking for much more than that. You were looking for evidence of what surely would have been an illicit love, and how you would have gloated if you had found it. You would say, all the talk in court then was real. Instead you have to say the talk is no more than idle chatter. Ah, what a shame! And I have to say that fact alone pleases me a great deal. It is good to know that we have confounded to you all for once.

Charles was not actually immature in his outlook, but much given to romantic thought. He had a vision of himself falling in love with a princess and living happily ever after. He did not seem to think that any rose garden came with thorns. I could not bring myself to enlighten him. He enjoyed his romance, even if it was all in his head, too much for me to disillusion him. It would have been unkind. I knew well about the thorns, having experienced them many times already, but to take away the illusions and dreams of a youth with the responsibilities that he had such a young age, I felt would have been unkind. So I kept myself or the information that I had, everything I had been through, thinking that in this instance experience would be a better teacher for the young Prince of Wales. There is nothing like learning firsthand about life.

Court life can become mundane after a while, the same round of entertainment, the same people making demands, the same walls enclosing us all in that hotbed of chitter-chatter, gossip, innuendo, and outright demands. I became bored. There is only so long that you can hold a dream in your head without it needed to be replaced by something far more interesting. Especially when the dream cannot, in any way, shape or form, become reality.

I needed adventure. I needed a new project. I needed a new challenge. I am afraid that George Villiers was ever in need of new territory to conquer. Having 'conquered' Charles, I need to find new outlets for my creativity and my restless thoughts. And so, I went King James and suggested that the Prince of Wales and I go to Spain so that he could court the Infanta. I felt she would be a worthy bride for him, but the King made it clear that he was not in favour of the proposed marriage. However, he did not allow that fact to stop us going. To my surprise, he was all in favour. I believe that he thought some travel, some time away from England, would be good for his son who needed education on diplomacy abroad. It was all very well being a master diplomat in your own court, when diplomats and courtiers and messengers came from other countries, but there was a considerable difference in being a master diplomat in someone else's country, in someone else's court. I agreed it would be very good for Charles to experience such a thing but I did not want a full scale mission to Spain. I wanted to do something different. And so having gained the King's consent to a journey of this kind, I began to plan. I thought it would be rather fun if we were to go incognito, just to see how people react to us. Charles was well used to the English acknowledging him as the Prince of Wales and granting him or respect in so doing. In another country he would not have such status, he would have to work a bit harder at proving that he was a worthy person. And if we went incognito, he would have to work even harder.

So what began as a game became real. Charles was enchanted with the idea of costume, of disguise, and asked his squire to find him something suitable. I was not very happy at having to wear something that did not flatter me, foolishly I had overlooked this in my plans. But then I thought; it is only for a short time, Villiers, what is the matter with you? Well, what was the matter with me was despite the fact it was a short time, I deployed not being able to wear my beautiful clothes.

I need not have worried. We only made it as far as Gravesend before we were arrested and had to reveal who we were. And then I could resume my normal role of flamboyant, expensive, jewel laden clothes which suited me much better.

Paris was beautiful. I thought the city was enchanting, but I realised very quickly that Charles only had eyes for a certain Princess Henrietta Maria. I had to get him away from there because the intention was he was to court the Infanta, not Henrietta Maria. This was my main difficulty with Charles, his romantic inclinations often tended to get in the way of any commonsense he might have acquired. And so we were on our way to Spain soon as I could arrange it. Charles talked at some length of the beauty of Henrietta Maria, but as we progressed through France and into Spain, he stopped speaking of her and instead began to speak of the Infanta, which pleased me very much. It was what I had in mind. I knew well this was an adventure, nothing serious, but it was good to be out of England, away from all the conniving, backbiting, intrigues of court. It was just good to be able to be ourselves, to be welcomed everywhere we went, to be treated as if we were both Royal, and I admit I enjoyed it very much.

The Spanish court welcomed us, if with reservations. That was very obvious in their attitude to us, "you are most welcome but only on our terms." Nothing was actually set, but it was very much implicit in the attitude. I could accept that, because this entire escapade was nothing but fun. Although we indulged in many long drawn out tedious discussions on what could be done for the Catholics in England, the concessions that needed to be made for them, all of which held no interest to me whatsoever. Charles took it all very seriously, debating points of law and religion, which quite surprised me. I had no real comprehension of the depth of his knowledge. But I also knew that he had no intention of implementing any such changes in England. It would bring against everything his father and he had been trying to do. The Church of England could not be disrupted for the sake of a betrothal treaty.

It was not very long before the complaints began to be voiced about my so-called behaviour, but if you put dark eyed, dark haired handsome young men my way, what do you expect me to do? Ignore them? It is more than any able-bodied man can do. And I did not. There were enough willing men there to keep me very happy for some time. It was others, those who did not like it, who made the complaint. Charles remonstrated with me about this and I said it was their problem not his. He agreed. He had enough to do courting the Infanta, with whom he had fallen violently and totally in love. To the point when he would have signed any treaty, agree to any conditions, provided he could have a year's betrothal with his new love. I do believe in the end of the King of Spain signed the agreement just so that we would leave. We arrived in February, we did not leave until October, by which time we had both wreaked enough havoc between us to last us the rest of our lives! And so we packed our bags and got on the ship to sail back to England and I had the pleasure of seeing Charles tear up and dispose of all the treaties he had signed. In that moment I knew that the Infanta had no chance of becoming Queen of England. And that suited me right well.

Our homecoming was spoiled by the fact that King James was dying. This we knew the moment we arrived, we only had to look at him to see that his days were numbered.

And so it was. With what seemed like the minimum of fuss King James slipped quietly out of this life and we all turned to look at King Charles. At first he seemed shocked, as the realisation that this really had happened dawned on him. And then I saw, for the first time, what I later thought of as his 'King' face.

From then on we had a king, not a prince. It baffled me for some time, until I got used to it.

But that, in itself, is another story.

Chapter Three

Villiers. He had to speak of Villiers. Should he right now confess, before he thought of the one whose name sat well in his mouth, that he feared for his sanity at this time? He felt as if he was torn, for he wished to think of these things and yet he was afraid that by thinking of them, even to himself, he would bring on the mantle of madness, for who would wish to walk the path of memory so? Yet he did and it was a burning desire to do it, one to which he had, of necessity, to give way for there was no peace to be found without it. He also needed to confess that his duplicity had returned to haunt him in his darkest hours. He would peel back many, many days and undo the words once spoken to this one and that, when he said one thing to one person and another to another and they come back, as all falsities do, to haunt him at this time of truth, even if the truth was only to himself with none to hear but the ashes in the hearth.

Villiers. Back to the subject which he had begun to explore. Villiers. Handsome, charming, seductive, manipulative, fun, if he could say such a thing. The devil personified in one tall, elegant, costly person.

When Charles grew to manhood, at least in his father's eyes, plans were made for him - without his consent or even his opinion being sought. The king had decided and that was enough for everyone.

Simply put, the king wished Charles to marry a Spanish princess. The Infanta was said to be beautiful and willing.

Father dissolved Parliament as it did not do his bidding and as king he expected it to.

He was trying - on many fronts - to use diplomacy in order to bring about changes within Europe, to stop the war here and halt the confrontation there and bring countries together. England and Spain unified by marriage would have suited him well. But – no one was interested in such a union. Other than Father, that is.

Villiers came up with a scheme, he proposed that Charles and he go to Spain incognito, see the Infanta, woo her and win her over and persuade her father to let the marriage go ahead. The question had to be asked now, with the other question of why it had taken so long to ask it, why did the king agree to them going on such an escapade? They could not have gone without his permission, the Prince of Wales and the king's favourite could not just take off for the continent without anyone knowing. What did he have in his mind when he consented to what was really a boyish adventure, looking back on it now? Or was it no more than a way to get Charles out from under his feet for a while? He had never ever understood the way his father's mind worked, he was ever calculating, could Charles even say devious in his thinking. Some of his planning seemed convoluted and even strange. Many times it did not work and caused problems in that small fact. Charles wished now he had learned from his mistakes, but do people not all think they know best?

The proposed journey to Spain was an adventure for Charles. For the first time he was going to do something that, on the surface, was not royal; they were going incognito. They chose odd names, arranged for strange clothing and false beards to be supplied to them. They talked through the route they would take and the fun they would have when they got there. Charles became so excited by the whole thing he could hardly sleep and ate even less than usual. Villiers became concerned that Charles would not be well enough to travel and encouraged him to at least rest during the day and eat a little more. They talked of it for hours, days, weeks, before they set off. They talked and they laughed and Charles knew he would follow Villiers no matter where he went, for he was everything Charles was not and he thought and hoped that what Villiers was would affect him in some way. Not that he could increase his stature in any way or change his looks or physicality, but it could change the inner person, the Charles who was shy, who did not speak clearly, who lacked courage but who had convictions he was determined to stand by, no matter what happened.

Looking back, he could see the faults Villiers personified and was grateful that none of it did affect him. He was in every way his own person, his life had been his mistakes, his fault, his destiny. He did not blame Villiers for anything. If Charles chose to listen to his often flawed advice, that was his fault, not Villiers'. He did his best to advise both king and prince. More fool them if we listened and acted upon that advice, he thought with a touch of bitterness.

They set off in February, in bitter cold weather, wearing layers of padding under their clothes to further help disguise them. They travelled on frozen roads with great care, not wanting to have an accident, either themselves or the horses, and jeopardise the whole enterprise. Charles was in exceptionally high spirits, he was free of his father's influence for the first time in his life, although he had at that moment failed to see he was firmly under Villiers' influence in every possible way. Everything was new, the small villages they travelled through, the larger towns where they were stared at as if they were truly foreign, all this added to their sense of adventure.

They decided to stay over in Gravesend before taking a ship to Spain but their odd behaviour, a mixture of furtiveness and high spirits, roused suspicions and before they had ventured very far into the town, they were arrested. Charles was affronted that anyone dared lay hands on him and take his horse away, which further added to the mystery of the two men as far as the officials were concerned.

The Mayor was not in any mood to be friendly to the two strange men who had ridden into his town, until Villiers took off his disguise and announced, in his most haughty voice, "I am George Villiers, duke of Buckingham, and this is His Highness Charles Stuart, Prince of Wales."

The quality of the clothes concealed beneath the disguise, combined with their natural aristocratic air, served to reinforce the truth of what Villiers had said. Charles was overcome with a mixture of resentment at being treated like a common criminal and a strange sense of excitement at experiencing something he would not otherwise have ever believed could happen to him.

"Sirs, the hospitality of the town is yours to use whilst you are here," the Mayor stuttered, aware he had almost caused a most serious diplomatic blunder. Slightly mollified, Villiers demanded lodging, food, wine and a roaring fire for them both, not necessarily in that order. The Mayor took them to his own home, where his servants hurried to provide a good meal and prepare a chamber for the two men.

In truth, Charles was pleased to have a night's lodging which was reasonably luxurious, very warm and comfortable. The disguise was all very well, but it did mean that they did not have their usual standard of luxurious accommodation. That was something Villiers had managed to overlook during their planning. In some ways it was a good thing that the deception had been uncovered, it meant more comfort, but it did mean that the fun had been taken out of it.

Next morning they boarded a ship going to the continent. The weather was bad, the Channel was a seething mass of waves and the ship rolled heavily under a gusting wind. At this rate, Charles thought, we will both be ill before we arrive -- Villiers was not a good sailor -- and the Infanta will not be very impressed with either of us.

It was a rough journey. The ship rolled alarmingly, Villiers became very sick and Charles somehow found his sea legs and was not at all ill. He was proud of himself for that.

Somehow they survived, the ship docked in Calais, they were given horses and an escort as befitted their standing in life and so, in easy stages, to allow Villiers time to recover fully, they made their way to Madrid. Along the way, many people came to see them as they passed by, some with apparent wonderment, some with obvious approval that English Royalty was paying them a visit. That pleased Charles very much, although Villiers wished to distance himself from what he called the 'rabble'. Charles was bothered by this reaction, which he thought was entirely unfair. But it was he thought he kept to himself, it was not a good idea to antagonise his companion whilst they were in another country.

Spain was warm, colourful and had many pervasive and interesting scents; the spices, unusual flowers, in his eyes anyway, dust and warm earth. The flowers were the things he admired the most, again, though, not saying anything to his companion. He wished he could have flowers like that in the gardens of the palaces he lived in.

Madrid was a fine city with beautiful buildings, open squares, wide roads and people who welcomed them. They were taken to the Palace where the Spanish king welcomed them, seemingly warmly, but there was a distinct reservation in the greeting. It became obvious in a short time that they were not that welcome, that a proposed marriage between Charles and the Infanta was not part of the Spanish king's plans.

For his part, Charles fell madly in love with the Infanta, finding her an enchanting person to be with. She was beautiful in a darkly exotic way which made her different from all the English girls that he had seen. This made her even more interesting in his eyes, but they were not allowed to bring much time together and he could not really get to know her. He consoled himself with the thought that if he could persuade to the King to allow the marriage, he would be able to win over the Infanta and make her his own.

There were many discussions, many proposals made, which would have bound Charles in a treaty which would have, among other things, granted concessions to Catholics in England. This he knew would never be allowed, his father would never agree to it.

But Charles wanted the Infanta for himself and so he agreed to do everything that the King asked. What the King did not know was that Charles had had no intention of following through with any of it. At least, that is the way Charles and Villiers saw it at the time. Later he considered that the King may well have known he would not follow through -- the whole episode was actually a face saving device. The King did not wish the marriage to go ahead, therefore he put obstacles in the way, knowing that Charles would not be able to carry them through and so the marriage treaty would fail. This way the King would not appear to be at fault. Nothing could come back on him diplomatically, which was what it was all about.

But that understanding came later; before then Charles could only see what he perceived as undying love for the Infanta and was content to agree to a year's betrothal whilst he went back to England and implemented the concessions which he had agreed to for the Catholic population. All this was going on in the Palace in Madrid, to the accompaniment of many banquets, entertainments, much riding, hunting, and other activities to pass the time. Charles knew well that he could not take the treaty back to England and persuade his father to pass the laws that would be needed to implement all the conditions. He knew this, but continued to enjoy the hospitality of the Spanish royal family and household until it became obvious that they were becoming unwelcome guests. At that point they made their arrangements to return to England. Charles and the Infanta parted on good terms, as indeed he did with the Spanish king, despite his knowledge that the King was pleased to see them depart. He knew, from the servants that cared for him, the court and the king did not care for Villiers at all. There was a rumour his execution had been called for. All Villiers did was laugh at the controversy he caused, saying they did not know how to live.

The moment they boarded the ship bound for England, Charles ripped up and threw overboard all the treaties that had been signed in Spain. Villiers watched him do it and applauded.

It was October when they returned to England, a mellow time of golden leaves and a sense of the year dying. It was completely unlike Spain. In some ways Charles felt as if he was completely unlike the person who had left England in February, or at least that is what he hoped. He had been through many experiences, he had seen France and Spain for the first time with his own eyes. He had attended masques and dances, had eaten strange food, had seen beautiful and unusual plants, and exquisite buildings. He had also experienced homesickness, in part caused by his father's letters to him, letters which said he would be held hostage, that he would be hurt or even killed. The letters were almost paranoid in their content, but Charles took from them what he needed, written proof of his father's affection. At least that was the way he saw it and he clung to that feeling. Unfortunately when he returned to England his father's attitude to him was exactly the same as it had been before he went -- indifference. If there was one thing he craved in life more than a wife to love, more than the ability to speak clearly and grow in stature, was a moment of his father's affection. He did not ask for love, that was too big a word, too big an emotion for him to conceive in his dark mind. James was a cold, hard man who sought only to have that which he craved: total control of Parliament, the country and all who were subservient to him, including his son. Charles had never, from the moment he was old enough to understand until the moment he closed his eyes for the last time, felt that he had received the tiniest scrap of affection from him. He was just the second son who had become the first son and a disappointment in the happening of it.

It was during the journey back to England, in truth, that he began to seriously question why he had been allowed to go. Whilst France and Spain had woven their magic around him, whilst he had been courting the Infanta and engaging in negotiations for a marriage, he had not seriously thought about why Villiers had arranged such an adventure, why he had promoted it as a worthwhile cause to the king, why he had allowed himself to be disguised in an effort to leave the country without being recognised, what had been the ulterior motive for it all? The only thing he could conclude was that Villiers wanted time away from England, perhaps to escape a jealous lover, or to exert more influence over Charles without the King's opposition. If that had been the intention, to some degree it had worked. For he was under the spell of Villiers! Even when his logical mind told him that the infatuation was not good, that Villiers' judgement was often at fault, that he should not worship his father's favourite, still he did so and was incapable of doing anything else. It was as if Villiers had mastered the black arts and carried all before him with his radiant smile, his personality, his charm and his talented way with words.

What he did know, and was extremely grateful for, concerned Villiers' relationship with him. Whilst Villiers openly flirted with, courted and no doubt bedded many of the men he met in the Spanish court, he never once touched Charles, apart from a manly handshake now and then, even when Charles would dearly have loved to be held for a moment, when uncertainty swept over him, when his confidence was badly shaken by something. It didn't happen. It was as if Villiers kept himself on a tight rein the whole time, just as he had in England. Being away from court and all the restrictions that imposed on them both, he had ample opportunity, if he so wished, to change the relationship between the two of them. Instead Villiers had been the very epitome of a perfect gentleman, friendly, loving in an abstract way, the companion everyone needed when on a visit to another land. Charles thought that one day he would ask his friend and erstwhile advisor what had kept him at arm's length but then decided he didn't really want to know. That it had happened was enough.

Spain had been an adventure, a challenge, a diplomatic game wherein he knew he was a pawn and yet went with it for the sheer thrill of allowing the Spanish king to try and encircle him about with conditions, for both men knew the King did not want the marriage. Charles knew how much he did not want the marriage and knew too that there were others with ulterior motives who would have liked the alliance. Games, pawns, deceits, his adoration of the Infanta and letters from his father, outrageous letters of paranoia and suspicion. His time in Spain was good, when he looked back on it. It had been his own deception, the agreement to it all and the moment he set foot on board the ship to sail home and threw it all, every agreement, every signature, every vow, into the cold waters where it all sank without trace, he knew he had remained constant to his own decision. That felt good.

At that time he was king in waiting, a king who would have a Fool. But he believed he was no fool then. He would not turn away from his church, his faith or his country for a mere woman. Ah, but it was easy to say when the Infanta was in Spain and he was on his way back to England! Whilst in Spain, he found the decision extremely difficult to make, which made of the actual carrying out the act of destroying the treaties even more satisfying.

Ah, but there are those who would say he turned from all that was right for a man. Mayhap he did, if he did, could he not plead that the influence of his revered father laid that burden on him, for did he not consult Villiers on every aspect of his daily life and did Charles not find he did the same?

Would that someone had told him at that time that Villiers was a fool!

That too was a lie. He could confront the lies now and shoot them down, for they were not fit to be thought of. He knew, somewhere in the darkest recesses of his mind, that Villiers was not exactly a fool but a bad influence, that he would be better off relegated to a part of court where he could not dupe Charles with his words, his smile, his casual handshake and his perfumed presence. But Father adored him, Father courted him and Charles was mesmerised by the dazzling entity that was George Villiers, duke of Buckingham. Rich beyond belief, talented beyond belief, with the ability to turn any situation to his advantage, to put blindfolds on those who were under his spell so that they did not see his every fault, to cover them all in the magic that was his personality and so get his way in everything, he was master of all he surveyed. And he knew it.

For a moment he wanted to go back to the Spanish escapade. He had enjoyed it. For all that it failed, it had been an experience he would not have missed. Some people he liked, some he disliked on sight, most he distrusted. He asked himself, how was it that he distrusted the Spaniards but not Villiers? Because he was English? Some questions had no answers, it would seem. That was one of them.

He arrived back to England to find his father was, in every respect, a dying man. He came back with confused ideas and when a war with Spain was proposed, he agreed. Then he wished he knew why, wished he could peel back those days and restore sanity to them and start over again. He couldn't - and didn't.

Charles had seen his mother die. It had been harrowing and devastating. Now he had the experience of watching his father deteriorate and slide toward his end. The king was not an old man but he was old in his body for he had lived too much and loved too much and taken too much of the draught of Life. It had been the undoing of him. Charles vowed it would not be his way, not then, not ever. It was one vow he did actually stand by for the rest of his life.

Testimony of the physician to the court of King James I and Charles Stuart.

I know not of how much I can speak of my time in the court of King James, and so for the moment I will not give you a name. Not that it matters very much, it is what we have to say more than who we are which will be of interest to those who are looking into the life of Charles Stuart. There seems to be an abiding interest in this monarch, for at times his actions seemed in contradiction to the life that we expected him to live. That may appear to some to be a strange statement, but I know it to be the truth.

King James suffered from a variety of illnesses, shortness of breath, a condition of blood which seemed to be made worse if he consumed too many sweet items, he suffered many headaches, and pains in his legs from time to time. I would advise him often to reduce the amount he ate, because his corpulence was not helping with the condition of his legs, but as with most things with King James, he ignored everything I said. I tended to him when he had very bad colds which resulted in terrible coughs, which in turn hurt most of his ribs. But then again, I would leave compounds of horehound for him and find them still in place when I returned later. He would say he did not like it, say that it was bitter even if I disguised it in a rich mead, and give me many excuses not to take it. It was extremely infuriating to have a patient like this, one that you could not order about.

I would also look at the young Duke of York from time to time, in an effort to help with some kind of exercises to strengthen his legs. There was little I could do for him that was not already being done by the devoted ones that he had around him. Charles was extremely fortunate in those who had been allocated to his household, for they worshipped him in their own way, and did everything possible to help him. There was a good patient, he would take any potion I left for him and tell me, with great thanks, that it had helped considerably when I came by to see him again. I did not believe entirely that it helped to that degree, but I am sure it had some effect on whatever was troubling him at that time.

I had very little occasion to attend to Henry, Prince of Wales, who was always the picture of health, energy, and exuberance. It is my belief, which I could not express to anyone at that time, that he contracted some kind of fever from a thorn which struck deep into his hand. He asked me to remove it, which I did, but the hole which it left was very deep and looked very ugly, and although I dressed it for him, he told me that it ached and burned. I cannot say for sure that was the reason for his death, but I think it played a very big part. The reason I could not tell anyone was simply that I was afraid it would be seen as incompetence on my part that I could not control the fever. I know this is foolish, for since that time I have seen others who have contracted a fever by hurting themselves on a splinter of wood or a thorn in the same way. But at the time I thought it prudent to say nothing. Instead I nursed Prince Henry as best I could, and was there when he breathed his last, to my great eternal regret.

I continued to serve the household, tending to them all through their grief, giving calming herbs to the new Prince of Wales to help him through the funeral, whilst secretly deploring the fact that his parents were not going to be there. Charles seemed to mature overnight, it was as if by adopting the title of the Prince of Wales he took on a new persona, he became more Royal, and even his stutter began to diminish as he gained in confidence. His squire sought me out to find the calming herbs the night before the funeral, for he knew that his master would find it difficult to get through without a little help.

It worked, he was the epitome of royal dignity, solemnity and courteousness to all who attended.

When he returned from Spain with His Grace the Duke of Buckingham, he complained to me of problems in his lower regions. I feared he had contracted some foreign condition that I would be incapable of dealing with, but this was not the case. I found he had contracted something -- I cannot say with certainty what it was -- which was definitely sexual in some way. This surprised me considerably, because I believed the young prince to be virginal and innocent. I could not ask him, openly, where he had contracted the condition, but I could ask His Grace. I did, later, to be even more shocked when he informed me, with a smile that was full of sexual innuendo, that the young Prince had consorted with young boys whilst he was in Spain, as a relief from his inability to fully court the Infanta.

I chose not to believe it but the truth was, the Prince of Wales had a condition associated with sexual activity – it was easier for my conscience to accept he had consorted with women whilst he was there, even though I knew the Duke had no reason to lie.

I have kept this a close secret these many years but now I see the truth about the young Prince, later to be king, is being revealed. I am adding this small part to the narrative in the hope that he will be better understood as a complete person, not as just a king who led his country into war. Charles Stuart is more than anyone has known up to now through his words alone.

Part 2 - King

Chapter Four

He knew he had to think of that which still hurt after all the passing of time, the death of his father. Why should it bother him even now, he wondered? He knew full well everyone had to return to the Father in Heaven at the end of their allocated time span and that it came to all, both high and low. It came in ways most would wish they could avoid and yet everyone knew it was meant to be, no matter what. But the memory hurt, even after all those years. He said aloud, 'let me talk of it and perhaps in the talking of it the hurt will fade from my mind.'

It was but a small step into his memories to recall the dark room, the choking, stifling air, for no one thought of opening a door or a window to allow the sick man a last taste or a breath of coolness. He recalled the drabness of it all, for the court had changed: bright colours had been replaced by sombre dress, heavy greys, muddy browns or funereal blacks. The drapes on the bed were dark, thick with smoke, ash and dust for no one had been near the sick – the dying – monarch to take them down and shake them free of the accumulation of the dirt of the centuries which appeared to hang in every fold. Or was that merely his imagination? Was it not really so that the dust lay lightly on the fabric and the thickness and the age of it was nothing but a figment of his imagination? And why did he so let his thoughts drift and entangle themselves into knots as complex as any net ever knotted, if not to deny his heart and mind the truth of that which was really happening, the fact a monarch was drifting into death? Of all the things he recalled, that was what comes to mind the most, the fact he tried to deny what was happening by not thinking of what was happening.

He stood at his father's bedside, watching as the sick man's breathing laboured, fearing yet wishing that each breath would be the last, for the passing was painful beyond belief to observe. The room was full of people; a priest, his Father's attendants, courtiers, his personal physician, his secretary and hangers-on who were worried about their place in court when the order changed, when the person at the top had no time for them.

Were those people, those crowding, gently pushing, repulsed but fascinated people, there out of the goodness of their hearts and not just so they could say later 'I was there when King James breathed his last'?

A silent prayer left him: 'Dear God, I do so pray to Thy great goodness that none of what I thought then was portrayed or displayed on my face. I did not wish any of those people there, kind or otherwise, to know my thoughts. They were for me and me alone to consider, to agonise over and to regret later.'

He waited patiently, knowing that the time was short and wanting, nay, needing to be there when it ended. In truth, he had no choice, did he? Few kings are given the chance, the comfort, the solace, of dying in their own beds in privacy. So many are struck down by assassins, by poisons, by ill-timed moves in battle which allowed others to steal their lives. Others were taken, made prisoner and never emerged again from that prison. At the time Charles wondered what his ending would be when his time was done. Before the trial, he wondered what ending it would produce, what the verdict would be and whether he would be strong enough to walk through the experience. Ah, that last question was one he did not wish answered, even if anyone held the answer to such an intensely personal question.

It was possible, had he thought on it, that he would have known the outcome of the conflict and the trial, for all things were designed to do that which the persons in

58

power demand be done. They wished to be rid of him. They would be rid of him. He believed it would not benefit them in any way.

But he did not think on it. In truth, some things are best kept from our minds, he mused, for the knowledge would send us insane were we to know. For all that the fortune-tellers and seers, mystics and wise women profess to know the future, none tell with absolute surety what is our fate. He believed that was a great kindness of the Lord God Himself, for keeping the knowledge from His people ensured that they retained a degree of sanity as they walked the difficult pathway called Life.

In his sorrow and unease of mind, he thought: I fear for the way in which my life will end, that I will not be the dignified person I need to be. Kings must of necessity be dignified. I am not sure I am strong enough. I confess this now, but when the time comes to make that walk … with God's help I will retain the majesty of a monarch and be the epitome of courage and endurance in the face of overwhelming circumstances.

Memories. He recalled how he surveyed the face and sunken, aged figure that was once a proud king and much-loved father, even if the love was all one way. The figure in the huge bed, surrounded as it was by dust laden drapes and dusty people, was as far removed from his hedonistic father, the outrageous king who loved men and did not care who knew it, who scorned convention and did not care who knew it, as any courtier was from a devout monk or nun in their barren cell.

Time was short. He knew it by the atmosphere in the room: there was a collective awareness that the sands were fast running out but he could not say for a moment how he knew, or they knew, that it was so.

His father stirred very slightly, his eyelids flickered but did not open. Soon it would all be over, he told himself and he prayed to God it would be so. The waiting was as harrowing as the event itself. The thoughts raced on. How much I would grieve? That was an unknown factor; his father had been a liability and the source of many jokes as well as an all-powerful monarch whose rule extended over two countries. He had been revered by some and hated by others. Charles stopped to wonder for a moment if anywhere in the emotions which his father had generated there was that elusive one: love. Did Villiers ever love him or did he only use him? Did Charles' revered mother ever love him, or did she only use his position and his bloodline to suit herself? Did the sadly deceased brother love him or did he long for the day when he would stand before the people as their king?

For the first time since his brother's death Charles wondered if Henry had dreamed of kingship, had imagined power and position, had longed for wealth and fealty from England's subjects. In his waking dreams, had he tried on the crown of England and found it fitted well? If he had, what then were his brother's thoughts when the sands of his life had run out so very fast and so very soon? Charles remained in ignorance of what truly went on in his brother's mind and heart. He had never thought to ask and he wondered if he would have been told if he had. Sadly, he thought, we did not have the kind of relationship where we would have discussed such things. He was no more than the younger brother at all times. Henry was ever the king in waiting, even at a young age.

He had not thought these things before; they came strange to his mind. The strangeness was intense enough that the thoughts haunted him still, for there were no obvious answers. Maybe when we meet in Heaven, in His great domain, I will seek out my father, my mother and my long-buried brother and ask them for their answers, he thought. Until that time, I have only my thoughts and they are coloured by my own feelings. I did not understand my family when they were here and I doubt muchly that they understood me.

His thoughts ran in all directions, before there was little else for him to do but stand with clasped hands and solemn face by his father's bedside, waiting for the last breath. It was a sorrowful, solemn moment, one that would remain engraved in his heart for the remainder of his life. Those who were in the room at the same time stood with bowed heads but their eyes were bright, with avarice? With morbid curiosity? With an overwhelming need to know their future? No doubt all of these questions were present, and maybe a few more that Charles had not thought of. Not everyone had the ability to read everyone's heart. All he knew at that moment was that the room was thick of the emotion, not all of it sorrowful. His own emotions made it a sorrowful solemn moment, but he was fully aware that not everyone shared that feeling. Why should they? They were all servants in one form or another, none were there because his father had to truly cared for them, all had to be used in different ways. He imagined that the overwhelming feeling in their minds was; what will the next King be like? Will he be considerate, will he be generous, will he let them retain their positions, or would there be massive changes in the court. Even as Charles scanned each face in the room, he detected their various emotions and delighted in and not showing anything himself. He knew his face was totally blank, it was something he had perfected during his lifetime. With some people it was the only way to be. If nothing else, it kept them guessing. He wondered where Villiers was, why he had decided to stay away from this last emotional moment. It was tempting to believe that Villiers could not face the death of his patron and friend but Charles was unsure, uncertain that was the true reason for his absence. He knew one thing, he would never ask him where he had been at that moment -- and he never did.

He had not confronted these dark memories before, for dark indeed they were, as he have no answers and, without consulting necromancers, he could find none. Even if he did, which is against the word of and the commandment of the Lord God and he would not do it, would he trust that which was told to him? He believed that the Lord God held us without the knowledge of what was to come. So he remained without answers

So, observe the Prince of Wales, small figure, oft overlooked, clad in black from head to foot as was demanded by such a sombre occasion, standing by a bed in which a mortal man, still a king until the moment of his last breath and beyond, indeed beyond, was moving toward making his transition.

That was the vision he had of himself at that time, insignificant, unhealthily despondent, weighed down by guilt that he was not thinking of the transition or offering prayers for the passing to be smooth and for his father to be taken into the great loving hands of the Lord God, but brooding on whether his long departed brother ached for kingship and whether his mother loved him, her husband or anyone. Of a surety his thoughts were improper, impure and yet – he knew he could not have thought any other way at that time, for had he considered what was truly happening, he would have given way to hysteria or dementia. The Prince of Wales could not do that. Dignity, duty, devotion. Lessons forced home by years of tutors and governors. For, when the king took his last breath and went to his reward in Heaven, he would be the next in line. The thought was terrifying. It was all he could do to control his emotions – and his body.

A murmur rose from the back of the room and he watched as yet another person pushed their way in. The place was crowded enough, he remembered thinking with extreme irritation. He remembered the sweat running down his back. It bothered him and he was unable to do anything about it. Dignity was everything at that time, the passing of an era, the passing of a king, the mantle being transferred from one set of shoulders to another.

He could have sworn a sacred oath to the Lord God that he could actually feel the weight of the wool settle around him. It came with such tremendous responsibility, he was not sure if he could stand up under its thrall. It was surely too much for him. He could not stand the grief of losing his father and taking on his mantle at the same time! The prayer went up, 'Lord God look Thou upon me with mercy and compassion and give me some of Thy strength, that I may bear this great burden with the courage and understanding that can only come from Thy great self. Look upon this soul about to pass into Thy care and keeping. This is the soul of the king of England and Scotland, small countries in Thy great scheme but large ones for those of us who have to govern and control the people.'

Would anyone believe him if he had said there was a flash of light from a corner of the room at that moment? He recalled staring at the dark corner. No lamp shone there; no courtier in bright clothes and sparkling jewels stood there for none dared arrive in bright clothes or wear bright jewels. All wore jewellery of the deepest jet. Nothing earthly could have created that flash of light. With a heart full of devout love for God, he looked down at the still figure of his father. The Lord had spoken. The time was almost upon them.

What time? What life? From the moment he had returned from Spain, from the failed mission to court and marry the Infanta, life had not been anything but difficult. War with Spain had been endorsed by Parliament; although he found he could not fully comprehend how or why England had gone to war with a country which up to then had been an ally. Somehow Villier's hand had been in it, as it had with so many things, that he knew but he did not understand how or where. And because of this, he found no way of comprehending how it had happened, not with clarity and certainty. He agreed, yes, he recalled that he agreed to it. Had it something to do with our visit there? He could not fully understand the workings of the politics of the two countries without much heartache and so, he admitted, he left it to others. No, again that is untrue. He left it to Villiers.

Sometimes, even in later life, Charles could not see a way to manage without his guidance. At that time he felt, deep down, that all was not right, that things were not as he thought he saw them. His vision was not clear, his thinking was muddled and unreliable. It was even now and, much as he hated to admit it, he was not ready to take on the role of king - but he had no choice. It was as if everything was spiralling out of control, as if there was no time to breathe, to take stock, to stand back and ask himself how he felt about everything; his impending marriage, his father's passing, Villier's role in his life. One moment he was a carefree Prince on an escapade, an adventure in Spain, the next he was there, waiting for the kingship to pass from father to son. And in the process of all that, somehow the country was at war and somehow Parliament was upset and somehow he needed to curb Villier's excesses. Was ever a man so cursed with indecision as he was?

Memories. He would wish them gone, for they bothered him with their clarity, their intensity and their – he had to say it – burden. Without them could people not move on, unburdened by the past? But then again, if people had no memories how would they learn?

He told himself again to stop thinking foolish thoughts, to stand still and quiet and dignified and wait. His feet hurt and his legs ached and his back hurt and he was hungry and thirsty and wanted it to be over. He felt guilty for wanting it to be over and yet, looking at the laboured breathing and the ash grey face of the man who had fathered him, he wondered if he did not want it over too. But then, if he did, why had he not ceased breathing long before?

At that moment the sick man muttered under his breath. The physician moved forward, obsequious and yet authoritative, carrying what looked like a tincture of herbs in a bowl. Charles indicated that his father should be left alone. The one thing that was clear, above all else, was that he was beyond help and no interference, benign or otherwise, by a physician would make any difference. He watched as the man stepped back, the beginnings of a scowl wiped from his face when he realised, when he remembered, that the king was dying and the man by the bed who had just given him an instruction, unwelcome or otherwise, was the next king. It would not do to upset a new king, one everyone knew would sweep the court of hangers-on and debauched people, for he had made no secret of it. He was well known as someone who hated the salacious goings-on. They knew well he was someone who had every intention of clearing it all out as soon as he could.

The priest was muttering prayers and making the sign of the Cross over the dying man. Charles wondered if Father knew or cared what was happening, that his passing was being blessed by someone for whom he had openly said he had no time. He had always preferred his priests and others who surrounded him to be handsome, witty, debauched and amoral. This priest was one of the devout, caring types, unknown in Father's court. Charles was glad he was there; it was a small victory for him. The secretary, the Gentlemen of the Bedchamber and of the Body had wanted their priest, someone who had shared their excesses, to be there at the last. Charles had, for once, stood firm, told them that the man would not cross the threshold as long as he held the right of succession. In that phrase he told them everything: be warned, beware, your days are numbered if you persist in your ungodly ways. Muttering under their breath, they went away and allowed this priest to come, a godly man with a pure heart. 'So be it,' he thought, 'so be it. I will have my will and my way.'

Right then there was only one thing that mattered: the king of England and Scotland was passing from this world to the next. Not his father: the king. It must be done with dignity, with decorum and with all the ceremony that befits a king.

His father's eyes flickered open for a moment and a smile tugged the lips which had been tightly pressed, as if in pain. "Baby Charles," he murmured and then Charles saw a change came over him, the face began to lose its lines of age and pain and took on the appearance of a young man. The eyes opened wide and it was as if he saw something – or someone – wonderful, such was the radiance of the smile and the look. Then, in a flicker of a moment, he was gone. The life had departed from him so quickly it was almost impossible to say he had actually died. Charles touched the still warm hand, felt the wrist, realised there was no pulse and bowed his head. It was over. He felt empty. He felt empty as if his father's passing had taken something of him with it. Fast following that emptiness came a weight so strong he almost gave way under it, the sheer shocking grief of losing his father. He did not expect it for he had anticipated the moment for so long, endlessly expected it, from the moment he realised the Hand of Death had grasped him and would not let go its grip. But - anticipating and seeing the passing were two very different things.

The physician also checked Father's pulse, put a hand against his neck and then reverently closed the wide staring eyes. There was a sense of relief in the room that was almost palpable; the king's suffering was finally over. The last few weeks, months even, had been tortuous as he had fought for breath and tried to cope with the running of the country without the ability to even take care of himself for a day. Everyone stood in silence, absorbed and lost in their own memories and their own thoughts. Then reality broke through the mourning. His father's secretary turned to him and said two words: "Your Majesty."

It was the signal for everyone to come to their senses and greet their monarch. Charles felt himself lifted out of crushing deep grief by the acknowledgement of this new status. He was king. He was truly the king and he had a kingdom to command - after the funeral which had to be arranged. It was as if he grew several inches in stature in that moment, motioning to the hangers-on to leave the room, to allow those who had to see to the body to get on with their task.

Grief or not, mourning or not, a new era had begun. King James had died. King Charles had arrived. The world would soon know of the new arrival, he vowed silently, watching the priest praying over the body of his father. No longer the king, it was his father who had died.

It took him some time to realise the turnaround he had made in his thoughts, from 'not my father, but the king' to 'not the king, but my father'. Later he looked on this as a turning point in his decision not only to clean up the court, but to take the country firmly down the pathway of pure living, righteous living, devotion to God through the Church of England, to have an end to conflict and create peace for all subjects. Whether it could actually be achieved was another matter entirely, one he would discuss with Villiers, when we had the time…

Before then, he paused to wonder why the robe of kingship felt like a mountain as it settled on his much smaller shoulders. Was it ever thus, he asked himself? Did his father feel this weight? Did it disconcert him?

He felt for a moment that he had nothing to offer, nothing to base his life on, that he was empty, a mere vessel. Was kingship an imposition or a pleasure? Would he make a success of it or would he fail? And who was to judge him, the people or Almighty God?

Testimony of the Scribe, Isaiah Scratton

My name, for what it is worth to you, kind sir, kind madam, is Isaiah Scratton. I was scribe to his most treasured Majesty, King Charles. I worked with him and for him for many a long year, in the many homes he had and loved and worked in. Much work, oh much, much work for the king was ever busy with his affairs even when supposedly taking a rest for his health's sake. A man devoted to his people, even if it was from a distance. But for sure, that is how it needs to be, why should a king be as a common man? He is, after all, appointed by divine right of God, is he not?

I grew old in the king's service. I have the condition of the bones which causes pain and I grew bent and hunched over my desk. My hands show the stain of ink of thousands of words written for His Majesty, my fingers curve to fit the quill and will not straighten again, no matter what the physicians try to do for me. In truth, what do they know of the human body which has spent so long in the service of a king that it knows nothing else? My body has changed to suit that which His Majesty had requested of me – to be his scribe. My head knows nothing else, either.

Now he is gone and I am lost. Where do I go, what do I do? Who wants an old, old scribe whose whole life has been in the service of the king when no one seems to want to remember the king, let alone employ someone who was in his employ!

I worry too about the child Kit, he who was page and messenger and half-starved little thing who served me well, running between my desk and the king and bringing back that which His Majesty did not like to be rewritten yet again. He would hide in a bed of straw, he was that small, and be there when I needed him. Little Kit, where has he gone? Who has housed him, who has taken him on to run messages and be there to do service? I could cry, I really could cry. My king has gone, my life has gone, my little Kit has gone and the world I knew has changed and gone. Now that man, that Lord Protector, whatever he calls himself, has taken over and is busy changing the world for the rest of them, those who supported him and those who did not.

There are those who say to me 'Isaiah, why do you give the King all of your loyalty in this way? You know what he is; he is a man who would seek only his own way and no one else's.' I say to them, would that you had seen him from the beginning. Would that you had seen him as the tentative, shy but determined Prince of Wales, how he entertained and talked with the diplomats from many other countries, see how he coped with all the licentiousness that went on around court, around his father. Would that you had seen him when he first took on the mantle of kingship, as he called it one time, his insecurity, his lack of confidence, but all in the name of God his determination to be a good King. I doubt you will find such a man again if you were to search this land of England from one end to t'other. 'I am no different from any other man. I was just born a King'. He would say this but he would know as well as I do, that it was entirely wrong. The late King James, may God rest his soul, was a King who believed in the divine right of the monarchy, and this he passed on to both his sons. When the Prince Henry went home, may God rest his soul, all the emphasis of the divine right of kings was put on to his son Charles. He absorbed it as he absorbed everything that went on around the court. Do I not know of his father's tendencies towards men? Of course I do. And you will ask me, as someone who has observed his King so closely for many years, did his son had the same tendencies? And I will in honesty say to you yes he did, but not for men as much as for boys. Your next question to me will be, were these boys willing? For there is a fear among many that the King issues an order and they have to obey whether or not it is the inclination or their will. And I say to you they were willing. They were willing because he was a shy, undemanding, self-effacing monarch to some of us. And if I say to you I cried inside for I was never chosen, would you believe me?

What I must say to you at this time is that this King wore many faces. Some will say there were only three and indeed the great artist painted him with three faces and I did oft wonder why. I knew my monarch, my king, as a man who would in a moment change from being the supreme diplomat, to being a somewhat vicious and arrogant man when he did not get his own way, to one of intense sexuality and then I would know that his needs had to be provided for, but there was a fourth and even a fifth layer to this man in faces only glimpsed for the briefest of moments and only those of us who loved him devotedly would ever have seen them. These faces were in turn one of deep compassion, and the other of deep devotion.

If it were possible to ask Queen Henrietta Maria whether or not she saw that face of deep devotion very often, she would no doubt say yes, she did. Because, some of the few times which I saw this face was when he turned to her and to his children, whom he adored. I had not known in my life someone so loving toward his wife and his family. If he were not King, he would have had a most happy life with Henrietta Maria and those beloved children. Everything that my King did was centred around his wife and his children. They moved

70

from home to home, with great ceremony and processional, so that the children have a variety of places in which to live, a variety of animals with which to play, a variety of scenery to entertain them and to please them.

And if, at any time, there were rumours that the animals were used in ways which were not strictly in accordance with their status in life, if I may say such a thing, then I say answer that with your own conscience. For I am not about to admit such a thing to the world. Maybe others will, maybe they will have more courage than I, but I do not wish to taint my king with such a thought. Now you ask me, why have I said it in this testimony. Well, I say it because I know for the surety that others will and I wish to make my position very clear.

For me, King Charles was - and is - a fine King. Yes, he made mistakes and led his country into conflict, but was that a conflict not aroused by those in parliament who refused, for whatever reason, to make concessions with him on his demands? And will you not say to me now that perhaps my king should have made concessions too? Maybe he should, maybe it was only right that he should have done such a thing, but then again I say to you he was king. I say it with all the emphasis I can. Kings are not used to their will being thwarted in any way and why should they? Has not every single King up to this time battled against those around them who would stop in their decisions to do this and do that which they think is best for the country? And, in the majority of instances had that king not denied that advisor or disposed of them in some way? And do I not say in the depths of my own knowledge, that this is the right thing to do? A parliament is made up of members who represent the people. People do not have the power, the sight, the knowledge, that a monarch has, and therefore they are not in such a good position to say what is right and what is not.

Maybe you are thinking I am not such a good person to ask about my king. Maybe I am blinded by what I know of him and see of him, but you asked and I have said. This is how I see my king.

And at this moment I see through a veil of tears.

Chapter Five

The hour was late, but the thoughts kept running on and for the moment he was content to let them do so. The fire had burned low to nothing more than a sullen red glow partially covered in fine grey ash. There was a distinct chill in the air and the shades, whoever they were, who had been lurking in the great heavy drapes appeared to move closer, as if wanting to overhear or actually take part in his endlessly searching thoughts.

Memories. After his father's death, he moved with great speed but total discretion to take over what was then his court and his country. For a short time he felt as if he was completely in control of everything. The deference people showed to him made a difference to the way he saw everything, he was no longer merely tolerated as the young Prince of Wales, but venerated as king. The difference was amazing. He had to stop sometimes and tell himself 'this is a really me, this is really my new status in life, these are really my people. They do as I bid.' The sense of power was overwhelming.

He began by removing certain people whose conduct had distressed him beyond belief during his father's time. It was a simple matter, he sent out instructions that each one was to see him in his private chamber, where he handed them gold coins and asked them to leave. They did not seem surprised at being told to go, but they did express surprise at being told personally by the King. He wondered why this should be so, and whether he had gone too far in making the decision and saying it himself. And then he thought: what does it matter? This is my court. The truth was that he did not wish to delegate it to another, he wanted them to know how much he had disapproved of their conduct during his father's lifetime and he wanted them to know this without him saying it to their face. They got the message by him quietly dismissing them. Nothing was said in his presence, they did not dare, but he overheard them outside saying: 'we went too far with the old King. We should have realised that the son would be different. At least we leave with money even if we do not leave with dignity.' It was enough for Charles. He was satisfied that the message had been given, without him having to express his disapproval.

In their place he chose quieter, more sedate people, those who worshipped God first and Mammon second, as far as possible, anyway. He could only see so far into a man's heart, after all.

The whole atmosphere of the court began to change. With this change came a lightening of his heart, which was most welcome. At times a wave of grief would overtake him, he would look for his father and realise he was not there. He would begin to make a decision and hesitate, wondering whether his father would approve, and then realise it did not matter. It was his court and his country. The mantle of kingship did not grow any lighter, but it became a little easier to wear.

Encouraged by this new mood of modesty and piety, he moved on to replace certain members of the court whose task it was to advise, those of whom he was not sure of their loyalty or their direction. Word had it they had thought themselves safe, not having been removed in the first wave of clearing out but he made it obvious they too had to be gone. Ah, there were few who could stand against him at that time. Determined as he was to change things, none could gainsay his commands. He truly felt like a king – for a time, at least.

In all of this he did not consult Villiers at all. They were his decisions and his alone. For a while Villiers was an outcast at court, no one wanted to speak with him, unsure whether he was to be retained as a favourite or dismissed as the others had been. When they are not sure of someone's position in the court, the people tended to avoid that person. It was not a personal attack, it was a fact of life.

When Charles had finished with what he thought of as his clearing out, he was more secure in his role as monarch. Those who attended him were as pious as himself and as discreet, which was just what he wanted. Then and only then he invited Villiers into his private rooms and they resumed the friendship they had enjoyed earlier.

Somehow it felt as if he had never been away. Before Charles knew what was happening, he had slid back under Villiers' influence – wondering why he almost said 'control.'

Villiers proposed that he considered marrying the French Princess, Henrietta Maria. Ever cautious, Charles sought to learn something about her character and asked for her portrait, even though he had met her when passing through France on his way to Spain. He recalled the small pretty girl with a sweet smile and thought she would be a good Queen and consort for him. She might even be someone he could mould to his way of doing things and wondered if that was just a dream. Once he agreed, envoys were sent to France to arrange and organise the marriage. Villiers was right, Charles decided, no king should be without a queen by his side. In the volume of work which devolved on him after his father's death, he hardly gave any subject extensive thought; if it seemed right, he would do it. Hesitation was not good for a king, he knew that; he had to be seen to be decisive, even if the decision was actually taken by someone else.

Arrangements were under way for the funeral. That in itself occupied a good deal of Charles' time. The grave was prepared; the laudatory service written and guests invited from Europe as well as an extensive list of dignitaries from England and Scotland who had to be there. It was essential that everyone who had any standing whatsoever were invited. A feast had to be prepared for them, that too demanded his time and attention. Villiers was everywhere, a firefly, flitting from one task to another, dealing with this, arranging that. He took over the marriage arrangements, assuring Charles all was well, that there was nothing he needed to worry about. That was good but there was a nagging doubt somewhere in the back of Charles' mind that he should be taking more control himself, that he should not leave it in the hands of someone –

There the thought sometimes stopped, but other times he took the step into the forbidden territory of being unkind. Then the thought would continue - in the hands of someone not of his high standing.

Then shame would take over and he would turn to Villiers, praising him and giving him more control, more power, more wealth.

What grief he felt at his father's passing was mitigated somewhat by his sense of kingship, of donning the heavy mantle of the supreme position in the country, of being the one to whom everyone had to turn, sooner or later, for decisions. Yet inside he was aware of the aching loneliness and a desperate wish that he could go back to being the Prince of Wales, king in waiting, deploring his father's court yet comforted by the fact that he had no responsibility for it.

Responsibility was a bigger word than he had anticipated it would be.

Chapter Six

The funeral was a stately, sombre occasion as befitted the burial of a king. No tears were shed by anyone for a departed monarch who had never managed to engage the emotions of his people or of his staff. Even Villiers, James' firm favourite, did not seem to grieve overly for his lord and master. Instead he was busy being himself, ensuring everyone knew of his presence and his influence. The moment the guests departed, he was back in the role of marriage broker and arranger, seemingly loving every moment of it, too.

Charles brooded on that for a time, wondering how a king could depart from this life and seemingly leave hardly a ripple in the surface of that life. It was as if the transfer of power from one person to another happened without so much as a flicker, the only change being the size of the person who now wore a crown and who was planning both a wedding and then a coronation. In his mind, his father had been a huge character. In reality, had he been so big? What would history make of a reign that seemed studded with flamboyant hangers-on and an outrageous lifestyle more than policy and progression for the hard-pressed English? Wars which were unpopular, policies which were against public opinion, what would history write as his father's obituary?

It was time to put such thoughts to one side and think of his future, starting with his new wife.

Henrietta Maria was a doll.

Was it impolite to say such a thing about his wife? Why, who was to hear him? His wife did not know of his feelings in that way, she knew he had a deep love for her and that was good. Truthfully, that was all she needed to know.

Another set of memories was being revived. It was good; it was helping him come to terms with events in his life. If he kept on at this rate, his memories would catch up with the day he was actually living and there would come a time when he would have nothing to remember that had not already been covered.

He recalled that he stared at the French Princess with an astonishment that he could not hide. The big question was, why? He had seen his new wife before, was it perhaps that she had seemed larger to him then, surrounded by others, courtiers and her ladies, mostly of the same height and shape, at a time when Paris had been more attention distracting than the pretty young Princess?

He had ridden to Dover with a sense of tremendous excitement filling him, for his bride was coming to England. A Queen was coming to help him with his life, to be with him during the interminable banquets, someone to liven up the court with giggles and colour, with ladies and with – love? Could that be? Ah, how he looked back on those innocent days and wondered where was his heart, his mind, his sensibilities.

He rode with Villiers and a retinue of armed guards, followed by horses laden with clothes for the royal party and gifts for the City dignitaries. They arrived the night before Henrietta Maria's ship was due to dock and were féted by the dignitaries of the City of Dover. It was one of the interminable banquets he so hated, where he had to sit through endless courses and be polite. There were drawbacks to being king: if one does not seek a reputation for rudeness or surliness, one cannot not depart from a banquet half way through, even if the minstrels do not please, the food is not enjoyable and bed calls in seductive tones that it would be good to lay one's head on a pillow and lose oneself in sleep. It would not be diplomatic to mention the company, to mention the dull but good and well-meaning men of the city! He recalled his thoughts, if only his bride was there, it would be a livelier and more interesting banquet, but she was not and he had to endure it as a king alone.

By morning, his sleep having been deep and good and the bedchamber everything he hoped for, he had forgiven the city elders for their dullness and, after breakfast, went up onto the roof of the castle, the better to see his wife's ship arrive. It had been Villiers' idea and a good one, a true bird's-eye view of the arrival of the fleet of ships bringing the French Princess to English soil. Charles walked out into the grounds of the castle and told everyone he was going to climb on to the roof.

The panic this instigated had to be experienced to be believed. They argued, they shouted, they cajoled, they pleaded with him not to climb onto the roof. Never had they thought of such a thing! It gave him much secret amusement. They fussed and huffed and all but wanted to physically restrain him from going up there but they could see no way of doing it, so they had to let him go. For Charles it was another small victory. He kept recording them and they bolstered him and he needed that. He felt he had to show he could, even in such a little way, get what he wanted and do what he wanted. He kept asking himself, am I not king? Can I not do as I wish? The answer was 'yes' but for others it was 'perhaps, maybe, possibly...'

From the castle roof he could see such a long way, such a wonderfully long way. The Channel lay flat and calm, the surrounding countryside had a beauty he had not fully appreciated when riding through it. He was glad he had decided to climb up there, to see so much, to appreciate so much. He watched as Henrietta Maria's flotilla came into the harbour and strained his eyes to see whether a tiny person, for from that height everything and everyone was tiny, was looking toward shore. The ships looked like toys a child would sail upon a lake or the moat. When they neared the harbour, he got back

79

down to ground level without difficulty just as the gangplanks were being put in place. He could almost sense the relief from the city dignitaries. They escorted him to the stage which had been especially built for him, draped in purple and gold, to await the arrival of his wife. Around him stood courtiers and dignitaries, a welcoming group, he thought, but then, looking back on it, it occurred to him to wonder if they were intimidating. He was used to these people, his new wife was not. He did not think on it at that time.

He held the picture in his mind of the tiny ships looking like toys and there, walking toward him, was a doll. It was as if the toy ship had spilled out a doll which had taken the form of Henrietta Maria, his Queen, his wife. She looked fragile, unapproachable. He felt if he touched her she would break and yet he could not stand back and act as if she was nothing to him. He stepped off the stage and reached out to embrace her. Once down on her level, she did not seem so tiny but still a fragile beautiful little creature who made him feel awkward. He became aware of an overwhelming sense of tenderness for this small, pretty child-like woman, but he had to stay strong, act like the diplomat which was what everyone expected.

She curtsied and smiled up at him, a tremulous smile that was on the verge of tears. He could not read from her eyes whether she was happy at seeing him again, whether the prospect of actually being his wife was pleasing or abhorrent to her as she was so full of unshed tears. He did not know her at all and so could not detect her true thoughts; he had to hope that she was happy and pleased to be his Queen. Her stumbling speech, which revealed her lack of self-confidence, touched his heart and he wanted, longed, to reach for her, wanted to hold her and tell her it was all right but he was aware of protocol. Always the protocol, always the rigidity of court convention. Then she broke down in tears and his resolve melted away with them. He welcomed her into his life - if not his heart - at that time. He felt tenderness toward her, but as one would a child, a frightened child who needed comforting. He greeted her entourage with a few words and then allowed them to take her into the castle and give her food and wine. There was time to rest before we went to London. She seemed animated when she returned to talk to him, colour had returned to her face and her hands moved in time with her voice as she talked so much that he longed to trap them in his larger hands and hold them still for a moment, wanted to say to her, 'you have no need to put on an act for my benefit, my dear wife, for I know we will settle to marriage together and be happy, given time.'

He was full of joy that his wife had arrived, that they were setting out on a life's journey together, one that would take him into new realms of responsibility and, he hoped, happiness. Then he looked up to see Villiers observing her with one of his sardonic smiles and Charles wondered what was really in his heart. He had arranged the marriage: did he approve, or did he regret her coming? Did he think this beautiful doll would come between the two of them? Did he think he could control her – and in that thought Charles realised what was at the root of many of his problems.

Villiers believed he controlled the king.

In that moment Charles saw that Villiers had supreme control over Charles' father and probably dictated much of his policy. At his bidding the country was at war when it need not have been, at his bidding Charles had asked Parliament for money to fund that unwelcome unwanted war – for whose glory? Certainly not for his. No king who created an unpopular war could be popular with his people. It was an enlightening moment and he stored it for the future, to turn over in his mind at night when the servants had departed and the bed curtains were drawn against the dark and the cold. For it was then, as now, he gave free rein to that which troubled him, that which haunted him, that which hurt him and when he asked the dark to help him resolve those issues. It was effective, it was therapeutic, it was calming even if it deprived him of sleep at times. In the past he had endured comments and snide remarks from Villiers. If he thought on it, that was about the standard of the conversations they had anyway. Charles solemnly asked himself now why he endured the man for so long - and had no answer.

The marriage was formalised at Canterbury with a great ceremony which was dignified, colourful yet restrained. Henrietta Maria was the most fragile, beautiful, tiny thing imaginable, committing herself in a clear small voice to being his wife for eternity. Charles admired her stately demeanour, her gentle way of accepting those who came to pay homage to her, the words she found for each person who deferred to her. He found his estimation of her rising by the hour and it surprised him.

The dignified marriage ceremony seemed to suit his new style. He overheard talk, people saying that it seemed as if he was ready to conform to the advice offered by those around him, from those who did not worry unduly about being in Villiers' favour and what a relief to his mind that was! The problem everyone had to deal with, which he knew full well, was that no one knew what thoughts were rapidly chasing one another beneath the calm, almost implacable face that he presented to the world. He thought of it as his 'king' face. It bemused people, they could not tell what he was thinking and that worried them. They were so used to reading his father's expressions and gauging his needs before he spoke that when they came up against his blank look, it sent them into utter confusion. It was something Charles enjoyed but dared not let anyone know that he did.

He tried to act as if marrying Henrietta Maria was the most wonderful thing that had happened to him so far in his life - and in many ways it was. For the first time he had someone who was truly his, no nursemaid or tutor to share with another, no courtier flattering them for favours for themselves or someone else. His wife was his and his alone. And yet…

The truth was that that dreaded the thought of sharing his life with this tiny person who seemed to radiate power and control, two things he did not wish to concede. He had waited a long time for the chance to take charge of the court, as he saw it, anyway, and did not want to give any of it away. He had not appreciated at that time how much he ceded to Villiers. That came later, much later.

In truth, he was terrified. He had the task of trying to placate both his new wife and Villiers. No one needed to tell him that they would be at loggerheads in the shortest possible time. It didn't need a scrying mirror or soothsayer to tell him that, it was writ clear in Villiers' behaviour and the flashing looks Henrietta Maria gave him even as he stood by Charles' side during the ceremony. It was as if he could feel the antagonism as a living physical thing. He was sure that if Henrietta Maria had her way, Villiers would have been banned from the ceremony, from the court and from Charles' life, but she did not dare suggest anything of that magnitude, being new to this country and to the court. Nothing was said, not then, not later, when he was no longer in this life, but Charles knew it as clearly as if it had been spoken aloud during the wedding ceremony itself. His wife had the most expressive face when her deep emotions were stirred.

A king needs a queen. He remembered thinking this as the formal words were spoken which bound them together as man and wife. Man and wife. How mundane that seemed compared with the reality! King and queen, and the queen no more than fourteen years old. Was he supposed to bed her? The truth was; he could not, for she was too young, too delicate and he was altogether too afraid. He wanted to talk – but could not talk – to Villiers about it for he would surely have laughed and dismissed the fears as nothing, would have gathered up some Court wench or other, deposited her in a bed somewhere and demanded Charles practice on her. He could not and would not. Why was he so intimidated by those around him at that time? Where was the resolve he needed to run this country as he wished, not as they wished? He said this still and it had been – how long now? So long! Ah what years, what years!

Somehow, during those twisted difficult thoughts and complicated emotional hours, he accepted that he was married to a doll. He sat with her through the magnificent feast, watching her pick at the unfamiliar courses, wondering if she would acclimatise to the English way of life easily, wondering why he thought he should marry someone not from England, apart from the need to enhance treaties and maintain good relations with neighbouring countries, that is. He managed to overlook the fact that he had gone to Spain to court the Infanta who, had the negotiations succeeded, would have come to England with precisely the same problems as Henrietta Maria. Sometimes, he thought, it is not easy being king. As he came to that conclusion, he realised he had held the highest honour in the land for less than six months and already knew it was not easy. It did not bode well for the future.

But looking at it from another angle, as his father had taught him to do many times, she was young, pretty, determined – the jut of her chin and her general demeanour told everyone she would not be a quiet, submissive little wife – and was well used to court life. She knew the niceties of diplomacies, how to conduct herself at a banquet, how to hold her own in polite conversation. The rest, how to run the household, supervise the servants and other duties would surely come later, when she had been there for a while.

Yes, there was much to commend his new Queen – if only he could still the doubts about her tender age - and the obvious need for her French entourage. They seemed to be everywhere, chattering among themselves, fluttering around Henrietta Maria, attendant upon her every wish, her every word. He found himself resenting them immediately, found himself frowning slightly at the prospect of coping with these strange people who knew his wife better than he did. Jealousy is a worm that eats at the mind, this he knew and decided he would have to guard against it.

More doubts set in as he watched courtiers flatter and attempt to charm her. Was she old enough to be a proper Queen, or was this just a game to her?

The celebrations began to flag, the minstrels, musicians and dancers were visibly tiring and people were creeping away to their beds, after making their obeisance to the new Queen and bride. Charles came to the conclusion that during that time he had stilled all doubts. Henrietta Maria had handled the flattery and the charm as if she had been doing it all her life, with a quick word, a jest, a smile and each time turned back to smile and look at him as if he was the only person in the Hall. That endeared her to him in a way no words could ever do.

He saw her eyelids drooping with tiredness and gestured to her ladies to take her to her bedchamber and help her get ready for bed. He went to his chambers, where his esquires disrobed him and gave him a night-shirt, aired before the fire. He was glad to be divested of the elaborate robes he had worn throughout the day, for they were heavy and overly warm. He waited for a short time, granting Henrietta Maria the courtesy of privacy, before going to the chamber himself. As he entered, the last of her servants hurried away, carrying her wedding dress and mantle. He saw her unfamiliar items on the chest, a hairbrush, some powder, her jewellery, and felt his heart turn over. This is what it meant to share; this is what it felt like to have another person in his life. Strange possessions on cabinets, strange servants around the place. Or so it felt, in any event. It was all so new, so out of routine. He noticed her prie-deu in the corner, her prayer book open at the right page, in all probability ready for the morning. His attendants were with him, standing around trying not to look as he assimilated everything that he was seeing.

Henrietta Maria was lying in the large bed, looking even more like a doll, the heavy drapes and coverlets swamping the tiny figure. His heart went out to her but he had to maintain protocol and dignity, something she was well used to. He wondered what thoughts were going through her mind now that she was about to be alone with her husband for the first time. He dismissed the men, extinguished the candle and slid under the coverlet alongside his wife. It was the strangest moment of his life, up to that time.

He had that day been formally married, committed, bound to a stranger. All that he really knew of her was her name, her nationality, that she was tiny and bold, that she held strong opinions, was self-assured and yet, he was convinced, remained a terrified little mouse under the bland face she turned to him during the service. That face was quite unlike the looks she had cast at Villiers, for she had made no effort to disguise her dislike, nay, her contempt, of him. He, in turn, had done little to disguise his feelings for her. Charles knew she was strongly Catholic, the new additions to the room had already made that perfectly clear. He hoped that in time he could convert her to the English church, to his mind the only true way of worshipping God. He hoped that in time he could find out what really lay beneath the surface of the little woman who had become his Queen.

They lay quietly together, neither speaking. It felt strange and yet normal, tantalising and yet familiar. A warmth, a subtle perfume, emanated from Henrietta Maria. He sensed her fear, too, what did this new husband want of her?

Nothing. In that moment, as he felt as though he had picked up her thoughts, he decided to do nothing but kiss her chastely on the cheek.

"Goodnight, my dear wife," he said quietly. He felt her sigh of relief and sensed her smile.

"Goodnight, my dear husband," she said, just as quietly. The tension drained out of her. She seemed to melt into the mattress. Within two or three heartbeats her breathing had deepened: the day had caught up with his new wife and she was fast asleep.

He laid awake for what felt like hours, hearing the soft breathing beside him. It was a whole new experience, sharing his bed with a wife, with a person he was entirely and completely responsible for from that day onward. He wished he had pre-knowledge what joy she would bring him, the happiness he would find in her love and caring, the family they would have, the delightful days and nights they would share. He wished, in the loneliness of this cold shadow-laden room in which he was passing the last night of his life, that he could have foreseen all that, it would have made the early days much easier to live with and through! But the Lord God, in His wisdom, does not allow anyone to look into the future in that way, He gives them the task of living through each day as it comes, for good or bad, and asks only that they follow His pathway. He wondered why men found that so difficult to do.

That wedding night he found himself wondering what Villiers was doing, what he was feeling. Was he jealous, drunk, was he alone or cavorting with a courtier somewhere? A pang of jealousy shot through him, sharp as indigestion. For all his need to be there with his new wife on his wedding night, he knew full well that he would prefer to have been drinking with Villiers, even if he was shocked by some of the language he used and the stories he told when in his cups. To do that made him feel...

Like one of the men.

There, it had been said, even if it had only been said in his mind where no one could know about it.

There were times, oh how many times, that he felt like a callow youth, unable to use the coarse words, unable to find a vulgar rude rhyme to match some ditty the others were composing, the oaths some of them used when the quarry escaped and the hunt returned home without a kill. Then he would ask himself why he wanted to be like them, why he wanted to use coarse language and invent filthy rhymes and knew the answer even as he asked the question: to be accepted, to be part of the group, to be one with a group and not be the odd one out, not be 'Baby Charles' any longer.

His father had a lot to answer for.

But then ... oh look at it from another direction, approach it from the cleaner side of life. He went to Henrietta Maria as a virgin, an innocent, clean and untainted. He used no gutter language, he knew no vulgar gutter-snipe rhymes. He would not, no matter what provocation, use such words in the presence of his wife without thought, for it was not in his nature to do such a thing. If he could not do that when in the presence of men, then he would not do it in the presence of his queen. He went to her with a clean body and a clean mind and he went with the love of the Lord God in his heart and soul.

'We will learn how to be man and wife together, when the time is right,' he thought.' It might not be tomorrow, next year or even the year after. It mattered not. I could wait. I would wait. She was so young! She was so innocent! I could not take that innocence and corrupt it so soon! Who was to know? I could say in the morning 'yes, we laid together' and in God's sight we did just that, for was she not lying here beside me? Were we not lying together? In truth we were.'

Once he made the decision to do nothing, he found his tumbling thoughts finally stilled and he was able to join his wife in sleep.

Testimony of Queen Henrietta Maria, Wife of Charles Stuart

Have I not asked for and do I not welcome this chance to speak of my darling husband? In truth, I do.

I first saw this handsome, shy, very young man when he and that arrogant posing individual, Villiers, stopped in Paris on their way through to Spain. They were on some adventure or other, just the two of them – supposedly – if you ignore the retinue of guards and servants who were with them. Villiers seemed to have brought half his household along and I recall we found it difficult to accommodate them all. Charles paid court to me and I was flattered for I thought he was someone I could like very much. It was a great disappointment to realise that his heart and mind were set on the Infanta, I did not think I could be better than her and it was with a heavy heart I bid them farewell when they moved on.

Imagine then how pleased I was when negotiations began for me to become his wife, the whole situation with Spain having gone wrong somewhere. I didn't ask, it didn't matter, I was to be married to the king of England and that was good enough for me.

Did I love him? You seek the truth from me? Ah yes, I see that the truth is what is in this book about my husband and that is what you will receive from me.

Did I love him? Not at first. How could I? I was but a young maiden when I was packed off to England, when the negotiations were finally completed and oh! did I not think they never would be done with their arguing and their discussing? I was nervous and slightly seasick and very homesick before we got half way across the Channel. When we reached the shore and I saw the guard waiting, saw the stage set up with its drapes, saw this slender serious man stood there and thought "Holy Father, this is my husband and he is a stranger to me!" I wanted to turn and run back onto the ship and demand the captain set sail for France immediately. I couldn't. If nothing else I was a royal Princess and knew my place and my duty.

Charles got off the stage and came to meet me and that small act of kindness was enough to destroy my self-control. I babbled a load of nonsense and burst into tears, feeling the most dreadful humiliation and shame that I had given way like that. But it didn't seem to matter, he was tenderness itself, such a perfect gentleman, guiding me to where we needed to go, what we needed to do, speaking with my entourage in good fluent French to make them feel comfortable. I began to see that there were good qualities to this new husband and I vowed to be a good wife as far as I could, while I learned all his ways, his needs and his personality.

I liked his shy smile, his soft voice, his eyes which were full of emotions I would have to learn to understand if I was to be that good wife I had vowed to be. I wondered at his body, was he strong, would he be ill, would I need to have doctors around him ... I cannot tell you now how many foolish thoughts went through my head. I was in England, I was a Queen, I was married to this man who, although he seemed very nice, was a stranger and I was expected to live the remainder of my life with him however long that might be. Oh the thoughts! Oh the nightmare of that first day, when everything was strange, the food, the strong wines, the coarse laughs of the men he said were his knights. They seemed rough and uncouth, the language harsh to my ears. He introduced them to me but their names meant nothing. I could not absorb the names and match them to the faces.

But I was aware of the brooding presence of that Villiers person. He I knew I hated with a deadly hatred for when he looked at my husband he looked at him as if he were his possession. No, I wanted to shout, he is mine!

I did not like England. I did not like the English court. No one spoke a language I could understand, their English was hurried and came with dialects and I could not understand them. What is a young person to do in those circumstances but speak French and talk only with my own people?

You see, my husband, the king, was busy with so many things, government, papers, meetings with this one and that, discussions on this point and that, he had little time for a wife who did not understand what was going on. All the time that Villiers was prowling, I have no other word for it, doing his best to make sure the king did what he wanted which was not always what I wanted. I was not able to fight him; he was too influential and too powerful for me. So I retreated into my own world and there was the problem.

Confrontation had to follow, one day, as sure as the night comes down at the end of the day.

And I saw the other side of my otherwise caring, gentle husband.

Chapter Seven

It was idyllic. For a day or so. They walked together through the court, they ate together, they sat together to listen to the minstrels of an evening, she laughed at the jokes of some of the courtiers and he accepted, just, the fluttering attentions of her ladies. How else could he describe the constant sound of silken skirts, of fans, of high-pitched girlish laughter, no, forsooth, giggles! Of the questions to Henrietta Maria in lisping French, not the clear accent-less French he had been taught but a rasping, lisping almost unintelligible language from which he perhaps understood one word in five. It was inevitable that he would feel excluded. He knew full well in his own heart that the language they spoke was the natural one of all native born French peoples and that, being English, he had been taught a purer more stylised version but – knowing this and accepting this were two very different things. He had found something in himself he hardly recognised, an intense and possessive jealousy. Oh he knew well that he was jealous of Villiers when he came, he knew that ... but that was different, that was –

Now he asked himself, was it different? Could he not be truly honest with himself in these dark hours when the moon had surrendered itself to the embrace of the darkness and taken its presence from the night sky, when the stars had hidden their faces from the earth as if not to view that which is to come? And was he being foolish in the extreme with fanciful poetic thoughts that were as far from him as the moon itself, however far that might be.

He needed to be honest. It was too late for anything but honesty, truth and clarity in all things. He knew his heart and mind contained a streak of savage jealousy that surprised and shocked him when it was revealed. He

92

was jealous of the French people around his new wife for they interfered with his court, his queen and his way of life. It sounded so petty now, so very petty, considering all that had gone on since. And all his fault, all his fault!

He despaired of sorting his thoughts this night. He despaired of making sense of his feelings after all this time, but thought he would continue his 'story', his journey through his life. Whatever provoked me to start this, he wondered? What came from outside to persuade this king to walk the path of his life? He was almost wishing he had not begun but having begun, he found himself so caught up in the memories he was unable to desist or even to resist. He could not summon someone to help him to his bed, to draw the curtains, extinguish the candle and leave him to darkness. He decided he would prefer to sit there by the fire, to watch the logs drop into ash, to see the ash build in the hearth as his memories built in his heart and mind. He felt as if he would collapse under the weight of the memories if he continued thus, but he had to! He was driven to walking the pathway of memories, no matter what!

Then, proceed, oh foolish king, foolish man, stupid man, fit only to take the place of your Fool after all. Proceed.

Charles looked around, wondering where the voice had come from. No one had entered the room, nothing had disturbed him but his own memories. Was that his voice of conscience? If so, it had been quiet for a long time in the silence of his soul. Where had it been all these years, when he was arguing with Villiers, with Henrietta Maria, with Parliament, with – just about everyone who walked the earth, or so it seemed. A slight exaggeration, he thought, but it's the way I feel. Well, the Lord God knows I have been arguing these past few days with a lot of people who had no intention of listening to me.

But enough, enough! He stirred in his chair, as if irritated by his own thoughts, the intrusion of the censoring hectoring thought which brought him back to his memories when he had hoped to move away from them and grant himself a little peace.

He found himself thoroughly irritated by Henrietta Maria's entourage of French ladies, priest and servants. He felt as if he was walking into them everywhere at Court. He found they were endlessly interfering in the preparation of food, trying to arrange for his new Queen to eat what she had at home, rather than what she should eat in her new home. He found them endlessly at their Popish prayers, with Henrietta Maria attending Mass and confession and following the calendar of the Roman church, with no effort being made at all to accommodate her husband's stated wish that she make a commitment to the Church of England.

It seemed to him that his Queen had been lifted bodily from her own Court and placed into his without so much as a token of interest being shown toward anything to do with England. The English courtiers quarrelled with the French attendants, the French physician tried to argue with the English one he had appointed for her and the whole atmosphere of Court became fraught with tension and underlying aggression.

This was not what he had visualised when the proposal had been made; he had imagined a compliant queen consort sharing his daily life, learning to speak English and helping with his day to day decision making, worshipping alongside him, taking some of the burdens from his slender shoulders. It wasn't happening and he didn't like it.

He tried reasoning with her, but her answer was that she felt lonely and homesick and did not like the English way of doing things.

There was an additional problem, one he felt he could not share with his wife, or with Villiers, for both would have been mortally offended if he had; some of the entourage were obviously homosexual and after his experiences with his father's Court, this grated on him and he wanted to dismiss them from his sight, from his home, from his life, just as he had with all the others. But his life now included Henrietta Maria and they were with Henrietta Maria's entourage…

As if to deliberately complicate life, Villiers, having brokered the marriage in the first place, seemed determined to destroy it. Charles could see his subtle hand in the disputes and knew, only too well, that his friend and confidante was both jealous and power hungry, a dangerous combination. And yet … and yet as always, he found himself incapable of dismissing him, of sending him out of Court and away from all the politicking he was doing. Charles knew Villiers was wrong, knew it in his deepest heart but he also knew he was incapable of sending him away. It would have been like sending part of himself away and he could not do it.

He resorted to prayer.

That sounded heretical. Anyone overhearing his thoughts would be entitled to have said, 'Your Majesty, you an upholder of the fine tradition of the English church admit you resorted to prayer?'

The response would have been: 'But you see … oh I must make you see … a king needs to be of a certain mind set. A king needs to be determined, to make up his own mind, to be decisive and firm, and I was not. I resorted to prayer.'

Sometimes worries overtook the mind to the point when there was no room for logical, sane thought. No room for quiet consideration of how to deal with matters when there was so much crowding in demanding attention. Sometimes there seemed no clear way forward. The decision to resort to prayer came as a shining light into the dark murky depths of the confusion.

It went further than that. He was on his knees before the altar in his private chapel, where he beseeched the Lord God to give him strength to do that which he had to do, work at making his marriage come back into being, curb or control Villiers in some way, not allow the Catholic element to take over the Court but to bring them all into the light and faith of the Church of England. His head hurt so much that it felt as if his brain was trying to burst out of its bony shell. He knew his sanity was at stake, knew he had to make a stand in all these things, as only a King could do. As only a King should do.

And there, in the privacy of his chapel, he said, "But I do not wish to be king." He said it so softly that only the candles and the wall paintings heard him. "I do not wish to be king. I do not wish to hold this great office, to make these decisions. I want no more than to revert to being the second son, the loving, loyal, devoted second son. Here I am, fatherless, motherless, brotherless, a married man with a wife who does not want to take on the ways of her husband's court, but to retain that which she knows and cares about, the French Court and its ways, to remain within the Popish church, to speak French at all times…"

Then it was as if a voice spoke to him, clearly, precisely. 'Send the French home. Reclaim your wife.' Charles looked round but he was alone with just the heavy smell of the guttering candles on the altar. The paintings had not moved; the only movement was the flames as an errant draught found them.

'Send the French home. Reclaim your wife.'

The words made perfect sense. It was not the answer to Villiers' ever-increasing influence but it was a start. He got up and felt a new confidence surge through him. It was as if the shining light that had directed him to go and pray had lit up his mind and cast out all doubts. He looked at the altar and the guttering candles. At the right moment, he decided, he would dismiss the French from his Court. 'Why at the right moment?' he asked himself. 'Why do I not go and dismiss them right now?'

'Because...' That seed of self-doubt was back, the one that said 'I must not upset Henrietta Maria.'

But whoever spoke to him knew that there would be a crisis. Whether it was the Lord God or one of His ministering angels, he did not know, but he did know they had foreseen a crisis. I will do it, he told himself. I will!

For all that, he spent much of the night in his own bedroom, staring at the hangings around his bed, practicing his words, his speech to Henrietta Maria, laying out all the reasons why her entourage had to go. He could see in his mind her acquiescence to her husband's will, see her sad face, knowing she would be upset, but determined to go ahead anyway. She would understand – in time. Then his determination would falter and he would begin to sweat, wondering if he could go through with it, or whether he would spend the rest of his marriage - and his life – in thrall to the French and the Catholic influence in his court. This he could not tolerate, he knew that.

The events the very next day hardened his decision – and his heart. Henrietta Maria did not so much ask as inform him she wanted to appoint French courtiers as her household officers.

His reaction should have been anticipated by his wife, had she been less concerned with her entourage and more concerned with his dislike of all things French taking over the court. Unfortunately she hadn't taken any of that into account, she had been wrapped in a French world: religion, language, courtiers and servants and Charles knew, but did not fully accept at that moment, that she had managed to overlook the small fact that her husband, the king of England, disliked what she and they were doing.

In hindsight he realised that in part this was her youth, her immaturity and in part her great homesickness. It must have been extremely hard for her to accept a new way of life, a new way of worship and a language she was uncomfortable with. How much easier to slip into speaking French with those around her, to worship in a Catholic chapel, to follow the path she had always walked.

In turn he knew he should have considered the homesickness of the young girl he had taken as his wife, given consideration to her need for familiar things, language and friends around her, but he only heard Villiers' jibes and knew he was tired of the French taking over.

The result was inevitable. It was said, albeit in jest, that his explosion was heard as far away as the boundaries of the City.

He exploded. He declared that as she was his wife, as she lived in his court, in his country she would do things as he wished, not as she wished.

Henrietta Maria had an easily roused temper of her own. He didn't know that at the time, they were too newly married to discover such basic things in each other's character. If they had, they would have been more careful.

The resulting row was heard by most of the court and all of the household. It was conveyed by gossip through the town and brought great amusement to Villiers. He goaded Charles with sly comments that he was allowing a 'slip of a wife' to dominate him. He had not heard all the row or he would have known that Charles gave back as good as he got but he knew that in the end, he had his own way. After all, was he not King?

In return for the jibe, he ordered Villiers to remove all the French from the court immediately. Even in the giving of the order Charles felt good, clean, strong, determined. Everything he had always thought he should be and could be but knew deep inside he wasn't.

Henrietta Maria changed from ranting and raving to wailing and entreating but he held the vision of stumbling over fluttering ladies and men, of priests chanting their strange words, of the scent of incense and the click of beads. He dismissed them all from the court. Eventually, after tears, discussions and more heated words, a few retainers were allowed to stay but the others were sent back to France.

For the first time in what felt like eternity, there was an element of peace. Charles had experienced little of that since his father's demise and even less after his wife arrived. It was good to feel a sense of calm as he moved about the court, even if it was of short duration.

Chapter Eight

It didn't last. He was acutely aware that it took Henrietta Maria some time to learn to live without her friends and associates, time in which she often found a quiet corner in which to weep with bitter loneliness and heartsick despair, but she would dry her tears and mutter a few prayers before going on her way. Everything she did was reported back to Charles by his servants. He was troubled by her tears but hoped that in time she would be reconciled to the English way of doing things. There was much to do, much to prepare for. As Queen she was expected to be ever present, ever regal and to watch every word she uttered, for fear of someone pouncing on a mistake and spreading it around court. He had grown up with the need to watch every word, every expression, but Henrietta Maria had lived a freer life in the French court. It was hard for her to control her emotions to that degree. He knew that she also carried great hurts. The violent argument she had engaged in with her husband had been broadcast to all and sundry and it had upset them both, deeply. There was no privacy, no sense of decorum from those whose task it was to care for the royal couple. She was still very young, very determined, headstrong and inclined to sulk. Her hatred of Villiers was obvious to all. To her his morals were despicable; his hatred of her, combined with jealousy, was guaranteed to feed her feelings. As long as Charles continued to champion him, listen to him and have him around as friend and companion, it continued to upset Henrietta Maria and so the course appeared to be set for the relationship between King and Queen to be destroyed.

It was what Villiers sought, above all else, it seemed. Charles knew full well that the relationship he had with his friend had been soured by the very marriage which that same friend had brokered: the dichotomy amused him in an ironical way, when he gave himself time to dwell on it. He might be indecisive, he thought, but he knew the human heart and knew Villiers' extreme jealousy and need for power. He recognised it as a part of his friend's persona, an integral part, there would be no changing Villiers, no matter what anyone said or did.

So Charles listened to one and listened to the other, trying to decide who was right, who held the wisdom in their words not touched by hatred and jealousy. That was difficult: they were both guilty of the same emotions. Villiers had always been there, had been James's favourite and now Charles', it was to Villiers he looked for counsel and he watched, helplessly, as Henrietta Maria grew even more distant and full of hatred for the magnificent, handsome but totally - in her eyes - despicable man.

The redness of the embers was dying away, covered in the deep layer of ash the log had deposited on it, slowly stifling it. Charles stared at the hearth, easing the stiffness of his legs where he had sat too long with them stretched out in front of him without moving, and saw in the smothering of the embers an analogy for the way he felt his marriage was going at that time. He had been beset with problems of all kinds, Henrietta Maria's sorrowing looks, Villiers' constant scowl and snarling voice as he complained of the Queen's activities, of his secretaries and advisors demanding he make a decision on this or that. His days began with problems and ended with crises. In between he suffered raging headaches, stomach upsets, pains around his heart which worried him and over it all, a continuing sense of inadequacy. He felt he could not reach out to anyone for advice, everyone seemed to be pulling on him in some way or another. All he wanted to do was find a quiet corner and stay there – preferably for the rest of his life.

England was at war with France, as well as Spain.

He recalled, how he recalled! Was it not engraved on the sinews of his very heart? Contemplating the darkness behind his eyelids, overshadowed by the darkness of the drapes around the bed. Such nights were a vivid memory for they happened so often and the feelings he had were so intense he remembered them as if it were last night. He recalled how he laid awake, the nights he shared his wife's bed, listening to her soft breathing, reminding him of the woman he had yet to possess, wondering where it all went so badly wrong. It was nights like these which made him have his own separate household, where he could be relatively free of the clinging wife and her needs, where he could talk to Villiers and others without her hatred interfering. And where he could sleep – when he did – at night without being aware of another person in his bed. But he also knew, for the sake of his marriage, the need for an heir for the throne and the way it would look to the outside world, that he had to share a bed with her from time to time. No one need ever know they had never been one as man and wife. He was not about to tell anyone, nor was the Queen.

He was back to the same endless tumbling thoughts. How could they be at war with the two countries who were once allies? Who were the Huguenots in the great scheme of things that he could - and had - committed English soldiers to their cause? By day he was the king, all-powerful, all decisive, all knowing. By night he was Baby Charles once more, indecisive, lost, clinging to the driftwood of memories to carry him through. And repeating endlessly, if only… if only…

If only Henry had not died, if only Father had lived a little longer, if only Henrietta Maria had been older, wiser, more commanding, if only I could stand up to Villiers' machinations…

And there, in the darkness, did he not admit to Villiers' machinations? And did he not decide to do something about it and did he not, come day and a new set of decisions to be made, allow the night one to go quietly back from whence it came? He did, he could not deny it. He did, day after day and night after endless night.

Lack of sleep made him irritable; night demons chased him through the day. He spent time at prayer and found no solace. One day was particularly bad. He had not slept at all, or so his weary eyes told him, and his limbs ached as if he had the ague. "Was ever a king so beleaguered by devils and demons?" he demanded of the wall paintings in the chapel, there being no one there, no living person there, to talk to him. The paintings had no answer. He confessed to himself he would have been surprised if they had. An answer, such as he had over the French invasion of his court, came but once in a lifetime, or so he thought.

Enraged with himself and with life, he stormed out of his chapel, to find a group of courtiers and his secretary outside the door.

"Your Majesty, would you-"

"Your Majesty, could I entreat you to-"

"Your Majesty, your visitor-"

He pushed past them all, knowing he was stone faced, and remained silent. They fell back in the wake of his obvious anger. Villiers approached and was ignored. It was a moment of quiet triumph, to see his face as his monarch cut him dead. He knew there would be many courtiers who would have seen, have gloated over this seemingly small act and would read into it more than was there. Enough: it would give them something to talk about, as if they had not enough to talk about already, in dissecting each other's character, reputation and standing in society.

The gardens were a refuge, a sanctuary from pressure. Plants did not require courtiers to support them, did not need new laws to make them grow. They lived and died according to their own natural laws. Walking through the grounds, looking at the silent beauty of each type of flower, he could find that elusive calm. For a time even the wars with France and Spain - and the problem of financing them – had receded to the back of his mind. Gardens had become his passion, his great joy, dating from the time that he had been in Spain and seen the glory that plants could create in an enclosed space. He had arranged for gardeners to work in each of his homes, providing the glory that he wanted. Walking among the flowers, shrubs, and strong growing trees, he was often able to find that element of peace that he sought.

He knew Villiers had superb gardens because he employed an outstanding gardener – one of the Tradescant family - and he envied those gardens. His were good but not as good. That would not do. Why should a mere duke have a better gardens and gardener than his King?

As he walked the narrow paths between the flowerbeds, hardly seeing the plants for the fury in his mind, he noticed what looked like a flower coming toward him. It was Henrietta Maria in a gown of the palest of blue silk edged in silver and embroidered with seed pearls. By a miracle, no one was with her. It only occurred to Charles later that she had contrived it to be so, that she had banned her ladies from walking with her, for usually she was not alone. Her narrow tiny feet, encased in satin slippers, seemed to glide over the gravel, making no sound at all. She approached him, fragile as a vanishing dream, and rested a slender white hand on his arm. He had never known her make the first approach. It surprised and pleased him muchly. He felt his anger go out through his boots into the gravel, where it belonged.

"Husband. Come, we will take food together and talk."

The quietness of her voice, the sure way she spoke, the calm she radiated reached him in a way no one had for many years. Blinking back tears he hoped no one else would see, he put his hand over hers and together they walked back into the hall. Henrietta Maria had arranged for wine, for food, and most important of all, for time when they could sit quietly together and talk with no one, not even the most lowly servant, within earshot of their conversation.

In truth, little was said. It was enough for his wounded heart and mind that his wife had made the effort to dispense with her ever-present retinue to come and find him, to arrange a time of peace for them both. They made small talk, they smiled a lot, they looked into each other's eyes and both saw the dawning of a new relationship, albeit only a spark, but sparks could be fanned into flames, given the right encouragement. He wished the time could last. He remembered thinking suddenly, he wished this could last, no more interference, no more troublesome Parliaments to thwart his desires, no more difficulties with treaties and wars, and no more difficulties at home. He wished for a happy marriage, for a family, for joy to come into their lives. He could wish but he knew at times he would wish in vain. The Lord God will give that which is in His power which He knows is right for us, His humble subjects, he thought. If it is His wish this king should suffer the trials and tribulations of kingship, then it has to be. It would seem that was His will, why else would his brother be taken at such a young age and his father not allowed to reach his dotage? But for the moment, he could pray to Him for a time of peace. He will surely grant that.

It seemed the prayer was answered - for a while. Villiers kept his distance, but not for that long and certainly not long enough. Soon he was busy whispering in Charles' ear and yet again the uncertainty of direction was there, disrupting his peace of mind. Henrietta Maria tried to counter Villiers' influence but she was a mere girl compared with Villiers' wide experience in the ways of converting his monarch to his way of thinking. The tiny spark that needed encouragement was quietly doused.

Charles stared at the fire, thinking, I see it now. Why, in God's name, did I not see it then?

Testimony of George Villiers, Duke of Buckingham continued

Well, it seemed I made a mistake in promoting the marriage to the French Princess as a Good Idea. I rarely make mistakes, this one rankled with me. I did not think the wench would take such a violent dislike to me, would work against me. There were the two of us competing for little Charles' attention and both failing, for a while, until I overcame the silly woman and pushed her into the background. I had a very good idea that doing so would throw her into the arms of the Frenchies with which she surrounded herself and that would annoy Charles so much he would have to do something. I half hoped it would be to send her home but realised that would not happen, you did not dispose of a queen that easily. Not since the days of the great Tudor had anyone thought of deposing a queen because of – well, not very much, really. Charles had no reason to get rid of her, so he did the other thing instead: he got rid of her hangers on. Oh did we not endure weeks of weeping and wailing and gnashing of teeth! But did we not experience a period of relative calm because of it? The queen began to anglicise herself – not before time, many said, myself included. Me, I was back in full favour once more, where I belonged. And there I stayed, keeping her well in the background and disrupting any hint of a husband and wife relationship developing. One thing I knew and was pleased about, they had not laid together. She was virgin and as far as I knew, so was he – insofar as women were concerned. You still seek the truth? It isn't pleasant but when is truth pleasant? Lies are so much more acceptable to keep the day to day relationships running smoothly, are they not? Especially when one is a consummate and expert liar. But no, these testimonies you demand of me are the truth. So I will give it, raw and unvarnished and without the taint of a lie.

He found his release with the boys who served him and the animals which were kept at the various homes.

I desired him more than ever as he grew into his role as king and took it out on those I courted, night after night after night. I was fortunate; I had enough money to pay them off if I went too far.

When we went to Oxford, I had a whole new hunting ground for partners. I had a good time. Charles didn't. Was that my fault?

Ah but I was in favour enough to be on his side when he dissolved Parliament because they wanted to bring charges against me. Me! The person who was practically running the country, did they but know it, for the person they called king was at times nothing more than a mere puppet in the hands of those who knew how to manipulate him. Which I did. God knows I had enough practice – first his father and then the son. Whispers in the ear, notes passed during meetings, a simple 'why don't we...' and they did just what I wanted, both of them. Like father, like son. Ah, but it was so simple. Life looked set to be good –

Then I met the maniac with the knife.

What can I say? A life set to be good ended in a moment of someone else's madness. I swear to you my last thought was - I never did get my hands on that body which I desired so much.

Chapter Nine

Was ever a king so plagued with his Parliaments, he thought? Come to that, was ever a king so plagued with his advisers? "I do swear," he muttered to his secretary, "I would do better without Parliament. Would that I could dismiss them all and rule alone." The secretary knew better than to comment, to remind His Majesty that it was not a very good idea, that the people, especially the members of the parliament, would not like it very much. He knew that full well but in moments of exasperation it was the only thing he wanted to say, to demand, almost.

"Sire, the parliament has moved itself to Oxford," the beleaguered secretary said quietly, knowing this too would produce an outburst. "They wish to avoid the plague, Your Majesty, as you yourself should consider, and Her Majesty too."

"Stop lecturing!" Charles waved at the papers on the desk. "Sort these out, tell me what they are, tell me what to sign, then tell me when I can get to Oxford. We need money, damn it, money to fight the French and the Spanish and I will have it, one way or another!"

"Why, Charles, I didn't know you cared so much for our cause!" Villiers had strolled into the chamber without knocking, indolent, self-satisfied, confident in his standing with his king not to have to obey the normal rules of etiquette.

The sarcasm was not lost on Charles. He glowered at his friend and scratched a signature on the papers as the secretary indicated the contents of each one. "We have to go to Oxford to get our money. We didn't get very far here and then the cowards turn and run!"

"Because of the plague, dear boy, the plague, that illness that is out there – among the common people." A wave of an elegant languid hand, the beginnings of a knowing smile. "Oxford will be good for us, new faces, apart from the damned Parliament, of course, new places to hunt, new loves to conquer."

"For some, maybe, but others remain loyal and faithful, I might remind you."

"Oh, as usual you will take the petite Henrietta Maria with you, to cramp your style. I am glad I have no need of such womanly attentions."

No, Charles thought, more be the pity, for then you might be a more generous and forgiving person, George Villiers!

The court went to Oxford.

It was a whirlwind time of worry and work. They had to pack their wardrobe - and for Villiers that meant a packhorse for each day, or so it seemed - they had to summon an armed guard, they had to make arrangements for provisions and places to rest along the way. It was as much a royal progress as a journey to see and speak with his own parliament and he resented it. Every part of it, from issuing the orders through the journey to the confrontation itself. He resented it and hated it and longed for it to be over. He wanted to be in London, despite the risk of plague – and the risk was real enough. He did not want to talk with those members whose sole object, it seemed, was to deny him the money he needed.

Now he sat there, alone, looking into the dying embers of the fire and saw beneath the burning log the ashes of the relationship he had with those members. He did not see then that he had antagonised them so much they had no time for him. He did not see then that they resented Villiers so much that to have him there meant disaster for any words that came out of his mouth. He could see it now, too late, too little, too late!

They refused his demands for the tonnage and poundage. He was furious but all the pounding at them made no difference. The wars were unpopular, the finances obviously tight. He was given two small subsidies that went precisely nowhere, a mere drop in the ocean of his needs to continue the war. He was given a hostile reception and there was talk of impeaching Villiers. Vague rumours, mere straws in the wind but oh he knew they were there, as he did everything which was connected with or concerned that man. Villiers was like a succubus, that evil demon that lies beneath a man and draws of the man's energy. And yes, he knew full well that a succubus was said to be a female demon. He knew it full well, as much as he knew his friend's sexual inclinations, which is why he chose the word. He was not there, he would never be there again, but Charles was aware of his shade at times. How it haunted his days and nights! He was afraid he would never be free of the memory or the presence of George Villiers, 1st duke of Buckingham.

'God grant me relief from his memory for a time, I beseech you!' It was as if the cry was torn from his lips with all the agony with which he had earlier said 'I do not wish to die!' It said much about the depths of his feelings for George Villiers. Even though many years had passed since Villiers had assassinated, the memories associated with the glamorous, flamboyant, devious yet intensely loving man were as fresh as the time when he was killed. There were many in the court who had known and loved Villiers, who had been intimately involved with him, people who seemed to have been able to set his memory either to one side or to the back of their minds. His name was never mentioned after his death in Charles's presence. Charles himself was incapable of doing that. Villiers had come into his life at a time when he was extremely impressionable and so had made an extremely deep impact on him. Even though Charles had turned to Henrietta Maria after Villiers' death, even though the marriage had then become strong, there had been and still remained a small part of his mind that mourned the loss of someone he considered to be his greatest friend. The question, which was never asked or answered, was: did Villiers feel the same about Charles? Or was it purely a ploy on his part to stay in the good books of his monarch? If he had not been assassinated, would he have stood back and allowed Henrietta Maria to be the Queen consort Charles wanted her to be? Some things could not be answered. And, at this late stage of his life, it really didn't matter.

Charles dissolved Parliament that August of 1625. No one would impeach his advisor. If anyone had to send him away, it would be the king himself. And the king had no intention of doing that. Villiers well knew it. He knew it as well as he knew Charles' name. Had he not spent years cultivating the art of manipulation, first with the father and then with the son? And did he not do it so passing well that neither of them could throw off his yoke of surreptitious machinations? Charles had taken many long years to see through the smoke screen Villiers had thrown up to disguise his real motives for all he had done. Now he could see it clearly, at a time when it was too late to make use of the knowledge. Would that he had seen it at the time!

Parliament was recalled in February of the following year. It seemed a lifetime ago now and how many lives had been lost in the meantime? That was something that ate at his conscience endlessly. He thought if he removed those agitators who spoke the loudest that parliament would accede to his will. He did - and they didn't.

A smile crossed Charles' face. He was recalling the time when he went to Parliament, wearing his finest outfit. He appeared kingly in stature at that point for his shoes had been specially made to make him look taller, that he might look the average man in the eye. This was important to him. Being so much shorter than others added to his lack of self-confidence. He stood in the great Hall, addressing an unwieldy mob of members, as he saw it, wondering why and how these people had become representatives of their constituents. They seemed to have their own reasons for being there, not all of which were entirely honest, at least in his opinion. The atmosphere was one of deep suspicion, there was a good deal of shuffling and shifting of feet, which was somewhat distracting. Charles did his best to ignore it, knowing that he had to appear at least confident in what he had to say. When at last they quietened, he began to speak.

From the chair in which he sat, staring into the darkness of the hearth, he recalled his speech, in such detail that it surprised him. He had not realised he was able to remember it at all, but then it had been for him a momentous occasion which probably had a great deal to do with the way it had impressed itself on his mind.

He reminded them of the time the parliament had persuaded his father and himself to break off the treaties which were in place. He said to them that they had everything their own way, according to their own wishes, and just when he felt that he could not retreat from anything which he had set in motion, they began to change the parameters of the situation. He declared to them that it was not a Parliamentary way to do things nor was it a way to treat a King. As Master Coke had told them, it was better to die by a foreign enemy than to be destroyed at home. He declared that it would be better more honourable for a King to be invaded and almost destroyed by foreign enemy had to be despised by his own subjects. There was a veiled threat in the statement that Parliaments were in the power of the King, as far as their calling, sitting and dissolution was concerned. What he had tried to say was, that if the parliament could agree with him, they would be allowed to continue, but if they did not, they would be dissolved.

The atmosphere in the parliament turned icy. Blank faces vied with unfriendly looks but not a word was spoken. Had there been words uttered, he would have been able to refute them, but he could not argue with silence. In the end he had to leave. It was, in every way, the beginning of the end of his relationship with parliament.

He walked out of the hall, his back straight, his head held high, and went back to St James' Palace. There in the solitude of his room, he threw cushions and kicked furniture and worked to dissipate the anger he had been experiencing. It would have been too dangerous carry that anger into a decision making time. That had to be done in the calm and peace which only came when the anger had gone away.

He dissolved that parliament in August 1626. It was becoming a habit. He felt good about it, wrongly, of course, but at the time – oh, at the time it was the only way he could see out of a predicament.

Ask me now, ask me this night, he thought, what I should have done and I will say: I should have listened to others, not to Villiers. I should have taken notice of the balance of power that was there for the seeing, but I was blind. Ask me now why I leaned toward someone described as a parvenu, ask me and I have no answer for you as I have had no answer for the first part of this walk through my memories. Have I not said, in complete honesty, I have no idea why he had such a hold on me? Did I inherit it from my father, a weakness, a need for a stronger, more devious mind, to take a hold of mine?

Ask me now why I called that last parliament in March 1628 and I will say it was my last chance, my last attempt to mend the bad relationship we had fallen into – and it failed. Dismally. They did not like anything I had done, forced billeting of troops, what was I supposed to do with them? And so much else they did not like. I cannot tell you how it felt –

It was a time for honesty and for heartfelt declarations of what it was really like. No pretence. He knew full well what it was like, how it felt, how it angered, how it hurt, how it bemused and bothered and how they blustered and demanded and forced him into agreeing to a Petition of Right.

What hurt most of all was the fact they felt they could not trust his word any more. And the truth was; he did not blame them for that. Not for a single moment.

But he could not tell them so, he could not admit this, for to lose face before the parliamentary members would have been disastrous for them all. So, when they began to attack Villiers yet again, parliament was prorogued. End of session. End of problems. End of arguments. He did not know that the end of all he held to be dear at that time was to come. If he had, would he have acted differently? Ah, would that anyone could see that which is to come! Would people not live their lives differently? But then, would that not be the easy option? Does the Lord God Himself not ask that his people live their lives according to His laws so that they do not have to reproach themselves with such things?

All the difficulties were traced to Villiers. And in August of that year, Villiers was dead. It was said a disturbed naval officer stabbed him with a table knife. Of all things, Villiers would have hated that, for he so admired and needed everything of good quality around him all the time. A table knife, a cheap thing, was a bad way for him to die.

Charles knew he was being a little facetious in thinking that, no way was a good way to die but he found a sense of irony in the fact that Villiers had been struck down in such a fashion. And in truth, he harboured a hatred for Portsmouth ever after, whilst knowing it was not their fault they had a malcontent and disturbed person in their midst. How would they have known? But men do these foolish things, cling to that which is irrational, it is part of the process of grief. And Charles did so mourn the loss of his friend. All that brightness, that vivacity, that flamboyant beauty and arrogance, gone in a moment of insanity. George Villiers, duke of Buckingham, was no more.

All these years later, that fact still brought a smarting to the back of the eyes, as if tears would flood once again for the relationship which he both loved and hated at the same time.

Testimony of Jeffrey Hudson, Fool to Queen Henrietta Maria and favourite of King Charles.

From the moment I leapt from the – thankfully cold – piecrust into the life of Queen Henrietta Maria, my fortune was made. I did well enough before that, but to get into the royal court was something I had not dreamed of but was very pleased to be there.

The first thing I realised was that the Queen was not happy. I might have been tiny but God gave me a brain and a mind and a sense of observation a full grown person might have. A Fool needs all those things to survive in a world where Fools are a-plenty and you have to work hard to keep your position. The Queen liked me, a lot, I was a novelty but I was also a companion to her, we could and did talk on many things. But she was a very unhappy woman. She talked to me as if I was a woman, talked to me of things only a woman needed to talk of. She asked me once why the king did not lie with her, did he not want children? I said I would find out. Now that was a big promise to make – not that I used the word 'promise' to Her Majesty, you understand, but if I said to her 'I will find out' it was treated as a promise and I had to find out.

I went to the physician first. I could talk to him; he was a sharply spoken man who said what you needed to know and no more. When I went to him, I said, straight out, because that is the way he preferred it, 'is there a reason the King does not lie with the Queen? She wishes for children.'

He thought for a moment, the eyes went dark and the brow furrowed as if it would never again be clear and straight, as if the furrows were carved into the skin. I wondered if he would answer me.

'Does the Queen know you are speaking with me?'

'No. I said only I would find out. I said no more than that.'

'Then tell her this, which is the truth. He has a condition which I am working to clear at the moment. When it is clear, he will lie with her. He does not wish to infect her. I leave it to you to phrase it as best you can.'

Whilst I had no idea what the condition was, it seemed logical to me that the King would refrain from touching his wife if there was fear of infection but I did not understand why he did not tell her himself. There seemed to be a deep chasm between them that had not been overcome. I suspected the root cause was His Grace the duke of Buckingham, a man I distrusted. He was always good to me, throwing me a coin or two and asking if all was well with Her Majesty. I had no complaints, just a feeling and they were rarely wrong. A Fool learns early on to live on his wits and so I had developed the art of reading between words to see what someone really meant. I did not think the duke of Buckingham truly had the Queen's interests at heart – but I did.

I told the Queen there was a small medical problem with her husband and when it was better, he would lie with her. I saw her face light up as if I had given her the biggest present in the world. From then on she was even more devoted and loving to the King, when he was with her. Ah, would that he would have been with her more!

I did notice that after I told her, she was with him so much, she was at his elbow more than not, she handed him things and at times he did not know she was there, thought only it was a squire or a scribe or a page or even little Jeffrey who had given him whatever it was he sought. But then he would turn and look and a smile would reach his eyes, those dark, dark eyes that held so much mystery and yet could flash with anger in a moment. The King had more faces than anyone really knew. He was cold, he was the King, he was loving with those he cared about, including the duke, he was – should I say this? Ah, I know others have asked the question, how much do we say and how much do we conceal? There is now no need for silence, the man's body was separated from his head – I wonder why I said it that way round?- and he can no longer speak. We are doing it for him so that the world understands something more of that slender, handsome, difficult man who became our king and who was brought down by those who could not accept the Divine Right of Kings. I say no more on that subject. I do say, though, that his 'loving' face was for there for many a young person in the court. And not a one ever said no.

Then we had the news that someone had done the duke to death. I could not, for a moment, say I was sorry.

Chapter Ten

"Buckingham is dead."

Charles sat at the table, holding a cup of wine, wondering whether he should drink it to add to the wine already consumed, trying to decide if it would dull the pain of losing his advisor, his friend, his comforter, his mainstay, his own personal demon. Why did it hurt so much to lose the demon who had plagued his life for so many years? Because it had been removed by one assassin's knife? Yes, in that lay the truth, the bare cold stone of truth. No kernel of truth here, but a stone, a cold hard stone. Buckingham was dead. He was dead and not by Charles' doing, not by his sending him away, not by his decision. Once again someone took the decision for him. Would he have ever sent Villiers away? His logical mind said yes, his heart said no. Would that he could be strong! Would that he had gathered his nerve together and told Villiers to desist from the foolish wars, to stop seeking glory, did he not have enough power, enough influence, enough wealth to satisfy any man? It would seem not, for he wanted the fight, he wanted the glory, he wanted –

In God's great Name, what did he want? To rule England without the authority of the crown, so that he could duck out of anything which went wrong?

The next question was, what did Charles do now that Villiers had gone? Who did he turn to, who did he consult, who did he seek counsel from?

"I know he is dead, Charles." The calm words came from the little person by his side, the one who seemed to be his shadow, the one who was there each time he turned around, the one with a word, a look, a smile, a cup of wine, a presence that was rapidly growing on him.

"I say it to believe it."

"Believe it," she said in response, taking his hand and gently running her fingers over the veins. "See here, see how you have life in this flesh, how your breath still comes, how your voice is still here with me. His flesh is stilled, along with his voice and his thoughts. He can do no more ill to you or for you, in his name or in yours, Charles. The man is gone from our lives."

"You sound almost pleased."

"I am not pleased that you sorrow. I am not pleased that someone you leaned on has gone."

"What did you mean, he can do no more ill to me or for me?"

"Villiers was no friend, my dear husband. He sought only to please himself and reinforce his own wealth."

"Even if that were so, which I dispute, should you be pleased he has gone?" It was almost a demanding statement, but Henrietta Maria stood her ground.

"I am pleased that there can now be peace, for he caused us to fight and he caused others to fight and he caused wars between our countries and with Spain. Charles, we need peace in this country, we need to build trust between us and our people."

"Our people?"

"Our people. I will start by offering my condolences to his family and we will express our joint grief at his death to Parliament. Then we shall see how the people accept you."

He recalled that the tiny Fool had appeared at that moment, full of irreverent jests about Villiers which, despite his misery and grief, Charles found amusing, even though he had spasms of guilt at laughing. He told himself not to be stupid; Villiers himself would have done the same thing. But Henrietta Maria's words stayed with him, bolstered him and gave him a new confidence for the future. He almost forgave Jeffrey Hudson for his interruption at that time. He knew well that you could not control a Fool, they made their own rules when they came to live with a monarch and his Queen. He had to admit, though, that the Fool's observations on Villiers did help to put him in a different light in Charles's mind. For that he was very grateful.

That night in his room, before he went to his bed, it suddenly occurred to Charles that John Tradescant no longer had an employer. Charles decided there and then to ask him to come and take over as his personal gardener and to create a new garden in the home known as Oatlands which he and Henrietta Maria were planning. With his help the gardens would be outstandingly beautiful, if the same flair and dedication was brought to the task as the man had given to Villiers. No matter the cost, he would have his beautiful landscape. He wondered, briefly, why he should think of that when his friend was so recently dead and wondered too why he felt as if a huge millstone had been taken from his neck.

So clear, so unbelievably clear, was the memory of that conversation with Henrietta Maria! He recalled the sense of wonder that consumed him, that his wife should use the words 'our people': all the time she had been with him, she had referred to 'her' people and never 'our' people. But then, he had been so consumed with the problems of the wars and how to finance them, the problems of appeasing and placating Villiers and fighting the Members of Parliament, trying to dismiss the troublemakers and only finding more trouble, he had not stopped to consider that his wife might be changing, might be accepting England as her home. He was surprised, shocked and delighted to find she had a different frame of mind. He also knew that she was, in her heart, glad that Villiers had gone, for he had been a destructive element in her life.

In the sanctity of her rooms, with no servant present to overhear and report back to willing ears, he did something he did not think he would ever do. But in that moment it was the truth, bald, unadorned, naked truth.

He said: "Henrietta Maria, I love you."

He remembered how she stood, silent and shocked, but the shock was one of pure delight and unadulterated happiness. It showed in her wide open eyes, full of the light of love, in the great upturn of her mouth, in her blush and in the outrush of breath that reached him.

"I never, ever, thought to hear you say that, husband," she said finally, just when he thought she would remain speechless. "I can say in truth before the great God of all, I have loved you from the moment I set foot on English soil and saw you standing on the stage, then breaking tradition and coming to greet me, but my sadness at leaving home and my difficulties with Villiers prevented me from ever thinking I could say this to you."

"The great God took something from me but He has given me something in its place; the love of my wife." He took her hands and then gathered her into his arms properly for the first time since their wedding day.

And that night, for the first time, they lay together as one.

Testimony of John Tradescant, gardener to the King of England

Plants be my life. The glory of them in bloom, the sight of them in leaf, the setting of them in the right place for shade and light, for the soil which be right, the keeping of the bulbs safe until they can be in the ground, all this is my life. To find a man like the duke of Buckingham who had money and enough to spare to spend on gardens that are a blaze of glory is a gardener's dream. To find a man like the duke of Buckingham was surely every man's dream for he was a good friend, benevolent, full of compliments, easy with his manner and with his time. I thought to find none better and the heart was fair ripped out of me when he went down under an assassin's knife.

I feared for my livelihood too, for who could afford me? I was not about to give up everything unless I had to. If that sounds mercenary, then so be it, for in a time when every man was looking out for himself, I had to do the same. My employer, my benefactor, was in a grave many years before his time because of a madman. My future was, to say the least of it, unpredictable at that moment.

I waited it out, though, sure that the Lord God would give me a hint, a clue as to where I would go next. He had led me to the duke, of that I was sure and I waited on Him telling me where I would go to next.

I did not dream it would be to the royal Palaces.

I cannot tell you how my heart leapt to get the news that King Charles required my services for his new gardens at Oatlands and for the other palaces he kept and where he liked so much to walk among the flowers. I went to him and offered him my loyal services, which of course he could order, being King and all, but it seemed like a good thing to do, so I did it and he smiled at me. I have to say now that if you never saw the King smile you missed a great thing. He was solemn most of the time, wearing a look that disguised much of what he thought and felt; it was a blank face. The duke used to call it 'his king's face', he used to say it to him. You see, when these aristocrats are together, they don't see minions, no matter how much those minions are held in high regard. I knew the duke thought a lot of me because of the wonder of the gardens I created for him but when the King visited and they walked and talked, they acted as if I was not there, not I or anyone who worked with me and so I heard the way they spoke to one another. The King would be dismissive of the duke and the duke would say 'I don't know what you're thinking, Charles, you're wearing your 'king' face again, the one I can't get past.' And the King would say 'that's why it's there, George!' and I would think, he was right, who are we to know what a King is thinking or feeling, unless he decides to let us know?

So you see, when the King smiled at you, it was sunshine in a dark day. His dark eyes would light up, his face would change to that of a younger man, his demeanour would change and you would feel yourself the happier for having seen it. Sounds foolish of a grown man to say such a thing but it was true and it happened many a time when he walked in the gardens I created and he told me of his pleasure of the plants and the flowers and the trees.

Them that brought him down, them who should have known better, them that brought him down will not rest in peace come their time to go to their eternal home, for they executed a sovereign king and broke the hearts of many.

Mine was one of them.

Chapter Eleven

The fire was all but out. The chill pervading the room crept into his flesh and made him shiver, as much as his memories did.

He found a new joy in life. He felt himself to be a proper man for the first time. He understood passion, knew the giddy heights of joint ecstasy, the depths that this brought to a relationship and all in all that he was a contented man. John Tradescant brought new ideas to him for the gardens and with him, a man who perpetually had dirt under his nails, who wore shabby dirt stained clothes, but who had the talent to make anything grow in any soil, or so it seemed, and with him Charles found even more peace. They talked for ages about where to plant the trees, where to make the paths, with Charles listening to the gardener as he used to listen to Villiers. But this time there was no ulterior motive, nothing but the desire to create beauty out of blandness. He did not think there were greater joys to be found, but Henrietta Maria's first pregnancy took the joys to a new height.

Sadly, that joy soon came crashing down.

The child born of their union lived but one hour. Henrietta Maria had been so proud in her pregnancy, became so pretty as the child grew within her, she was so much the adoring Queen; she had delighted everyone with her happiness. But the pains started suddenly, before her time, in the early hours of the morning. She screamed her panic and her ladies went running. Someone roused Charles and he rushed to her room, to find total chaos and confusion all around her. Tears, shrieks and blood were his confused memories of that frantic and worrying time. No doctor was available, the local midwife was summoned and helped bring a fragile tiny boy into the world. It was all over very quickly; the child was hastily baptised as Charles, duke of Cornwall and died without opening his eyes.

The transformation was total. Henrietta Maria went from the joyful expectant mother-to-be to a crushed, devastated woman. The joy which had filled her when the midwife held out the tiny crumpled red-faced boy for her to see fled as she realised that the child would not live.

Charles had been allowed to remain at the bedside to see his new-born son. Although he feared that the child would not live, it being so small and delicate, there was always the chance of a miracle. He supervised the baptism and left the women to their tasks. Henrietta Maria broke down and sobbed in his arms as if her heart was breaking while he fought back his own tears and tried to be strong for her. It was useless to say at that moment 'we will have more babies' for the one she had was lost, would be buried without having known anything of life. When she fell asleep very suddenly, exhausted from labour and grief, he let her gently fall back onto the pillows and tiptoed away. He needed to be alone to confront his own grief, not to display it in front of others. It was not seemly for him to do so.

He went to his chamber and poured wine, sitting still and staring into the goblet as if it held the answer to the world's secrets, the great mysteries of life and death. He believed the Lord God had blessed their union, for the pregnancy had come about so soon, had been so free of troubles, not once had she complained of pains, of sickness or any of the other vagaries he understood most pregnant women suffered and yet the child had been taken from them within an hour of arriving in this life. Would anyone have the answer if he asked the simple question 'why?' or would it forever be something that they would not know? Or was it, as he believed at that time, that the Lord God sought to chastise him for all his past misdoings? Was He punishing Charles for allowing

Villiers to be in a place where he could be killed? Was He angry with Charles for allowing Parliament to stay unsummoned? Was there anything else he could have done, should have done, given her this food or denied her that?

Or was it simply His will that the first child should not live? The ache in his heart was of such intensity that it was almost a pain. He drank and it did not touch the pain. He needed his wife and could not disturb her sleep, for her grief was great and her need to recover from giving birth so violently was paramount.

He needed respite from that which plagued his heart.

He needed to subdue the frightening memories of the blood, the hysterical tears and sobs from his distraught wife. He had never realised how messy and painful the act of birth could be. Or how dangerous.

He spent the rest of the night in Henrietta Maria's chapel, the one he had built for her, praying to her statues, her saints, for her safe recovery and her ease of mind. He said nothing of his own need for peace but his heart was quietened by the prayers. It was there they found him the next morning, exhausted, hungry and thirsty but quieter than he had been for many a long, lonely year.

Like the good servants they were, nothing was said to the queen and she did not know what he did. Some things were best kept as secret as it is possible for them to be. But others knew and they whispered behind his back that he had secret Catholic tendencies. These whispers reached him, as every such thing did, and for a moment he regretted it. But then, he thought; a chapel is a chapel, a place to speak with God. It was no one else's affair which chapel he chose, the Queen's or his own. But it was damaging to his reputation as a staunch supporter of the church as set up for England. It was yet another burden for him to carry. He wondered how many more there would be. Villiers dead, people squabbling over his estates, parliament not obeying his will, and now a child that had not lived. Henrietta Maria would find it extremely difficult to cope after such a dreadful loss, he had to spend time with her and help to console her.

He vowed silently to go and speak with her about this new project, the Oatlands gardens, in the hope that it would divert her thinking of the child which had been quietly buried. She was young, he told himself, and there would be other children, if God willed it.

He wondered if it was irreverent of him to think of John Tradescant at this time, when he had so much to grieve over, then decided it was not, that all he was doing was giving the man employment. With that, he satisfied his conscience and looked forward to a whole new project, one of beauty, of timeless peace and tranquillity, which would be the balm his troubled mind sought at all times.

Chapter Twelve

Henrietta Maria, after her convalescence, quickly regained her health, strength and vitality. She laughed and joked and flirted with Charles, inviting him to her chamber, plying him with drink and making sure that if she became pregnant again very quickly. This, he thought, was as much for his benefit as hers. Neither of them spoke of the departed child, neither of them spoke of the name they would give to the next child which arrived, but in his heart Charles knew that he wished to name his next living son after himself, just as he had done with the first born. It was a tradition and he wished to keep it as part of his life.

The Fool, Jeffrey Hudson, was despatched to France to bring back a midwife which Henrietta Maria's mother had recommended. He did this, not without difficulties, for Flemish pirates captured his ship and it took the intervention of the Governor of Calais to restore him to the Queen, who was absolutely distraught at the thought of not having her Fool come back to her.

Maybe because of the advice and assistance of the midwife, maybe because this time the child was whole and healthy, the pregnancy went its full term. Henrietta Maria was full of health and confidence that the child would live. At the last moment, as his son was born, Charles wondered if it was an ill omen to call their son by the name of the one who had so quickly departed this world, but he reminded himself that the first living heir needed to carry the name of the father. The second Charles who arrived in this world, squalling, kicking and full of abundant health, was given that name. The Lord God had smiled on them for the child was as unlike his departed brother in every possible way apart from the fact he too was male. This son was strong, determined, unprepossessing - but Charles had every hope that he would grow into something resembling handsome in later life - and was very much the delight of his admiring devoted doting mother.

And Charles called - and then dissolved - the third Parliament.

In the privacy of his chamber, he ranted and raved against the members of Parliament. He shouted to the poor squire who was trying to minister to him: "what am I to do? Am I to stop living? What is the breath of life that I seek still, do I not draw breath continually and does my heart not beat steadily still, despite all that the world has tried to do to me? Have they not tried to control me, to imprison me, to denigrate me, to take from me that which I am – king of England? Would that they could see me now, those Members of Parliament who so derided me, who refused my demands, who demanded in return such things as I could not and would not deliver to them! Would that they could see me now, ranting and raving in this way. Then they would call me fool." The squire looked frightened and tried to edge away toward the door. Charles went after him. "I'm sorry," he mumbled, "I did not mean to worry you. It's merely that those members of Parliament have aggravated me to this point. You are dismissed. I will attend to myself this night."

When the squire had gone, Charles felt the anger flood out of him and he reviewed himself as he must have been seen by the squire. Charles Stuart, the fool who thought he was a king. His rantings had been illogical, manic, it was no wonder the poor squire had looked frightened. He was no doubt wondering what had gone wrong with his King.

He sat down abruptly in a large padded chair, stared at the all but dead hearth and muttered: 'Charles Stuart, I find you this night to be the same kind of fool you once thought of as Buckingham. Villiers. George. The man who did so much damage, who caused so much sorrow, who created such disastrous divisions between myself and my wife, myself and some members of my court, England and France and Spain -

Oh God, am I losing my mind? Look where my thoughts have gone! From my second born and first living son through dissolving Parliament to Villiers! Am I truly going mad? If I am, then tomorrow, all will truly be lost!'

Calm, he told himself. Calm. Make no sound but the breath and the blood which continue to operate and to flow regardless of how he felt. Calm. He tried to order his body: stop trembling, my hands. Stop quivering, my legs. These are a king's orders and I shall be obeyed! It took a while but then his body obeyed and he became still.

In the sanctuary of the room in St James's Palace in which he was that night walking through the memories of his life, Charles admitted to himself that Parliament was a thorn he could well have done without. Because of that, because of his determination to rule alone, for a long time he managed to dismiss all thoughts of Parliament from his mind and his life. He resolved to do so this night too, turning instead to thoughts of his family who meant so much to him. The joy he found in his offspring was in part because they were solely his, a coming together of Henrietta Maria's warm and pliant body and his own had created the wonderful children on which he doted. For the first time in his life he had something which was not second-hand. No one else had played a part in the creation of the children. To others this might have seemed a very small point; to him it was extremely important.

His children were, in every way, his delight. They were the delight of his wife, too, and they became a close and loving family. He was not good with dates: he knew that his beloved daughter Mary arrived the year following his son Charles, but later, in the winter months. James, named for his sorely missed father, came two years after Mary. Another two years went by and his pretty Elizabeth arrived. He remembered the snowstorm at the time of her birth, he remembered thinking she was a snow princess. Should he bring to mind the loss of his daughter Catherine, so difficult born, so soon departed this life? Poor Henrietta Maria endured such travail to bring the child into the world and the child so soon gone. They did wonder at the ways of the Lord God to bring such pain and sorrow into their hearts. But then he thought on this fact, that He did this to make the loving couple care for their existing children that much more for, despite ill health which affected them all from time to time, whether they be royal born or otherwise, they thrived and they gave Charles great and lasting pleasure.

He knew too the family was well-endowed with servants of all kinds, to deal with this and that, to take care of this and that. He knew he did not at any time say 'there are too many people here, how can I pay for them all?' for the money was found and the servants did their work and the children thrived. He had to say the care they received from all helped them to grow in strength of body and of mind and they all became fine young people. Even the little Snow Princess, with her troubled legs, grew and prospered with care.

He paused for a moment, studying his very thoughts, the words that should emanate from his mouth but which were coming from his deeply troubled unhappy mind instead. He sought for a few moments to bury himself in pleasant memories; to remember the good times with the children, their growing up, their movements from one Palace to another, how they enjoyed Greenwich and Richmond, how they loved St James', how they admired Whitehall but somehow it was never the home the other buildings were. The households the children had, the servants to help them maintain a life that was suited to their royal status, these things were right and proper. He had no doubt that paying for so much was right.

His own household was rigidly controlled and he insisted he would have it so. Formal, yes, regal, definitely. Nothing could be further from the life his father lived than the life he lived. Every one there knew their place, knew when he would rise, when he would eat, when he would ride, when he would go to prayer, when he would go to sleep. He would have it so. It suited him well to have a controlled household and as he thought that, he realised he wished always to be in control. That was why he had no Parliament to attend, no arguments with people who would not see his point of view. That way he could control his country and his life.

During this time of peace, and it was a time of true peace for him, he was introduced to the painter Anthony Van Dyck. From then on his court, his homes and his palaces were filled with the great portraits he so admired. He had artists come, work was done and paintings were collected. It was a time of great beauty, a sense of peace, of great love, and a feeling that everything he sought had come together. It had been a long time in coming.

The fire had all but died out, which left the room in a greater degree of darkness than it had before. Despite the flickering candles still, it seemed to the haunted man as if they were ghosts in the room, ghouls who looked sad and weary, waifs who sighed and sent the drapes rippling with their breath, others who knew what was to come and who looked distressed, a mirror of the distress which he himself was enduring. He stopped to consider the rambling thoughts, wondering why he had diverted from the clear pathway he had been walking up to then. So orderly, those thoughts, no diversions, no deviations, nothing but the highway that was his life's path and yet quite suddenly the thoughts had tumbled and twisted, crashed and fallen, throwing themselves at the corners of the room. He was tired, very, very tired but sleep was as far from him as the great Moon he had seen from the window earlier, that unreachable orb that controlled every life and yet had no knowledge of those lives. Cold, unfeeling, in every way the epitome of the atmosphere in the courtroom during the trial. For in God's name, if they had retained one particle of feeling in their hearts, they would not have found him guilty! Or so he believed, anyway. A man walking the pathway to death has to hold on to something, he thought. It was a small deception after all.

Going back to thinking of the time of joy and happiness with Henrietta Maria, he admitted that the great love he shared with his wife grew beyond anything which he had ever dreamed or hoped would happen. And in that he found final solace for the death of Villiers. The shining extravagant light that had been George Villiers, Duke of Buckingham, had continued to linger despite his having been dead and buried for some considerable time. Charles had overheard courtiers mentioning him disparagingly when they did not think he was listening and this, plus his own vivid memories, contrived to keep Villiers alive in his mind. No one that charismatic, that flamboyant, that influential, could ever be fully said to have died. Putting thoughts of Villiers to one side, Charles fully committed himself to his relationship with his wife. He listened to her in many things. He admitted she was not always right but she was more sensible with her advice than Villiers ever was, even in his most sensible moments. He still had heartache from time to time with grief for him, for he had been the most influential person in his life, albeit that the influence was not as beneficial it should have been. That mattered little; it was the intensity of the relationship with someone which dictated whether you missed them passionately when they leave this mortal world. It had been an intense relationship. Charles had missed him intensely because of it. In the semi-dark room, he mused, if there is a true afterlife, then Villiers are will know this and he could almost sense the sardonic smile with which he would greet that knowledge.

Having diverted, and having vowed he would be honest in his thoughts, he forced himself to return to the metaphor he so disliked but had to confront, not merely approach.

The moon is unreachable; it controls our lives but has no knowledge of our lives.

In this instance, this time of truth, he told himself he would admit that was how he had lived his life. He knew the people were out there, the peasantry, the nobles, the courtiers, the knights, but he distanced himself from them all, holding close only those he cared for, his wife, his children and his trusted servants. No others were allowed a part of his consideration or his caring and his attention without actually demanding it and in that they knew full well he was king and they were of lower rank.

Did his people, his subjects, live in hovels? Did he care? Of course he should have cared, but did he? As he moved from palace to palace with his family, did he really notice dirt, disease and discord among those who lined the roads and paid him homage as the royal procession passed?

He confessed, in this secret quiet time in which he was thinking, that he did not. He saw only the silks of his own clothes, of that covering his wife and his children, the quality of the harness on the horse he rode, the quality of the horse itself, the amount of servants and men at arms who rode with them. He saw not the common people. He saw not their needs, their fears, their longings for a settled country and peace at all times, freedom from Popery and heavy taxation, from martial law and unwanted soldiers billeted on them. He saw none of this, he saw instead the grace and majesty of royalty, of kingship, of supreme rule by one person, divinely appointed, of supreme dictation of one law: his.

In that, he realised, he and his people were as far apart as the moon and the earth were at its farthest point in its orbit. And he did not see it.

He sometimes wondered just how much of a fool he had been.

Testimony of Queen Henrietta Maria, wife of King Charles

Would that we could have been no more than husband and wife together in a country house somewhere, with a large estate which could be turned into beautiful gardens where we could walk and sit and the children would play without fear of someone coming and disrupting our walk, our sitting or the play of the children! Would that we could have taken ourselves away from everything which bothered my husband, the constant visitors, the demands of the nation, the people, the ever-present need, it seemed, for money and the need to raise taxes which upset the people. Time and again my husband would turn to me for advice on this point or that and I would give it. Sometimes he would agree, sometimes we would argue for I knew well that we saw everything from very different viewpoints. I knew that he would have given much if I were to convert to the English church but I could not, it went against all my beliefs to do such a thing. I was born into and brought up in the Roman church, even for my beloved husband I could not set it to one side and pretend I could worship somewhere else. I knew the people disliked this, but what did they know of my feelings. My beliefs? Should I have worried more about them?

My concerns were first, my husband, second, my children and third, my family. Everyone else came after that. Oh, but I did not realise how wrong my advice was or that my arguing with my husband and his advisors was ... I thought I was helping, I believed I was right.

I did love being pregnant, I did love presenting my husband with children he could fuss over and love – and love was something he had in abundance. He adored his children and gave them everything he could. They had their own servants and rooms, they had all the clothes and toys and treats they needed, they had tutors and ponies and books and companions. Most of all, they had loving parents who truly cared about them. I do not think many children could ask for more than that. When I saw my beloved husband looking tired and strained, or angry from confrontations with those who would so argue with him, I wanted to rage at them to leave him alone, let him be, tell them he had enough cares on his shoulders to weigh down several people, let alone one man who was trying to run the country as best he could with those who constantly wanted to usurp his authority. Who did they think they were?

And then, what did I do but argue with him myself ... no wonder he grew tired of people and spent so much time in his much loved gardens, walking and talking with that old gardener person, discussing bulbs and tulips and trees and shrubs. It pleased me that my husband knew so much about plants but annoyed me that he should talk about it with someone else. That is foolish, because I had no interest myself and he knew it. Oh Henrietta Maria, what a mixture of conflictions you are!

We are talking about truth here, truth about my husband but this is a good time for me to talk about the truth as it refers to me, too. I have things I must get off my conscience.

I knew that I was a second choice. I knew that Charles would have loved to have married the Infanta, had she not come with so many conditions about Catholics and their status in England – which I applauded, I have to say but knew well that the English would not tolerate – and so he married me instead. I am not used to being second. I fell in love with this good looking man who happened to be my husband and at all times I wanted to be first in his eyes, in his mind, in his heart and in his soul. I resented anyone and anything who came before me.

One such was George Villiers, duke of Buckingham who, as it happened, arranged the marriage and then resented it, terribly. He took a dislike to me the moment our eyes met. I knew it, I saw it, I resented it and that resentment went to hatred.

I used to dream of Villiers being out of our life. I used to think how much better life would be if he were not there, whispering his evil into Charles' ear, trying to turn him against me, trying to destroy all that we were trying to build in the way of a marriage.

My dream came true. He was taken out of our life but those who remained were as bad. All of them who clustered around him, Strafford, Hyde, all of them. They tried to lead him away from the course he wanted to take, tried to tell him he was wrong. How could they? He was the King of England, he knew what he was doing!

Didn't he?

Chapter Thirteen

Charles knew, from the words given to him by those who no longer cared if he lived or died, that his wife's Catholic leanings were at the heart of some of the problems which had arisen. He only saw it as a concession to her happiness, her well-being, her peace of mind, to allow her a Catholic form of worship if it pleased her. His one desire was that she would come over to the true Church, the one in which he worshipped, which he constantly told everyone. But his love for her was so great and had been so great that if she did not wish to do that, he was content to let her go her own way and worship in her own way. All that mattered to him was that they both approached the same God in the same light, that they needed His divine strength to help them in their role as King and Queen of England. He knew, from the words given to him by those who no longer cared if he lived or died, that his autocratic rule had divided him from the people. This he frankly disbelieved at the time; he had never felt part of the people so how could his rule divide him from them? And they, he was sure, held no love for him. This he knew, this he fully appreciated, this he understood now was just one of the mistakes he made. But if he looked at the total of the mistakes made during a lifetime that could be deemed to have been a mistake from beginning to end, that one was a mere grain of dust.

He sought to be honest with himself. He, who had been used to entertainment of the highest level, minstrels and book reading, choirs and learned discussion, was spending this night thinking about his life, his beloved wife, his children and his mistakes. How the mighty king is fallen! But it is a necessary thing, he decided, for he had to come to terms with that which he had done before the morning, before what was be his Armageddon.

To do that, he had to walk pathways he would rather avoid, confront memories he would otherwise have left concealed behind dark doorways, think on issues he would have walked away from and deal with sorrows he had thought left behind.

Briefly, for it caused too much pain to dwell on it, he had to think to himself once and for all that the children who died young: the beautiful little Anne and the lovely little Catherine who had no life at all, had never left his heart. If he did not mention the children, it was because he did not wish to bring them before the world. They had their place, his son Charles would inherit the throne one day, one far off day, his son James he believed would go on to do great things. His daughter Mary had her prestigious marriage partner to lean on. All would do well, he prayed. Those who had gone ahead of him and who were already in Heaven, he would hold and give his love to them when he got there.

Onward, Charles, onward! This was not the time for drawing back like a wilting flower from that which was unpleasant. For was not this next part of his life that which set the pattern for the rest of his life, to bring him to where he was now?

The king needed money. What monarch did not need money? What could he do but tax the people more to give him that which he needed, income to run the country? So he asked for ship money from everyone, on the basis that everyone would benefit from the protection of the ships. The people did not agree, the people rebelled and then he began to hear murmurings against his Queen, about her enticing the children into Catholicism, about her leanings to the Roman church, about all manner of things he could not tolerate. Who were these people to criticise the way his family and he lived? They were nothing, they were no one! They were not royal, they had no royal blood, so who did they think they were? And so his angry thoughts ran on – and on – and on.

He conceded that his visit to Scotland was to seek help from the Scots. He also admitted to being surprised by the reception when he returned. He also admitted to an overwhelming anger that the Parliament refused to agree to his demands. He could see no way out of the predicament in which he found himself. The populace, the rabble, the knights and noblemen who were turning traitor on him, he despised them all. They sought to impeach his Queen, his wife, his love. How could they even consider such a thing!

And then it really all went wrong. Just how wrong no one could really have foreseen, could they? Mayhap he should have done. Mayhap his own judgement was at fault. But it was as if a great surge forward had begun and no one and no thing could stop it.

They walked toward civil war.

Part 3 - Fighting Men

Chapter Fourteen

It sounded so simple when said like that, as a statement of fact, not a venture into disaster. It sounded as if the two sides took two steps and there they were, confronting one another. It wasn't quite that simple, but then life never was truly simple, was it?

It started with the Scots, who did not like the book of Common Prayer Charles wanted to be universally used, who rebelled, who started all sorts of riots and killings and problems, combined with his inability, yes, he could say it clearly now, for it had to be said, his inability to put down the uprising. It surprised and worried him. He could see no fault in the Book of Common Prayer, he could see no reason why they should not accept it – after all, it was his wish and was he not their sovereign king?

Then there was the lack of money for the soldiers, the refusal of Parliament to grant him any more funds for fighting, the court cases over the ship money and somehow, in the middle of all this, his reign somehow fell apart. He thought he was supreme monarch, he thought he could control everything: parliament, treaties, taxes, finances and war. He wondered how many kings before him had thought the same thing. His words were ignored; the parliaments were a shambles. He dismissed them. He sent them all packing. He believed in himself. What he did not do was listen to the tiny voice deep inside, the one sent by the Lord God Himself to warn that we were mere playthings on this earth compared with the vastness of His Kingdom and His realms, that we should listen to Him and not to ourselves. Whilst Charles worshipped Him with his heart and soul, he did not listen to Him.

The room had become cold, ice cold. The last embers had been smothered by the thick falling ash, just as his hold on the country through his parliaments had been obliterated by bitter disputes and entrenched positions on both sides. He had become acutely aware of a huge gulf opening up between the people and the monarchy and he could see no way of bridging it. Not without giving up his ingrained belief that a king was supreme, divine, his will at all times should be obeyed. Parliament and, it seemed, the people, wanted to - and indeed were – taking the opposite view.

Now, in the solitude of these hours of silent contemplation, he asked himself the question: did he want to do anything about bridging it? Did he not, in his arrogance, in his conceit and single-mindedness, did he not believe it was for them to come to him and not him to go to them?

His restless questing mind shouted, must I answer these questions? Do I need, truthfully, to go that deep into my mind, to settle my conscience before – whatever is to come?

The questions were there. Whether anyone would get answers was another matter entirely. He was not sure he was ready to answer. Who is asking these questions anyway? Are you one of the Lord God's chosen ones, an angel come to help me settle my heart and my mind before I begin the greatest challenge any man can face – the walk to the end of my life?

It was almost easier for him to believe an angel had arrived than for the entire exercise of walking his past to be no more than a figment of his imagination.

Laud.

He heard the word as clearly as if someone had spoken it aloud. Laud. That man, that problematic man. What damage did he do? Truthfully? Little. For he did only that which the king asked. Charles had asked for the complete prayer book to be restored. He asked that the communion table be at the east end of the church. He asked that people bow to it. He asked that in every respect the original way of worship was restored. Some called it Roman, he called it restoration. In such a division was conflict. But he would have his way, was he not king? Did he not expect his subjects to conform to that which he ordered? Of course he did.

In the calm that was the time of relative peace in England, he believed he had his way. Foolish Charles! Would that he had listened to the tiny voice deep within which said 'oh foolish one, what makes you think they are obeying your every word without rebellion?' He did not account for the many who had left these shores for other parts where they could worship according to their own rites, he did not account for the Scots who would not accept his words. He did not account for discontent building among his people, for he had no thought for the people. He saw only that which he wished to see: his beloved wife, the children fast growing and the coffers full of taxes that were unpopular but enforced.

And someone dared whisper the name of Strafford.

Ah, but that tore his heart out even now! The man was his supporter, his counsellor, his advisor, arrested on the grounds of treason. Treason! From a man like that!

Strafford. Lord Deputy of Ireland. He brought Charles tax money, advice and for a time he did good work. Unfortunately his tactics did not work with the Scots but when did anything English ever work with that benighted country, he asked?

Parliament had Strafford arrested for treason. Parliament sought to indict him but the grounds were flimsy and the evidence missing or non-existent. The treason claim was changed to an attainder.

Why then did he personify the absoluteness of monarchy to the people? Because of his place in the House of Lords, because of his standing with Charles? He swore his friend would not suffer. Strafford begged

144

Charles to reconsider and allow him to die so that the king could become reconciled with his people. A dream, a foolish empty dream that had its roots in a sort of Utopia where people would understand that kind of sacrifice. They didn't.

'God knows what I would have given not to have signed that warrant!' Charles thought suddenly, feeling a darker, deeper chill go through him than the cold room had generated. 'I will give myself willingly to the executioner in recompense for the taking of that life. That gifted, wonderful life that should have continued for many years, which should have graced this land for many years. Let us not speak of Strafford. But oh my angel, whoever you are, whatever I think of in this time is nothing but pure pain. It tears my heart. It tears my soul. It brings tears to my eyes. I should have held out! I should and I couldn't and I did not dare and I didn't. Oh God help me for sending a pure man to his death! And how bravely he went! How bravely and how unbidden he went! To no avail. It made no difference. His was a sacrifice in vain.'

Lord God, he prayed intently, grant me the strength to do the same as he.

Charles vowed he would not disgrace himself in the morrow. He would not. Yet his heart quailed at the very thought – for there was much undone that needed be done, much recompense to make that had not been made. It was in his mind to ask, how many had said that before him?

The answer was - thousands and thousands. Ever and always it was over too soon, no matter how long anyone lived. Should we remain on this earth until we are old, until our bones creak and our voice goes, until our eyes no longer see and our legs no longer carry us, would we not still ask for another day, another hour, another minute, to set this to rights and that? Are not all people of the same mind? Charles knew he would, of his own heart and mind, ask that he set everything to rights before –

Before it ends, too soon, oh Lord God, too soon! Wilt Thou not look kindly upon this humble servant and allow him a few more years with his wife, his children and his friends? Or is Thy will such that I am to return to Thee sooner than I would wish? If it is, Lord God, if it is, Thy will be done, not mine.

And it seemed, in that moment, as if the ghouls and shades who filled the room closed in around him, touching him with their invisible ice-cold fingers and torturing him with the breath of the tomb. He shook uncontrollably, fighting the wraiths, fighting the ghosts of his own memories and his own disastrous decisions but most of all, the cold fires of hell in his heart at the certain knowledge that he would never see Henrietta Maria again.

Testimony of Thomas Wentworth, Earl of Strafford

Charles Stuart is a complex, intelligent, in some ways charismatic, yet troubled individual, who relied heavily on those around him rather than his instincts and abilities. This I blame to a very great degree on his father, who insisted and persisted in calling him' Baby Charles' which does not do much for anyone's confidence. If you add his physical disabilities and his stature, you have an individual who is extremely self-conscious at the best of times and to be given a public role with these disabilities made it three times harder than it would have been for anybody else. I know in his book he talks about Henry VIII being a second son who became a great king. This I acknowledge but Henry was strong in body and mind, had the presence and the charisma of a King, and was able to quietly take over and then stamped his authority on England. In fact I believe he knew he was born to be King, where Charles only ever wanted to be second son. Being given the kingship as it were, by the death of his brother, meant that he had to assume a mantle that was not really right for him. Unfortunately he had no choice but to take it on, there being no one else.

I first met the young Prince of Wales through attending court on different occasions and noticed his retiring attitude, polite, cool, dignified but never a hint of the person beneath the court persona which he assumed. I knew it to be a persona simply because we all did that and no one could be that calm, that detached, in what I think of as 'real' life and so it proved to be.

I wanted to argue with King James over many things, including some that were whispered to him by Villiers, duke of Buckingham, a man I freely confess I had little time for. He was a dilettante, playing at diplomacy and was dangerous because of that. I thought he did everything to enhance Villiers, not those around him and I deplored his sexuality too. I cannot help the way I am, it was something I found abhorrent and still do. To lie with a woman and with a man is beyond my understanding. I can just about accept those who prefer men only, it is the two way thing which offends. I argued with Villiers too, I made no exceptions when it came to matters which I held dear to me, the war with Spain was just one of them. The King ignored me, but that was the way he treated everyone. I did argue with Villiers, but again, it was to no avail.

The king's death affected the Prince of Wales considerably. I noticed that he became more subdued than before, and he seems to be making every effort to be more statesmanlike, to act as the King he thought everyone expected him to be. Unfortunately, it was not in his personality to exert any authority, he was often heard asking people to do something rather than telling them to do something. And always in the background, like an evil shadow, was the Duke of Buckingham. There were so many times I wished that man to the far ends of the earth. The difficulty was that Charles had appointed Buckingham to be his First Minister and so in going against the First Minister's wishes you were in effect blocking an act which the monarch himself wanted. But then, I asked myself, did Charles really want this, or whether was he doing it only because Buckingham asked him to arrange it? How much of what went on was Buckingham's machinations and not Charles's own desire. I was not alone in my thinking, there were many others who felt the same. It was a difficult time. We were in official mourning for the King, King James, and we were trying as best we could to help the new King into his role as monarch. We all felt that we were being blocked in this by Buckingham, who seemed to have not only the King's ear but the King's confidence too. It was a difficult time.

Charles called a parliament in June 1625 when I was representing a Yorkshire constituency. I felt strongly about the war with Spain, that it should not be happening, and I opposed the demand for war subsidies to be made on Buckingham's behalf. This was not a popular move. Just how unpopular I found out when Parliament was dissolved and I was appointed Sheriff of Yorkshire which effectively kept me out of the next Parliament that the King called.

I freely confess to you now that I objected most strongly to virtually everything that Buckingham did. This is not anything to do with his sexuality, but with his almost total domination of the King and of the King's thinking. Buckingham was also vindictive, when I refused to support the court in its desire to force money from the country, I found myself out of office and then when I refused to contribute to the loan as well I was imprisoned. This I knew was Buckingham's doing and no one else's. He did not like anyone standing against him. He had the King in the palm of his hand and he wanted the rest of us to be there as well. He found we were not as compliant as Charles.

It is difficult to say quite why Charles was so reliant on someone as outrageous as Buckingham because anyone could see that he was not a good influence and his advice was often faulty. I can only assume at that time that Charles was so insecure in his position as King that he would listen to anyone with a strong voice. It was quite obvious that Buckingham was a strong personality, he also had charm, flair, charisma, call it what you will he managed to impress himself -- I have to say this, impress himself on the impressionable. Those of us who were more worldly wise than the King were not taken in by all of this, which most of us saw as a flagrant and outrageous act. Yes he was good-looking, yes he had fashion sense and sufficient money to dress in the current fashions but beneath all this I felt there was a black heart which only sought to serve Buckingham and no other. Did I at any time feel guilty for thinking this way? No I did not.

It was a sad and difficult time for parliament when the lawyers among the members had to put together the Petition of Right. Charles was blatantly breaking laws everywhere in his drive to gain that which he thought he should have, by divine right; the ability to enforce taxes and loans, to billet soldiers wherever he wished, to interfere with property laws and just about any other violation of the Magna Carta that you can think of, a small exaggeration maybe but that is how it seemed to me at the time and certainly to other members of Parliament. My support for the petition obviously did not go down very well with either the King or Buckingham. However, once the King had accepted the petition I supported him in his actions. This led me to being branded a turncoat by the other members. My "reward" for this was to be created Baron Wentworth. I should justify myself here. I supported the king because he had at last done the right thing. I see nothing 'turncoat' in that. Do you not reward those who do the right thing? Of a surety you do. Just as you stand against them when you think they are not doing the right thing. I did not seek a reward but I admit I welcomed it when it was given to me. Would I not have been a fool to do otherwise?

My problem then arose because I wished to stand against the King in resisting are pretty taxation and imprisonment but without upsetting the Crown in doing it. It was virtually impossible. I actually started a movement for a bill which would have secured the liberties the populace sought as precisely as the Petition had, but the uncompromising nature of Parliament and Charles's own refusal to concede anything led to its failure. This was extremely disheartening. I found myself divided between the parliament and my monarch. It was not a good position to be in.

I also found that Charles had changed yet again. He was not so indecisive, but his thinking had clearly developed along the lines that his father had laid down, that is, the divine right of kings. Whatever he said he expected to be done. It seemed not to matter to him that it went against all the laws of liberty which this country of ours had fought long and hard to put in place. The Magna Carta was a turning point in English history, it said that the people had a voice and the King could not impose his will upon them without going through the parliament, something that Charles was obviously trying to do. I could see this, I longed to be able to go to him and say "this is wrong, your Majesty, you cannot do this to the people. It goes against all that is written into our laws. Do not listen to Buckingham. Think of your people." Sadly it was not something I could do. I was not in his confidence. I realised that his demeanour was changing yet again, he was colder and seemingly harder than he had been before. I wondered where the young hesitant Prince of Wales had gone, how it was that we now had this determined and stubborn and difficult monarch to deal with.

Charles' marriage to the little woman, Henrietta Maria, did go some way to softening his outlook, although we all felt he leaned too much still on the unspeakable Buckingham. At least Charles had something, someone, else to think about and that helped to some degree. Unfortunately her Catholicism was a problem, parliament did not like it, the people did not like it and only Charles refused to believe it was something that should be approached and diverted and dealt with. It was another example of his blinkered outlook on life, one that would never change, I am sorry to say.

Needs must that I be honest. Buckingham's assassination gave me much relief if not a degree of pleasure. To think such a fastidious and – I can only say excessively wealthy – man should be killed with a mere kitchen knife was somehow perfect. I hoped that Charles would then learn to stand on his own two feet, make his own decisions and become the king we all hoped he would be. Sadly not, word had it that he was controlled by his wife, who had as much idea about politics and the situation the marriage had created as she did about growing wings and flying. Am I speaking treason here? I must say this is my only chance to be totally honest about my feelings for my king and as much as I grew to admire him and have affection for him, at times he drove me mad with his inadequacy, his need to rely on someone he saw as knowing more than he did.

Charles was gracious enough to appoint me Viscount Wentworth and grant me the presidency of the Council of the North. I felt I could serve him well there and I have to admit, at this time of honesty, of leaning more toward him than toward Parliament, whose members were beginning to be more militant and I was not at all contented in my mind with the way it was going. When the serious breach developed between king and parliament, I had to decide finally which way I would go. I didn't take long to make up my mind, I went with the king. If nothing else it made me one of the two principal advisors to the king during the long period when he governed the country by himself.

Such a position of power is not given to many people and those who hold that kind of closeness to the monarch are usually those with the intelligence to guide and help. I say this without wishing to make myself grander than I am, but think of those who have been close to kings, Thomas More, Thomas Cromwell and others. Yes, I know the final end of their reign of power and I had no illusions about my own life and death. I planned to make the most of it whilst I had the chance. Fate, and kings, are extremely fickle and the populace even more so.

The post of Lord Deputy of Ireland was mine for the asking. I took it, I did the best I could, I was hated for it. Was ever a man more misunderstood than I was at that time? Only later could I begin to say, seriously, that Charles was more misunderstood than I. So be it, we do what we must to survive in this world. I did much to curb the excesses of the wealthy for the benefit of the poor but no one cared for the way in which I did it. In this my life mirrored my king's, he tried to do the same but no one cared for the way in which he did it. Ah but there are many who do not see it that way.

It was said I disliked the Irish. That is not entirely true, I thought as a race they had potential, were they only to become more English and give up their religion for the true faith, the Church of England. Then I could have dealt with them better. It is truly a shame they did not see it that way themselves.

What else can I tell you of my king? I was created Earl of Strafford, which was pleasing and I was most grateful for that. I worked hard to get him to accept some of the conditions of parliament, I tried hard to mediate but I soon realised the point of mediation had long gone. My mind was too sharp for the parliament which sought to impeach me on various grounds, what had they to fear from me? But the signs were there, this was the beginning of the end.

Charles made me a promise, that I would not suffer in life, fortune or honour. I knew well, in my heart and my mind, that if he were to keep to that, parliament would turn on him too. I offered myself as a sacrifice, they having made up their collective minds that I should die. I released him from all obligations to me and went to my death believing all would be healed between the king and his people.

In many ways I was right, in many other ways I was wrong. Nothing could heal the breach between king and parliament, king and people. It had gone too far, there was too much animosity between them all for a compromise to ever be reached. Because of that, the country went to war. Because of that the unspeakable was spoken of and then enacted – the execution of a king.

The king considers himself a fool. I say he was not a fool but misguided and led by the wrong people. The friendship we had, the service I gave, was from the heart. I can say no more, I can do no more but say to you, this was a fine man, a fine king who had the wrong advisors and the wrong pathway laid before him. The fact he was easily led is not a fault of his own but the result of his upbringing.

The fool is myself, Thomas Wentworth, Earl of Strafford, for believing that my death would resolve his problems. All it did was curtail my own life to please those who did not wish me to continue to live.

And that rests on their consciences to this day.

Chapter Fifteen

For all that the people did not care for him, for all that
the fine Englishmen that he ruled cared not for his rule
or his God given right as king, it was not they who
brought this country to the edge and then the abyss of
Civil War, but the Scots, he thought. May the Lord have
mercy on their souls for it is they who caused the scales
to tip in the direction of violence when they could have
tipped in the direction of peace! On their consciences,
then, must lie the souls and the suffering of countless
people torn apart in the conflicts that ensued. Why did
they invade? Could they not have stayed on their side of
the border and left England to their affairs? Why was the
imposition of the prayer book such a difficulty for their
minds to absorb?

Whatever the reason, they rebelled. And whatever
the reason, Parliament refused to support Charles in the
war. And Parliament refused many things, whilst
bringing up all that they held against him yet again.
Would that he could have stifled them all, would that he
was not forced to call Parliament again and listen to their
arguments and their complaints and their litanies of his
ill-judged decisions, in their eyes and minds, that is. He
knew full well many of those ill-judged decisions came
from the agile and fertile mind of his beloved wife and
he could see no wrong in that. They complained of her
Catholic leanings, his answer was and always would be,
his wife worshipped as she saw fit. He saw no wrong in
that, either.

Mayhap he was wrong to think of war, mayhap he
should have sought compromise but – there seemed no
compromise available to him. For their minds were set
fair for conflict, for war, they issued notices of array and
so Charles did the same. There was no specific moment
at which he said 'we are going to war' but somehow that

was happening and somehow people were choosing sides and somehow – he knew not how, he knew not the full workings of the minds of those around him – the realisation dawned that they had to fight. First they had to fight the Scots and then they had to fight those who would take from him the kingly powers, those who wished to crush everything he wanted. Those who asked for his wife's impeachment were beyond his comprehension. They were lower than the dust beneath his horse's hooves in his eyes. He had no time for them, no patience and no understanding. His wife was Queen, by right of marriage, by her heritage and her lineage, and they wished her impeached on the grounds of her Catholicism. He would have thought them to be glad she was a God-fearing lady who truly worshipped, who did not make a token acknowledgement of the Lord God and all that He stood for. Instead they looked to their own ambitions and did not like that which they saw impeded their progression toward riches and fine estates. Mayhap Charles simplified their desires too simply, he did not know, he could not say for he was not given the gift of seeing into their hearts and minds. He saw only his own.

He saw conflict. He saw divisions so deep no one could surmount them. He wanted a cohesive church; he ended up with a divided country.

It was not the first time people had taken up arms against their rightful monarch and logic told him it would not be the last. But in the long dark watches of the night, all that truly mattered was that the people of England were taking up arms against him. No other king, no past king and certainly he carried no thought for a future king, had faced such an uprising. They took up arms against him. It was personal. It was hurtful. It was unbelievable - yet it was happening.

And he said to Henrietta Maria,' if it is to be, it is to be. If God is with me, I will win. If He has turned His

156

face from me, then I will lose. Whatever happens, it is in His hands and His will cannot be denied.'

Testimony of John Pym, Member of Parliament and stern opponent of both King James and his son King Charles.

For a long time I have wished to tell the world how I saw these monarchs. At last I have the opportunity I sought! Thanks be to Almighty God for His great mercy in granting me this time and this benefit of having my voice heard! I will praise His name forever!

Now I have the chance, what do I say and where do I begin and who do I denigrate ... Villiers for a start, all Roman Catholics for a second, including the presumptuous little Queen who never learned to keep her nose and her voice and her opinions out of politics and the monarchs for a third. King James was bad enough, philandering and playing games with his favourites instead of dealing with the duties of Parliament and the country but – in the name of Heaven, where did Charles Stuart come from? With the Divine Right of Kings stamped on his forehead, in a manner of speaking, he stormed and raged and dissolved and resolved and generally caused utter chaos in Parliament and out. His unwarranted and unwanted taxes, his assaults on those who tried to advise him – apart from the terrible Villiers and his equally terrible wife, that is – were surely without precedence in English history. Should I, at this point, mention Strafford ... it seemed to me that King Charles appointed one bad person after another, money grabbing arrogant aristocrats who only saw their wealth and their estates and not the good of the country.

I have to say, if only a small part of what I heard of the King's sexual gambits, boys and animals, the one willing, the others not so, then the man was not fit to wear the crown of England. Yes, I am a Puritan to my very bones, I make no false claims here of any piety that is not part of my life. My God is everything, and to serve Him a man needs to be pure in heart, mind and soul and to refrain from all that is invidious to the Lord God with his body, too. I was faithful to my wife, I adored my children, I needed no other stimulus to take care of the carnal needs of a human living in this life at this time. God put us here to procreate and that is what we did. We did not need to do that which was unnatural.

I will admit that I fought with the King on many occasions, in Parliament and without, fights which were bitter and hurtful to us both. I tried to impeach his First Minister, he tried to arrest me. Battle lines were drawn long before he launched the country into Civil War, for which he may never be forgiven, certainly by those of us of a Puritan stance who deplored his lifestyle, his family and his Catholic leanings, this not taking into account any of the horrendous and unnecessary deaths he caused by his actions. All must be paid for at the seat of Judgement. I would not wish to be in his position on the day the axe severed his head from his body, a day when I rejoiced that the country had at last lost a tyrannical monarch who sought only to do his will and not that of the people.

May God have mercy on his soul – eventually.

Chapter Sixteen

He went to Scotland.

He went to Scotland with high hopes and no real comprehension of what he would say when he got there. He went and did not leave provision for himself back in London and his mission failed and he came back with despair and blackness around him such as he had never felt before, even in his darkest moments. He knew, when he considered his journey there and its dismal failure, that part of the blackness was the loss of Strafford and Charles' part in his death. He could not be done with seeing his hand write Strafford's name on the execution warrant. He could not stop wishing that he had snatched his hand back at the last moment and said 'no, I will not send this man to his death!'

He regretted many things. This night of all nights, he thought to say to the ghouls, whoever they were, whatever form or shape they took, whether they were his conscience, his un-conscience, his worst living nightmares or his guardians, this was the one thing he regretted the most. His hand, his own hand which he would cut from his arm were it in his nature to do such a thing, took up a quill and signed away a man's life for his own sake. Would history see it that way? Would history read into that act the truth of his mind and his motives? He could not say. Henrietta Maria held him close and said he had to do it. Mayhap he did but it made it no easier to bear. He was, for the first time, right glad this night that none could see there were tears, freely falling now, the first he had wept for that sad, unnecessary death. Tears were easing, slowly, the great weight, the stone which he had carried since 12th May 1641 was finally lifting. How could he have given the man his word and then gone back on it? How could he have ignored Strafford's plea to sign the warrant so that

Charles would be restored and the monarchy maintained? How could he have foreseen that such a thing would not happen and the death was no more than a sop to the people who could not see the value of the man himself?

'Thomas, this night I beg your forgiveness. You did what you thought was right for me and for the people. It was not your fault that they did not understand you or your motives. It was not your fault I gave in to pressures from others.'

He asked himself now, how many present on that fateful day were truly sad to see Strafford die? How many were there out of blood lust and a misplaced glee at the downfall of someone they perceived as being evil, against the monarchy, against England?

He also asked himself now, in truth, had he held out, would it have made one iota of difference to what was to happen on the morrow? He told himself in truth that hurt, no, it would not. They were out for blood and blood they had and they will have.

Change direction of thoughts. Change posture in chair, stiffening body and aching limbs but oh, how soon it will all be over and no more pain and suffering and heartache will be borne!

Irish. Rebellion. Deaths. Exaggerated, no doubt, but damage done, so much damage done that he could not begin to think on. And did it not play into the hands of those who would seek to bring him down?

An army was needed to put down the uprising in Ireland. It did not happen. Both sides were afeared the other side would use the army to take control. Would Charles give up control of the army? No. He could sign away many things but not control of the army. His insistence on this drew people to him, but the Grand Remonstrance took it all away.

All his faults were dragged out, all his mistakes were dragged out, the humiliation was beyond bearing. Demands for reform of the church. Demands for rights – demands for this – demands for that – all he knew was none of it was right and none of it could be agreed to without surrendering his rights as king.

He sent out an instruction to impeach five Members of Parliament.

It was stupid. It was foolish. He should have taken advice. But consider this, was he not king, even now? Was he not supreme in this land? Was he not the ultimate authority? He willed not to have that authority questioned, scorned, ignored. Some things were not to be borne and that was one. When he realised no one was going to do anything about anything, he took the bull by the horns himself. Literally. He talked long with his beloved wife and then set out for Parliament with an armed guard. Did he shock them by entering the Commons? He did indeed and it was only the first of the shocks. But they were gone; the five he sought to imprison had gone. The Speaker was arrogant and made his stance clear, he answered to Parliament and not to his King. It just got worse. He felt – inadequate, scorned, defied, how many words are there to describe the many emotions he went through? Henrietta Maria said all he needed to do was take away their leader and the other members would follow his will. Instead they had advance warning of his coming and left for places unknown.

And the next day, too, he found them still gone.

He never did discover who told them of the plan and gave them time to escape. Who amongst his counsellors and advisors had seen fit to go against the royal will in this way and make Charles look foolish? Who in his court disliked him so much that he could turn his conscience and his heart over to those who would bring down a king? It hurt him to think that anyone would turn against him in that way, people he had trusted, people he thought of as loyal. It was a sharp lesson, when it came to politics no man could be trusted.

Worse, he found people were shouting against him in the streets, the crowds were hostile. Where once they gathered to wave and shout greetings, now they gathered to shout abuse. Some even reached for stones to throw, but held back at the last moment, when armed guards raised their swords in threat. But the bleak, angry faces tormented him, as it was such an unbelievable change from deference to defiant. It was frightening and he began to fear that he had taken a step too far. Even if he had, though, he could see no way to reverse it.

The ghouls in his room were taking on the faces of the dead. There was Strafford, there was Villiers, there was – too fast, the face changed too fast to be sure of who it was. Were they real, or were they his memories crowding in and battering him with their overwhelming impressions?

Go back, where was I? He asked himself. The missing Members of Parliament, the foolish king standing in the Commons being openly defied by the Speaker and the other Members, his armed guard standing around uselessly, awaiting the order to leave for it was not so much uncomfortable as embarrassing to be so shamed before his own Parliament. They did not laugh but they might as well have done for all the respect he was shown.

Back at the palace, he realised he felt like a man standing on a cliff which was being assaulted by strong waves and the ground was moving under his feet and he knew if he does not step back from the edge very soon he would be in danger of being swept away in the landslide that was to come. But he was incapable of stepping back for his feet were deeply mired in the edge of the cliff and all that he could do was wait helplessly for the final wave which would destroy his foothold and carry him away.

Testimony of Queen Henrietta Maria, wife to King Charles

I watched hopelessly as our world fell apart. All our talk, all our plans, all our dreams were being taken away from us, one at a time. We were in danger, we were in serious danger for there were many who did not like me, as a person, as a Catholic, and many who did not like my husband, either. Was he a weak king? I thought not throughout our entire marriage. The servants were agitated, afraid for their lives, and did not wish to stay with us. I cannot blame them for that. My thoughts were for my children and my husband and I wanted a safe place for us to go. Where was safety when the world seemed set fair against us? The common people hated us, they shouted at us if we went out and so we shut ourselves away, so that the children would not be affected by this. It was unfair to include them in our problems.

I was very aware that the worry was taking a toll on my husband's health. His clothes did not fit him so well and he could not sleep at night, or so his equerry told me. I sought to have him sleep with me, but he said no for fear of keeping me awake. Ever did he think of me, this loving man. I so wanted to go to Parliament and tell them what I thought of them, but that would have been extremely dangerous and foolish of me. I knew that I was not very popular with my husband's advisers and his staff, even though I thought I knew better than them in many instances. They would not listen to me, they put aside everything I proposed and went on their way, which they said was the right way. I could not see that but if they were not prepared to listen to me, what could I do?

He came back from Parliament white, shaking, in the most awful rage, demanding that everyone left him. I went to him, held him and tried to stop the shaking. After a while he quietened I was able to ask what had happened. He told me in detail how foolish he had been left to look at how he resented it. It was the affront to his dignity as King more than as a man which had so deeply disturbed him. I think I knew at that moment his reign was through that I didn't want to accept it. Even as I thought that, I began making plans of where we could go, what we had to take with us, what the children would need, and was on the point of calling servants and putting arrangements in hand there and then. I stopped myself, for my husband's state of mind was more important and that is where I directed my attention. I called his physician who prescribed calming herbs which, when they came, certainly made a difference.

It was at that moment he confessed to me that he knew it was all over, too, and his eyes filled with tears. We sat holding one another, trying to gain some comfort from our mutual love and I believe for a while we did. As we sat, I began to think the unthinkable, that we might have to separate and that, I knew, would break his heart.

Chapter Seventeen

It became clear that there was danger, that those who supported Charles and worked with him were in danger, but more than that, his family was at risk from the crowds who had not understood the situation but had plenty of ammunition for their outrage from those who would bring him down. This he knew without anyone telling him, although they took every opportunity to do just that.

They left London. He had fears in his heart for Henrietta Maria, his beloved and adored wife, knowing how much she was held to be a problem, a Papist problem, in the hearts of many. He had fears in his heart for the children. He did not believe anyone would harm the royal offspring but he was not prepared to take any chances with their safety. He cared not for his own. His family was everything to him and he had to get them away from what might be a mob set on violence, for the mood of the city was fractious, dangerous, volatile.

They left London. Three words. Three words that encompassed a world of pain, hurt, disappointment, heartache and anger. Oh the anger! How it threaded its way through his mind, his sinews, into his beating heart and flowed with the blood through his veins. He gripped the reins so tight that by the time they reached their destination he could scarce unlock his fingers. It was the only way he could retain his dignity and preserve what pride he retained, determined that none should know of that anger. Not even Henrietta Marie suspected the depths of it but then she was consumed with her own concerns, her husband, the children, her homes and her attendants, not all of whom could go with them immediately.

They went to Hampton Court and there they stayed the night whilst deciding what they had to do. Again, a simple statement covering a sadness beyond belief. Abandoning their homes, their way of life, their friends, their attendants, for not all could travel with them, there simply was not enough room and he did not know where they would be making a home, all this hurt beyond belief. They did not sleep. The children did, for they were fair worn out from the journey and from the emotions which, no matter how hard anyone tried, could not be concealed from them. They had been uprooted in a hurry, they did not have all their known servants around them; they had not all their possessions with them. Charles arranged for them to have what could be packed in that short time and transported with them, the rest he said he would send for, when he knew what was to happen. A king on the run from his own people is not a situation that can be come to terms with overnight. A king was there to rule, supreme over everyone, including his Parliament. His word was law. His father had told him that many times and his dictates were obeyed instantly. Why then were Charles' ignored or defied? Was it because they were not in accord with what Parliament wanted in their entirety? Then people should have talked of it and come to a compromise or solution. But then, he told himself, when did he ever speak with Parliament without it degenerating into a full scale argument that had no resolution, nor could one be found, for royalty and Parliament were diametrically opposed to one another in their demands. They wanted concessions, he could not concede.

Plans were made over which he had no control, no say as to one way or the other, for his mind was in conflict and his emotions were torn up. He could not say yea or nay to those who advised him to let his family go to Europe, away from conflict. In the end it was Henrietta Maria's decision to relieve him of the burden of their safety. He hated it, in the sanctuary of their room he cried in her arms but it had to be, he could see

166

no alternative. The people were turning against her, she could be at serious risk of her life if she stayed and she would hold him back from all that he had to do.

They went from Hampton Court to Windsor Castle, from where messengers were despatched to make arrangements for a ship and safe passage. Arrangements were made for guards and companions to go with his beloved wife. The minute Fool, Jeffrey Hudson, elected to go with Henrietta Maria, saying she had need of him but in truth he had need of her, for he adored his Queen and could not bear to be parted from her. It was arranged that she would take the Crown Jewels with her, sell them and use the money to raise an army and put Charles back on the throne of England.

When the arrangements were finally made, they went to Dover and from there his heart took ship to Europe. Somehow he endured going down to the dockside and helping Henrietta Maria onto the gangplank and into the ship. Somehow he coped with the small arms of his children wrapping around him and then letting go, for a ship was an adventure and they were keen to explore. The sailors were deferential to him and to the queen, which helped a little. He knew they would be taken care of. One last kiss for his wife and he was back on dry land whilst the ship rocked gently at anchor before casting off and sailing out into the channel.

His heart and his youngest children went away on a ship which he followed with his gaze as far as he could. He rode along the cliff tops, watching the vessel moving away. It became smaller and smaller, a complete reversal of the time the toy ships sailed in, bringing the doll that was his wife aboard it. It seemed like yesterday but had been years of upset, from the time Villiers had engineered the discord between them, through Villiers' assassination and into the peaceful years of children and intense love, all thrown away because the king and Parliament could not come to an understanding. The

167

sails were unfurled, the ship moved faster across the water. Away from him. Away from his arms, his heart, his life. He had a terrible premonition that nothing would ever be the same again.

He waved his hat wildly, hoping they could see him, and prayed, oh only the Lord God knows how he prayed that the tears he held would not spill, that none would know how part of him had been ripped away and even as he rode, that part of him went further and further away. How would he manage without his confidant, his life, his love by his side? Who would he turn to for advice and comfort? How would he know how his family fared? How could he look to a future of conflict, for it was now written and writ large at that, there was conflict, as if he had not seen this coming so many years before, without that support?

Charles kept his two much loved older sons, Charles and James, with him. At least part of his family were staying in England, where they belonged. Oh how he resented the fact his Henrietta Maria had to leave! How it burned and tormented him! The Lord God knew it did still, as much if not more than it did that awful day when she left. His only consolations were that the Crown Jewels were with her and that she was safe. But oh, the thought of exchanging her safety for her presence was the dichotomy which tore him apart.

And oh the great plans which went wrong! The Crown Jewels were to help raise a Danish army but it did not happen and Hull, where he hoped for a stronghold, refused to open to him and the navy, for which he had fought so long, went over to the Parliamentarians.

Again he took refuge in facts and knew it. He knew what he wanted to say and how much he did not want to reveal how he felt. But the night demanded from him the truth and in facts there was no truth, there were only facts and they, which can be disputed, were twisted to suit the party concerned at the time.

So, feelings at that time. Feelings of loss and desolation as the ship disappeared out of sight. As the entire armed guard and those courtiers who stayed loyal turned away from the Dover cliffs and began the long trek north, finally arriving at the closed city of Hull where he had hoped for support and a base from which to campaign. Riding north with hope and aspirations, with plans to do this and raise that and send out arrays and call the loyal ones to him. Hull was the lodestone. Hull was closed, the gates fastened against him, clearly on the Parliamentary side.

Disappointment was a strong meal to consume.

He went to York.

York was a stronghold for him whilst what was fast becoming a Royalist party formed around Charles and those he had brought with him. He felt secure there, the walls were strong and the people were strong, too. There, voices were raised in support of Charles and they in turn were strong voices. It encouraged and lifted him to be with such people. There came word of those who would support him, there came the funds that began the campaign. There came the feeling he might be victorious after all. When the night doubts crept in and they did, of course they did, he felt the security of the city of York and thought: this might be my fight after all.

But in the dark lonely early hours of the morning, he was unsure, uncertain, worried about the future of the country, the monarchy and himself. He worried to the point that he began to feel ill and knew he could not go on like that. He spent hours, the night hours, in prayer and felt God was listening but not helping. It was as if He was saying 'you started this, Charles Stuart, you are on your own.' He knew this was foolish, of course it was. God would say no such a thing to an anointed king. But his uncertainty threw his doubts straight back at him and if God spoke at that time, he heard Him not because of the clamour of his own foolish thoughts.

He sent out orders from this secure base that loyal members should leave London. The orders seemed right at the time. Edward Hyde came to York, for which he was eternally grateful. Here was a man who moderated his demands, his words and his thoughts into a form that was more acceptable to others and did not cause too much aggravation for him. He needed that desperately, for without Henrietta Maria by his side he had great need of an advisor of sorts. Hyde was good for Charles. A royalist party truly was coming together, including some who had defied the king in the past. He let this go on, doubting their sincerity whilst grateful for their support. This did not make a good foundation for trust, he admitted to himself, but at the time ... he saw no other way but his own. He would have it then and now that he was - and remained - king and his word was absolute. Or should be. It continued to be a constant source of annoyance that he was ignored, bypassed, not given the chance to speak properly or the courtesy of being heard when he did do. One thing he knew for a surety is that when angered, which he was muchly during those days, his stutter all but disappeared. It was an offensive thing to him; it made him sound foolish at times and the look some people wore, a look of contrived patience as he struggled with words, only made it worse. Some people were not good at hiding their feelings as they waited for the sentences to be painfully completed.

He was told by informers that Parliamentary groups were forming and were even involved in skirmishes here and there with Royalists but nothing had been announced, as it were. No formal declaration of war had been made. Charles wondered why people were fighting but did not ask, it might have sounded stupid and he did so want to be seen as decisive for once. For all that, he spent time wondering what was causing the raised feelings so soon, had war broken out without his even being aware of it? Once again it undermined his confidence in himself and he looked around for something to boost that confidence, before he gave way to it and gave up.

Hyde suggested Charles go to Nottingham on a mission to raise more forces and encourage the men. It was the normal thing a king had to do and this time he did it with fervour and genuine emotion. This was his kingdom and it was at stake, or so it seemed to him at the time. On his journey, men flocked to his cause and Nottingham welcomed him with a great civic ceremony. He began to feel that the tide was turning in his favour and for a few days all was good.

But then things began to go wrong. Had he been the kind of person to be influenced by auguries, signs and other such fateful things, he would have read into that inauspicious start the fact that the conflict would not go his way. The problem was it was his fault, entirely his fault, from start to finish.

He wrote a proclamation of war and then changed his mind. Without Henrietta Maria to advise him, it was something he did frequently and often to his great disadvantage. With no time to rewrite the entire thing, he crossed out and amended and the Herald could not read the changes well. He read it as a jumble of words. None could understand it. He dismissed that small happening and ordered that the standard be raised.

It blew down in the night.

But no third thing happened and he went ahead with his plans. If that thing happening had occurred, even though he was not superstitious in any way, he might have thought again. Then again, he might not. In truth he was committed to an armed conflict whether he liked it or not.

The truth was, he did not like it; he did not wish to become embroiled in an expensive debilitating tragic war which would damage the country.

The truth was; he could see no way of avoiding it. The fighting had already started, each side had its principles and its stance and none could back down without considerable loss of face. He could not allow the monarchy to be so shamed. The parliamentarians had staked their considerable reputations on defying the monarchy. They wished to have a greater say in running the country, to the detriment of the king's rule. Charles could not allow that. They would not listen to him, because he could not agree to their demands.

Where else was there to go but armed conflict?

Was it not true that it was ever thus?

He needed to take London.

Ah, how simple were those words! How deceptively unbelievably simple that sentence was! And how he regretted thinking it would be a simple thing to do! Charles really believed that with the royalist army behind him, they could fight their way through the gathered forces and recapture the capital city. Then they would be in a better position to fight the war.

However … he had little money, only those who supported him were contributing and plate had been contributed to melt down but the Lord God knew it was insufficient to pay everyone. Those who opposed him had so many other places from which to draw their income.

The royalist army travelled as far as Edgehill. There they met with Parliamentary forces and he was surprised, even as he thought on it that long endless night, how quickly such armies were formed, drawn together, funded and equipped and set in the field to fight. There they confronted one another, gentry and peasant, Royalist and Parliamentarian as they came to be known. At that time Charles saw it only as 'Them – Us.' And the royalists, of course, had the right of God on their side, for monarchy, kingship, was God given, not people given.

He also found he was afraid. An army on the move was an imposing and frightening sight, so many armed men walking in step, carrying pikes, swords, battle axes and all manner of weapons, some wearing chain mail, some covered in armour, some riding the fearful destriers who seemed to have the battle fever in their very eyes and nostrils, judging by the way they pranced and snorted and had to be held on a tight rein all the time. Mostly, though, it was the men, those who walked with determined faces, that is, determined to give no quarter, to kill or be killed. Charles looked round at the men who made up his army, saw the quality of their weapons and armour, their mounts and their men and was afraid despite all that. He had never been in a battle before.

The noise was incredible, he had not bargained for the accumulated sound of screaming men and shrieking horses, of weapons hitting other weapons or clanging on armour, of the moaning of the wounded and the final sighs of the dying. The smell of blood and body fluids nauseated him but he could not leave the field, it would not be good for morale for him to ride away, much as he wanted to, much as he longed to.

The clash was violent and unforgiving. In those words he should have seen the pattern for the entire time of conflict in England. Violent and unforgiving. Had he known it would be a conflict that would set brother against brother, father against son, town against town, village against village, would he not have let that standard drop where it would and declare, no matter what, we must talk? In God's good name he now declared it to be so! But that was looking back and how clear it all was when looking back! How clear it was sitting there, as he was that night, looking over the memories, looking over the misery it caused, that it should not have happened.

If it had not happened, he would not be there that night, facing that which was to be faced, that which no man, no king, should have to live through.

But he was diverting, again.

Edgehill was unsatisfactory. Yes, there were casualties, yes there were dangers, yes the ball went close to him but still – even with royalist casualties and their casualties, it was indecisive and the battle ended without either side claiming a victory or being capable of claiming a victory. He felt ashamed that he should have been frightened, even though he knew that fear ran through everyone before they went onto the battlefield and the battle fever took over. He felt he should be above that, whilst reminding himself, again, he was only human, even if he did wear a crown.

A few weeks later they moved closer to London than they had done before. Charles was elated and then concerned, was his army strong enough to carry on, should they go to Kent and look for more support? Should they, could they, perhaps not and then again…

Uncertain of his direction, he ordered a withdrawal to Oxford, that fine university place of learning and elegant buildings. And there they stayed. And there they all but rotted that winter. He mourned and wept in his secret heart for Henrietta Maria, bemoaning the loss of her kind words and welcoming presence; he mourned and wept in his secret heart for the separation from his young ones. It was as if he had literally been torn apart. He could not stop his thoughts from turning to her, the one he missed, the one he loved so dearly. He would have given most anything to hold her for a time, to hear her voice and take her counsel on that which they were doing: fighting other Englishmen. It was not enough to have Rupert say 'they are only peasants!' for that he knew full well, but it made little difference. They were Englishmen, no matter their standing in life. They were Charles' subjects. For the first time in his life he acknowledged that peasantry were people in their own right. How many would say, too late, Charles Stuart, too late!

This long empty night, he thought; I believed we rotted that winter but in truth, that was not entirely correct. Christmas was held in style, with a Lord of Revels, everyone walked and talked and loved: in that some of the Royalist party consorted with women, that is, and those who were so inclined consorted with men. Charles walked and talked with those he trusted and how few they were only his heart knew. The truth is, although they were civilised people who walked the riversides and pathways of Oxford and he remembered what a beautiful city that was, they were in a state of suspension. They were awaiting conflict. They were embarking on that which was unbelievably damaging, a civil war. History had shown that a civil war tore the population apart. King Stephen fought his cousin Matilda and all but destroyed the country. Charles worried that he was in danger of doing the same thing. Even as he waited it out in the serene surroundings of Oxford, he knew it was dangerous, he knew it was a step too far. But he had gone too far to draw back. Everything said now he was committed, he had to go on, he had to assert himself.

All this, despite the news that the Crown Jewels were lost and no army would be raised. Everything would depend on him and those who supported him. It might not be enough. It had to be enough. There was no hope otherwise for him as king or the monarchy in England. It had to be enough.

His heart, his mind, his very soul cried out to the Lord God throughout the many services he attended that his beloved wife would be kept safe and his darling children kept safe from all illness, all accident, all threat to their lives and that they would be in each other's arms again before too long. The separation was a constant pain, one he found it hard to live with. He would lie awake in the long dark nights and long to go to his wife's rooms, to reach for the comfort of her, forgetting for that brief moment that she was far away from him and then the long dark night would become an empty one and the pain would shaft through him, more acute than any sword, lance or axe could ever be. None could or would see his tears for they were for him alone.

Chapter Eighteen

Charles' heart's desire was fulfilled in July of the following year when Henrietta Maria returned to England, bringing the children with her.

Ghoul, angel, whoever he was addressing the thoughts at that time, would surely see that his story read more as a chivalric romance than that of a king at war. But of a surety there would be many men who would write of the clashes, the indecisive battles – and how he wished they could have one decisive battle to show the Parliamentarians that they were men who could fight and win! – the casualties, the strategies plotted and carried through by his generals and others in command of the various parts of the Royalist army but none who would write of the aching loneliness of a king without his queen. If it had been an arranged marriage which had never turned into a true relationship, then the ache would not be there. But it had. And so, in the day and in the night he longed for the one little person who could put his world right.

He knew there would no doubt be many who would denigrate the Royalist side of the argument, many who would point a finger at a king who brought his country into conflict, but that was for the future. He knew full well, though, he would not come out of it as a king without a stain on his reputation. He also know full well he was not the first and would not be the last monarch to be tainted by his actions. Charles' much-loved and revered father was a good king, in his own way, but his court had been tainted by the unnatural love he held for so many of his courtiers and in particular for that arch-villain, Villiers. No, no, not now! His thoughts shied away from Villiers.

Instead he decided to dwell for a short time, a happy short time, on the period he spent with his wife. Oh but there was so much to talk of and so little time in which to talk of it, how they hurried through the political talk and got to talking of what really mattered: their adored children, their time together and how they would spend it, the love they had and – he had no need to say it: everyone knew full well what happened between a husband and a wife who loved one another.

It fair broke his heart to think she had been in England a full six long agonising months before she could go to him. Six months during which he had walked and talked and ate and slept and discussed and planned and all with the biggest part of his heart and soul missing from his body and his life.

Henrietta Maria spoke movingly of her terrible crossing, of the time with the Royalist army while they made arrangements to bring her safely to Oxford and to him. How he praised the men who took such great care of his most precious possession! He could not begin to describe the joy that all but burst out of his body when he beheld her face and held her close! It was - and remained - a moment of the greatest happiness to him. It comforted him even as he sat there, before a fire which was dead, a fire which had consumed that which it was given to consume, as life consumes that which it is given to consume, as the Civil War had consumed his life. As far as Charles was concerned, it had taken and destroyed his good name, his country and his people. It had taken his marriage and broken it, for he knew that night, he recognised it for a fact where he had clung to a vain hope, that he would never see his wife again. In His name, he thought, whoever is listening, he had to say that no matter what people did to him from that moment onward, nothing but nothing could have hurt more than that thought. The child of their union, his new daughter, his beautiful baby, what of her? How would she remember the man who fathered her? As a failure, as a disaster, as a proud king whose people turned against

178

him? And if the people turn against their king, does that mean he is a bad monarch? What would people tell her of him? He had no doubt his darling wife would tell her of the good things her father did, of the good person he was – but would that compensate for those who would whisper otherwise? Ah, of such things are heart-wrenching doubts, fears, disappointments and regrets made. So many regrets, so much doubt, so many disappointments and the fears, oh could he but speak of the fears. No, for that was something too deep within him to be produced and aired even to those who did not exist outside of his imagination.

For someone so small, he carried a large amount of guilt, unhappiness, resentment, even hatred which he had to lose for fear of going to his Maker with such a thing on his conscience and on his immortal soul, thus placing it in danger. So the trawl through his memories and life, apart from easing his mind and whiling away the lonely desperate hours, was his attempt to come to terms with all that he had done and to make his peace with his God in his own way before the end. He had known what that would be long before the trial, he had seen which way the straws floated on the river's surface; he could read the signs as well as anyone. His imprisonment, his gaolers, his treatment at their hands, all told him which way the straws were floating on that particular river. He had no illusions, no illusions at all. They were taken from him at the time of his capture.

But to return to Oxford, to the court there, small as it was, to his time with his wife who, as usual, began to take over and dictate policy. This he would not have minded but oh, she would argue so with those who were his finest tacticians and his finest general and the finest minds he could have to help him fight the war which had so unfortunately begun, seemingly without one positive step being taken to stop it. He could not stop her arguing, she had her way over everything and a strong opposition to all Parliamentary action was formed. He could admit it now; he went along with it for the sake of peace. Unfortunately he knew the decision was wrong, so very wrong. He should have been stronger; he should have taken the initiative and ordered more direct action. He should have, he should have; he asked himself, will I go to my grave saying these words? But what use is it to say these things so long after the event, so long since it all went wrong and Oxford was threatened and his newly pregnant Queen had to leave for her own safety? No use at all. That was something he knew. That was something he had accepted, as he had accepted so many other things.

How did Henrietta Maria feel when she said goodbye to him? Did her heart break as much as his, or was she more concerned with her pregnancy and her family? How could he even think of such things? Threatened by Parliamentary forces as he was, she carrying their child at the time, she had to go for her own safety. She was hustled away through England, looking for safe havens as she went. How did she feel, how did it affect her? Would he ever really know? He heard reports later that it was a most difficult time for her, more difficult than at any time before and of course this reflected in her confinement, the most dangerous she had ever had.

Charles knew how it affected him; it was as if every separation they had endured up to that time had been of nothing compared with this one. They knew they may never see one another again – they knew it in their hearts and souls - and they were right. He knew, despite his many attempts at bravado, that he would not win against those who would see him and his Royalist party gone from this world, this life, this God given rank that he held.

He knew from communications he received that her journey to the continent was hazardous, that they even fired on her ship! God rot their souls for wishing to end the life of his Queen! England's Queen! How could they, how dare they!

In the middle of all this heartbreak he took his courage, his sensibilities and his concentration and won a decisive and good victory in Cornwall. His forces routed the Parliamentarians to his complete satisfaction. He sat there with a smile, remembering the good feeling of knowing he was victorious, that although men had died, the Royalist army had overcome. He sat there with the chill of the air penetrating him, all but glowing with that particular memory. It was good that he had at least one major battle to hold on to, but it hurt to know that if he had but held his nerve, there would have been more such victories and possibly a change in the tide of fortunes.

He decided not to go through the many battles, the losses, the sadness, the disappointments, the setbacks. He knew all that had no doubt been recorded by someone, somewhere, just as his every move had been recorded by someone, somewhere. The only things left to him, things that were personal and secret, were his thoughts, his feelings and his prayers. Everything else appeared to be public property. That was something that displeased him considerably. He believed that his life, his actions, were his own. His wife and his time with her, was his own. His children and their upbringing was his and his alone. He was aware, could he not be aware, that every king was a part of history, part of the very earth that the land was made of, this England, this country – He said it aloud, said it to the ashes and the chill of the room, this country that his actions tore apart in a war that was so savage none shall be the better for having endured it. Not one person would remain unaffected by it. Not one person had managed to avoid being touched by it.

He knew, from his many lessons, from his reading, from his understanding of history, that in the past battles were isolated affairs, that a battle could be raging in one area and those living in another adjoining area would perhaps hear the sound of man-made thunder as the great cannons were employed or siege engines used and those persons would shake their head and carry on with their lives. Maybe they would see the wounded, the dying, the defeated as they fled or tramped from the fields of blood but no, it did not touch their lives.

The conflict which Charles set in motion, albeit unwittingly, albeit without malicious intent, albeit through no real fault of his own, was cruel, was all pervasive and divisive and hurtful in the extreme.

He prayed fervently: 'God grant that at no time will a war be so cruel again, that man will not fight his neighbour, his brother, his father or his son in the name of the king or of Parliament. God grant this one wish to a man who will soon be standing before the Throne of Judgement to answer and atone for what he had done in this terrible period of time.'

He wished, so much he wished with all his heart and soul that he could roll back the years and do everything differently, that he could tell Villiers he would make up his own mind, that he would ask Henrietta Maria to be a loving wife but tell her, please do not interfere with policy, that he was capable of handling that himself, of telling Strafford that he would live and holding his hand back from signing that execution warrant, that he would listen to those who spoke with wise voices and not those who spoke with forked tongues.

If only, he thought, he could do that, he would do so many things and he would not be there, in a cold room with a dead fire and guards at the door as if he would run, as if he would try again to evade those who hold him captive, as if he would try again to evade that which lie ahead of him. No, this he would not do, not now, not again. That time is past but to tell 'them' such a thing would be to tell it to the fast moving wind that carries the words and sends them scattering to the four corners of this earth. They would not believe him. He admitted, in this moment of candidness and in the secrecy of his own thoughts and mind, they were right to disbelieve because of past actions but they did not know his mind now, they did not know he was resigned to that which would happen.

They fought on. The armies fought at Marston Moor and the Royalists lost. Brave Rupert rescued many from that dreadful battle, all honour be to his name and his memory! He served Charles well, that valiant soldier and tactician. Would that he had had a whole room full of people like Rupert, how much better would the battles have gone, how much better would the whole war have been, but once again he diverted, as if it was all too much to bear.

He knew of his mistakes. He saw them as clearly as he saw the walls, the cold grim walls which held him there. It seemed for an eternity of time he had been looking at cold grim walls, at Oxford, at Uxbridge, at Carisbrooke. Cold grey walls. Hang them with tapestries if you will, beneath the trappings of simulated warmth are cold grey walls, he thought. He saw further than the outward coverings, he saw beneath them as he saw beneath the smiling faces and grim faces and indifferent faces who came and attended to his needs and then left again. One thing a man soon learns and that is to read death in another man's eyes. They did not need to say the word. He stared Death in the face.

Did it hurt?

It did. It hurt a lot. Now the hurting was such that he –

He lied to himself. It did. It hurt a lot. But the hurting was different. He no longer hurt because it was almost all over, but because of what he had done to England. Because of what he had done in a mistaken attempt to fight on, to wish for aid from others which came not to his rescue, to offer concessions to Catholics in return for help which came not to his rescue.

He hurt, in some ways, because of the battle of Naseby. Would that he had kept his senses and not allowed the army to be divided, would that he had been sensible and listened to those who counselled him not to send men away. He thought he knew best.

He had said earlier that if he could roll back time, he would do things differently, he would tell others to be quiet, that he knew what he was doing. He asked himself, in the cold light of the long dark night, did he know best during that war? Did he really know best at a time when he was homeless and rootless and at the mercy of others for what felt like a lifetime, staying where he could, sheltering where he was able, taking the hospitality of those who would grant it to him to keep him safe for a while longer, to let him rally the troops a little more to fight on a few more days, a few more weeks when everything, everything, told him it was done. The battles were lost. The war was over. It was finished. England had a new regime, one that he felt would not be to people's liking when they came to fully experience it.

Testimony of Prince Rupert

It is my belief that I was born to be a soldier. I had no other interest in life. I took every chance to be in conflict, to learn strategies, to listen to more senior commanders, to take notice of all that went on and on course to be in the thick of the fighting. I fought in various places on the continent and I knew that I was held in high esteem by my uncle King Charles of England. He proved this by awarding me an MA at Oxford and asking that celebrated painter, Mr Van Dyke, to paint my portrait. My uncle was extremely useful to me in many ways. I thought him a very good King, I thought he had the best interests of the English people in his heart, and I thought him a fine tactician out on the battlefield, but here I was wrong.

It is hard for me to say just where the Civil War in England went wrong. I was very keen to come to England and help my uncle and we had some resounding victories because of it. There are those who would say that it was not entirely due to my influence, but they are entitled to their opinion, I would not argue with them. I would say that during my presence in England at that time we had some resounding victories.

I do believe one of the problems of the Civil War was simply that there was a good deal of indecision. When there was a victory, it should have been pressed to its ultimate, to ensure that the best use was made of everything that went on. We should have swept from one victory to the next, whilst we had the parliamentarians on the run. It never happened. This is what we needed, and if we had been able to do it, we would have turned the tide and the people of England would have been with us. People are, on the whole, very much like sheep. They follow the leader. In this case, it was the winning side, regardless of which political stance they took. So it proved to be with this ongoing war. It was a great pity. There was so much that could have been done, had the royalist is been able to build on their victories. I am repeating myself. I am fully aware I am repeating myself, but it must be said. My uncle's indecision and some of the comments made by his other senior commanders and advisers, meant that I could not arrange for the army to do what I wanted it to do. Was I right? History will say that the wars planned out just as they should, that the parliamentarians had to win, that the royalist cause was lost, because of my uncle's determination to stand up for the divine right of kings, no matter what. I disagree.

In my eyes the people were wrong, they who took up arms against their King. Whether or not he agreed with the divine right of kings, whether or not they agreed that he was right or wrong to dissolve parliament and rule on his own, you do not go against a King's wishes. To go into conflict against your King is the ultimate treachery, in my eyes, and I was willing to fight to the death for my uncle for that very reason.

There were those among his commanders who would not accept my youth, my decisions, those who resented the fact that my leadership had produced those resounding victories, where their actions hadn't... and I sensed tremendous jealousy and resentment among them all.

Whatever anyone thought I was made Captain-General of the Army but I clashed regularly with other commanders who did not have my vision, my clarity of thought, my ability to see through that which was fog like surrounding a battlefield. Yes I lost battles, yes I lost cities, and countless men, but what did they lose? How much did I put fear into them, riding as I did with my dog by my side, fearlessly going into battle, taking all before me? Did I not justify my place in the army?

But where then were my thoughts for my uncle? They were in the decision I made that the Royalists were not going to win and I advised him to do what he could not do: seek a treaty with parliament. It was his only way out of the predicament that he could not take it, his pride would not let him. That is the way I saw it, although he insisted he believed he could win. That, I thought, was the cover-up for the fact his pride would not allow him to turn back the clock and make a treaty with parliament.

It all fell apart with great rancour and bitterness with a court-martial that had to be held to clear my name - which it did but it rained a relationship between my uncle and myself. Eventually I left the country and left him to it. There was nothing else I can do the trust had gone, the commonsense had gone, all that was left was an ongoing useless conflict that was taking life needlessly.

I heard of his subsequent trial and execution with the greatest sorrow imaginable. It could have all been so very different. He could have been a great King had he been able to give just a little, these people would have respected him, his parliament would have respected him to, but he could not take that step. That pride, that stiffness within him meant that he laid his life on the line, and he lost it.

I do not think I'd have had a sad day than the day I knew he was to be executed. I found it hard to believe that the people of England could do such a thing to their King but they did.

I can never in my heart forgive them for that.

Chapter Nineteen

A conference was finally arranged between the Parliamentarians and Charles and all those who advised him. Charles let them come, knowing they would not achieve anything but needing everyone to know at least he had tried.

They met in Oxford and they talked, but they would not agree to hand back any powers to the king. They left empty-handed; did they for a moment think he would surrender his sovereignty to them? Did they truly believe they could approach a king, placed in that position by God Himself, and expect that king to surrender to them? What fools they were, what fools they are! Where were their credentials, when were they touched with sacred oil and the crown placed on their heads? Those were questions they could not answer but still they sought to take the sacred role from him. Those who would sit in judgement on him, what divine right did they call on? None. There was none.

Ah, too late did he rant against them, for they had the final word. The Royalist armies fought here and there and in far flung places, they fought but they could not hold out against Parliamentarian forces which seemed more determined and better equipped than the royalists. Where did the money come from to equip them so? Charles sought every penny he could, melted plate as fast as he could, much as it grieved him to destroy such fine pieces, just to raise the money for the army he had.

And so he came, with an inevitability that could not be ignored, to Naseby. He asked himself as well as anyone else who might be in the room with him, those he could not see, those he was aware of – let none know of his visions for fear of them deciding he was insane – why did he divide his army? Why did he not go forward and crush the so-called New Model Army? What a foolish name, what a foolish decision! But he thought his men were strong enough to fight in the north and the south-west, he did not envisage the overwhelming force of the so-called Army.

He lost – everything. Men, munitions, the war. And he roamed here and there, being harboured where he could, experiencing hospitality such as he would not have believed from those who believed in him still. He knew he owed them all a huge debt of gratitude and eternal thanks.

It was an unbelievable time of heartbreak and bitterness. Being harboured, being hidden, to think he, a proud king, had come to that! It was difficult in the extreme to continually be smiling and cheerful and thankful and grateful – even though he was – for the hospitality and the support, there were times he wanted to shout and scream his rage at an unseeing, seemingly uncaring world. He felt himself to be dead inside, for the one he loved was far away and he was likely never to see her again. He knew, how well he knew, what a trial his wife was to those around him, those she would argue with, those she defied. She thought she knew best and in some instances she really did, but in others, he had to admit with a heavy heart, she did not and she should have kept quiet, as befitted her place. But he could not bear to stop her when she began her vociferous discussions with his advisors who deferred to her rank and quietly tried to defend their positions and stances in regard to the war and the situation in which they found themselves.

All this he knew. He knew it with clarity of vision only hindsight can give. But he also knew that he loved Henrietta Maria beyond all sense and reason, she remained his doll, his beautiful wife, his Queen, his children's mother, his heart, his soul-mate and he knew she lived and he knew he would not see her again in this life.

And so he thought, in truth and with the bitterest of despair, he was and remained a walking dead man for his heart was elsewhere and never would it be returned to him.

When Charles returned to Oxford, eventually, when the Parliamentarians had finished destroying his army and his hopes, the memories of walking there with Henrietta Maria, of being there with her, of holding her and loving her were so painful he wondered if he would ever stand upright again.

The papers, his papers, were captured. How simple a sentence was that, too … but more than that, his plans, dreams and schemes were captured and turned against him. Henrietta Maria wrote to him and still he and his wife did not agree on many things. She could not see his view, being a Roman Catholic as she was, and not Church of England, as he was. He had no help from her, even though he sought it.

More than that, though, was the embarrassment and the sheer rage he felt that his plans were exposed to those who would bring him down. But for all the feelings he endured at that time, he still had plans which they could not know as they were concealed within his heart, along with his hatred for them, for those who would challenge the right of a king to govern his people in the way he thinks best. And those who sought to impeach and harm his God sent Queen, too. He wondered if their spirits would rest easy when they returned to God's realm, knowing what they had in their black hearts and minds. Or if they would reach Heaven at all, whether the doors would be shut to them as Hull was shut to him.

There were some things he was finding hard to forgive. He knew he would be judged on them when he returned home but for now, he thought, God forgive me for not finding forgiveness for them in my heart. It is beyond my ability to do so at this time.

He was cold. The room was chilled and he was chilled beyond belief by his thoughts, his memories and his yearning for his wife and children.

He was haunted by another thought, too, the word 'haunt' was carefully chosen. He was sitting in the darkness and in the cold, wondering what his father would have to say of the way he had destroyed the country he said he loved. What words would he have for 'Baby Charles' now? What rant and rage would he show him for the mistakes he had made, for the ill-chosen advisors and the equally ill-chosen decisions which lost them the major battles? Ah, but he dare not venture into what he would think of his wife and Queen … for fear of his own conscience assaulting him. He almost thought, I could wish to speak with him for a few moments to guide me on the morrow, but no, he would have nothing to say on such a momentous occasion, that I know. He would probably laugh that sneering, contemptuous laugh of his which cowed so many of his courtiers, everyone but Villiers, of course, who believed he was not included in any of his father's rants at any time, or his contempt, either. Charles found himself unbalanced for some hours if he experienced his father's laughter or his rage, as if he had to rebuild confidence in himself.

And that was something he had never admitted to anyone at any time in his life. Not even to his beloved wife.

Charles surrendered to the Scots. It seemed logical at the time, create a division between the English and the Scots and sow discord amongst his enemies, of which there were many. He heard tell of the divisions within the Presbyterians, of the rise of the Independents, who sought for freedom of worship in parishes – as if that would work, he thought with derision – of divisions among the members of Parliament themselves. None could reconcile their thoughts with another, it would seem, or so it was reported to him. And was he not still the king? Still the supreme ruler of England and of Scotland and of any other land which belonged to this benighted country, ravaged by war and by people who thought of themselves, not for themselves?

The problem, in his mind, was this. He wanted a settled religion. The Presbyterian party was scared of the thought of radicals ruling their own parishes. The army could not be disbanded without pay and they were in turn not prepared to accept the Presbyterian regime. It ended up with him being unable to surrender the Episcopal Church and the Presbyterians unable to accept it. It was something they could not bring themselves to discuss, let alone accept. They stuttered and argued and talked around it without saying as much.

Then the members of parliament came with their proposals: that he subscribe to the Covenant, that he surrender control of the militia for twenty years and on and on and on, things he could not agree to. So he didn't. His requests to go to London were denied, but the arguments continued and he felt safe as long as they did so, for no agreement could be reached on his future if they argued.

Then they outwitted him by buying off the Scots and moving him to a new location. He was treated hospitably - but he was a prisoner.

In his heart he knew the fight was over but in his mind he felt there was a chance, provided he kept his head clear at all times. Oh, but that was hard to do! He fought the black thoughts which threatened to consume him, tried to keep his planning decisions in straight order whilst he awaited the outcome of what was – to him – an illegal detention. Not that anyone was prepared to argue that point with him, it seemed.

Charles was torn into three. He was a small person, this he acknowledged, he never grew as tall or as strong as his brother Henry. He bore little resemblance physically to his father, but notwithstanding his lack of stature and his other limitations of mind and body, God chose him to be king. He did this by taking Henry home to be with Him in Heaven, what clearer indication could there be than He wanted Charles to be King? But those who were supposed to work with him, his Parliament, contrived to take from him his Queen and his wife, his children and his liberty.

Part of him continued to mourn for his wife and family, part of him was broken by the fact, the horrors, of the divisive war they had fought and the third part of him was shackled and held and he resented it with every particle of his being.

He held fast to the thought that he could continue to pay one party off against the other and in doing so, he would reclaim his freedom and his throne.

He held fast – and wrongly, for they had other plans, other demands. Whilst they restored the independent members to Parliament, others fled and the sword dominated it all. Force not freedom, demands not discussions, it went on and what went on was often outside of his knowledge. A blindness seemed to come over him, he was not in touch with the true heart of the country or the negotiations. A sense of despair began to creep into his mind and would not be shaken, no matter how hard he prayed or how much he spoke or how much he was encouraged to believe otherwise.

Hampton Court became his place of residence –his prison, his gilded cage.

He was chilled through this night, even the wine he drank was cold to the palate when he wished for heat – and he noted that that he did not refer to the place as his home. For as sure as he was sitting here discussing his life with no one, and he freely admitted that in this late hour, Hampton Court was a prison and not a home. Comfortable, yes, with good food and good wine and much to entertain him, but he had no wife with him and no freedom. Whatever the surroundings, that makes the place a prison.

Those who brought him information, the courtiers, the servants, the grooms, many and varied were those who sought the news and items he needed, said that Sir John Oglander, he of Nunwell House on the Isle of Wight, was a confirmed Royalist and that he would welcome the King should he find a way to break free of the prison bars. He had also heard tell that the Governor of the island, one Hammond, was a devout Parliamentarian. He would be in danger if he ventured there but then again, he wondered if the Governor would be kind enough to allow him to stay at Nunwell House for a while. From there he could perhaps raise a Royalist group to help him make a permanent escape to the Continent, to be reunited with his wife and his heart. For all this Hammond might be Governor, Charles was still his king, he was still a subject and subservient to the king's rule and his orders. Or so he told himself. Sir John would have royalist contacts, people with money, people with influence, people who would rise up against the Parliamentarians and help the king become free again.

Hesitation was not worth considering. Action was needed. Whatever the outcome, he had to make some kind of move, for being held prisoner was damaging to his heart and soul, was adding to the depression he was feeling, was depleting his energies and his will to go on. That would not do. In the eyes of the Lord God and many in the country, he was still the reigning monarch.

Charles set plans in motion for an escape from his prison. He recruited loyal servants and men at arms who could be bribed not to talk of the venture, arranged for horses and a few supplies to be available and finally set the date when they would actually leave. All this filled him with a sense of excitement and tingling anticipation, freedom was so close and yet so far, success depended on others and not on himself but he thought he could do it, he could carry it off, he could be victorious. It was all he could do to keep his 'king' face in place when anyone visited him.

The November night planned for his 'escape' was both cold and wet but the exhilaration of being free compensated for that. He found the fact the guards were singularly lacking, as if someone had arranged for him to leave, to be suspicious. Mayhap they had, to give them the chance to unload a burden. Of a surety no plan is ever secret if more than one person knows of it. With a heavy wool cloak wrapped around his even more slender body, a felt hat jammed firmly on his head, he mounted a fine horse, waved to his escort and set off.

They rode flat out for the coast.

Riding all night in foul weather, with his equerries and guards around him, his heart singing for the freedom he had to ride through his country freely, his country, his people, his legacy, Charles believed he could win this battle. Then his thoughts ran in every direction, none sensible. He let them go for fear of tangling them up in sensible thoughts later. All that mattered at that moment was there were no walls around him.

They took shelter in an inn once they reached Portsmouth and Charles sent equerries to the island to confer with the Governor as to his intentions towards him. Foolish he might have been but he thought to clear the position with the man before entrusting him with the king's personage. It meant a day of being confined – again – but at least he was confined at his own wish, not someone else's and he had the added stimulus of knowing at least one person on the island, which was so close and yet so far, was Royalist in his leanings. And where there was one, there would be others. With that kind of anticipation, it was almost easier to pass the day waiting without getting irritated or annoyed.

A day later the Governor, Robert Hammond, returned with Charles' men and John Ashburnham, another Royalist, who met up with Hammond before he got to the king. Hammond seemed friendly, deferential, pleased to see him – at least on the surface anyway. He told Charles he would do him all the duty and service in his power. Charles chose to believe him, chose to think that once he was on the island, he could use his powers and influence generally to raise that royalist army he so needed. It was balm to his still troubled mind.

They took ship next morning across the Solent, which was running a high tide, making the journey somewhat uncomfortable. With his guards and private reservations haunting his mind, he docked, got back on the horse and rode to Carisbrooke Castle. The day was overcast but the sense of freedom still filled him and he viewed the towering edifice of the castle, poised on its hill outside Newport, with delight. It seemed a secure place from which to launch a counter-attack.

Everyone made him welcome, his retinue was absorbed into the castle buildings and Charles himself was welcomed by the Seneschal and taken to the Great Hall. There he could sit by the huge fire and warm himself after the long cold journey across the Solent and then to the castle itself.

"I'd like to spend some time with my friend Sir John Oglander," he told Hammond later, as they sat drinking mead and discussing the situation in England.

"Of course, Your Majesty," Hammond responded. "We know well of Sir John and his fine home in Brading."

Charles irritably wondered why he felt as if he had to ask permission to visit a friend but that was how it felt. He began to wonder if he had made a mistake in coming to the Isle of Wight, whether Hammond had told the Parliamentary forces he was there. It would be an ideal place to hold someone captive. Darkness began to shroud his thoughts and he became uncomfortable. He excused himself and, calling his squires, went to his room where he spent a sleepless night fighting his own thoughts. Was Hammond a true royalist or was he under the control of the New Model Army? Was this freedom - or was this another prison?

Nunwell House was beautiful. He said it unreservedly. It had elegance and style and Charles would have been glad to have stayed there for some days, but one night was agreed with Hammond, who he was more and more inclined to think was a gaoler and less and less a friend, so one night it had to be. Sir John was a charming and hospitable host, his household worked hard to ensure the King had a good dinner and the wine was excellent.

For him, the real purpose of the visit and the real pleasure of the visit was being able to speak freely in absolute confidence with someone he trusted. After dinner, mostly seafood and then a woodcock tastefully prepared and seasoned, they retired to Sir John's private room and there, in the security of the rich panelling and the heavy drapes shrouding the windows, they spoke long about his situation.

Charles knew, for he would have been told if it were not the case, that Sir John had never spoken of the words which passed between them. He said he would take them to his grave and this Charles believed.

They spoke of Hammond, of the doubts which Charles sensed behind his words, of the belief which had come to him overnight that Hammond had been placed on the island to entrap him. He had not seen it before he came, or he would have gone straight to the Continent instead of coming to the island. He only saw it in hindsight. Hammond's words were mealy mouthed, to put it bluntly and he added them to the fact that his 'escape' had been all too easy. When held in other places, he had been aware of guards on every exit and knew that every letter had been perused before being passed to him. If they did not realise he was aware of this, they were more stupid than he thought. But when the cage door is left open, do you stop to consider why? Do you peer round corners, looking for the missing guards or do you race off into the dark night, sensing freedom and liberty and release from all chains? What normal person would do otherwise! They took a chance on allowing him his freedom, not knowing for a surety which way he would go, but he also saw that they were astute enough to have anticipated his going to a Royalist island and circumvented it. The Royalist Governor had been replaced by this man, who no doubt held strong Parliamentarian views or he would not have the position. It had happened so fast that the hand of Cromwell and others could be seen in the hasty appointment. It was a well-planned trap. He had fallen into it. Foolish Charles.

He had believed that he could raise a Royalist group from the Isle of Wight and return to the capital with force to regain his throne. These were the plans he discussed at Nunwell House that night, full of good food, sitting by a blazing fire, holding a goblet of fine wine and listening to the wise words of a good man in a room which was beautiful and secure. He could not have asked for more. Well, in truth, he could, he needed a plan which would rescue his standing as monarch, a plan to displace those Parliamentarians who were holding all the power and all the money. It became obvious as they talked that it could not be done.

Sir John was obviously emotional, distressed that he could not help but in truth he helped more than he realised. By being a person with whom Charles could talk through his plans, albeit bad ones, he helped to show him where they would fail if he tried. It was better not to launch into something blindly and suffer the consequences than not launch into it and suffer the consequences. Enough blood had been shed for his cause, he did not wish to be responsible for yet more. The deaths lay heavy enough on his conscience as it was. Sir John had a good mind, a logical sensible mind, he discussed the plans with his king honestly and openly, which is more than many would have done, or had done in the past. Would that they had done so, he might have made fewer mistakes during his reign. Sir John had his respect and friendship for that alone but he went on to be a greater friend than that. His devotion to his king was complete.

They talked long into the dark hours and then Charles retired to the room set aside for him and his equerry. He did not sleep. He knew it was nothing but a prelude to the end.

The testimony of Sir John Oglander

I come with anger. I feel anger burning at my heart, in my mouth, in my throat, and I hear it ringing in my ears. The anger is directed against those who held my King in their power, held him against his will, and finally murdered him.

There will be those who will say that this was no murder. They will say that it was a sentence of the court, decided upon after a trial, and was carried out according to the law. I would disagree with them. The trial was a fiasco, the court had already decided my King's fate before he even set foot in the hall, whatever he said in his own defence was sure to be ignored. No witnesses were called on his behalf, his legal arguments were ignored. How can this be a proper trial? It was not.

It is one of the greatest honours any man can have, the opportunity to grant hospitality to a King. When his Majesty came to Nunwell House, there to eat dinner with me and relax for a while, to partake of my wine and the peace that my home gave him, it gave me a memory I cling to even now. If I had but known that when he rode away from me the next morning he would meet with the treachery of Hammond, I would not have let him go. I would have pleaded with him to head in the opposite direction, back to the port and to take ship to Southampton or Portsmouth and, with the whole of England before him, to have a better chance of escape.

I did not know.

Instead he met with Hammond, who took him to Carisbrooke Castle and there imprisoned him.

Oh I know it did not look like that. I know it was 'here is a good place to stay and of course you can visit your friend...' but the truth is out there. He was imprisoned. The sad thing was, he knew it from the moment he set foot in the place. Too late!

There are some things which are unforgivable. That is one of them. I could not go to Hammond and say "why did you imprison our King?" For he would have answered "I did the bidding of those who ordered me." In that he would speak truth. But, in some instances a man has to go by his conscience and not by orders. I would dear like to know how Hammond lives with his conscience these days. He held, behind castle walls, the anointed king of this country. I know full well that history repeats itself a thousand times and a thousand times in the past men have been imprisoned: aristocrats, Kings, holy men, criminals, the morally bereft and the insane, but in truth, we have not learned from such acts. One fact is clear above all others, a King is above all people in his land. All people are subservient to the

King. Therefore it follows that no man can imprison a King. To do so goes against all natural law. I would go further and say that to put a King on trial is against all natural law. The fact is that the King is anointed by those who do God's will. God's will is not meant for man to throw away as it suits him.

I have been a loyal supporter of his Majesty for as long as I can recall. I followed his unfortunate progress throughout the conflict but have to say now I was shocked and heartsick to learn that he had landed on the island. Whether he sought sanctuary at Carisbrooke Castle is not something I know. All I know is he came to visit me in my home and that was a great honour for me.

Let me go back to that day. His Majesty came right weary, travel stained, hungry and thirsty. I know not why he seemed to have such a need for food and drink. Did not the people in the Castle give him sufficient sustenance, were they trying to deprive him even then? I gave him a room, with an ante-room for his squire who took care of his king. When he had taken much of the dust from his clothes, he came down to the room where I waited, with mead for him to drink, whilst my servants saw to his meal. He spoke to me in a tired, dispirited way, of his regrets and his sadness at the conflict which had raged throughout the land. He said he wished it had never begun, but that he felt he had no choice. I pledged to him that night my loyalty and in return he told me he had never ever believed otherwise. I saw how he began to relax a little, Nunwell House has that effect on people. It is a quietening, calming home where people feel secure. His guards were at the doors so none could enter and spoil his evening. I gave him that which I could, a bag of gold coins. It was all I could do, for I had been much impoverished by the war, by the demands of my estate, and by some insufficient harvests. His Majesty professed himself to be content with my small gift and thanked me most sincerely for it.

We dined that evening on sweetbreads, whiting in fine sauce, oysters and prawns, cod gently steamed with shrimps and finally a dish of woodcocks. I also gave him wine. I know that his Majesty is not much partial to wine, but mead is not a good accompaniment for a meal.

We spoke long over our meal and the time spent afterwards, words which I hold in my heart to this day. Words I am not prepared even now to give to the world. In many ways they were his Majesty's gift to me, and I will not speak of them.

I will not speak either of the words we shared when I visited him every week during his confinement in Carisbrooke Castle. Could I call it anything but that I would, but the truth is there in the word I used.

I know how Hammond's men tried to overhear that of which we spoke, how they tried to gather evidence against his Majesty, how they contrived with various tasks to be around us as we walked and talked in the castle grounds. But when we knew they were there we spoke of nothing more than the weather, harvest, the condition of the castle itself, and other such mundane matters. When they became bored, they moved away and then his Majesty could speak to me of that which he held his heart. Those words too were a gift to me, and such gifts are not given away. Nor are they purchased at any price. And they never will be.

I looked upon my King as my friend, someone held against their will, needing friendship, companionship and compassion at that time. After all, was he not separated from all that he loved? The Queen was not with him. Much as he loved his children, it was Queen Henrietta Maria who was his heart and soul, and she was not with him. During this long and lonely time, I do believe my visits were the one thing which kept him from thinking too long about his future. At least, I would like to think so. That is a service few get to render to their monarch. I consider myself honoured.

But it was with a heavy heart that I realised the weeks were sliding away and that sooner or later he would be taken to London and all would be finished. We both knew it although we did not speak of it much. It was too hard to think on, he was a young man, not yet in his fiftieth year and I was old in comparison, being in my sixtieth years and yet at times he seemed older and wiser and sadder than I had been throughout all my trials and tribulations. I felt that, no matter what I had suffered, his suffering had been far, far worse and that had weighed him down and aged his mind beyond his years. I looked into a face that had grown haggard and lined over the time he was confined, confinement does that to a man; he begins to resent the entrapment and the guards set at every point. The failed attempts to escape only made it worse. As long as there is a plan, there is hope. Once the plan fails, the hope is gone.

And so I say now, in what is the truth to me anyway, they murdered my kind. And in doing so, they brought down eternal condemnation on their heads.

In my heart I continue to weep.

Part 4 - Fool

Chapter Twenty

Next morning, Sir John rode with Charles and his escort to Newport, a fine town of expensive houses and fine horseflesh, judging by those seen out on the roads. They went along tracks that ran between well tended fields replete with fat livestock. The island held a certain beauty that entranced him, even in the grim November weather. There was a quietness about the place that appealed to his inner self. But he was apprehensive of what was to happen – rightly, as it transpired.

They were met at the outskirts of Newport by the Governor with a group of armed men who immediately surrounded the king, pushing his men to one side.

Colonel Hammond rode forward, taking his hat from his head. "Your Majesty, please come with us." An order couched as a request. No question that he would do other than go with him. He had but a moment to offer his thanks to Sir John before his devoted servant and friend turned and rode away, his shoulders bowed with such sadness as anyone ever wished to see in a man. Before Charles could watch too long, though, the Colonel gave the order to move on and they made their dreary way to Carisbrooke Castle and the room which was to become his prison for more than a year.

During the journey not one person spoke with him. Not so much as a comment about the rain, which was then fast falling and soaking into everything, not a word about the prosperous town which they were passing through or the stares of the inhabitants who stopped to watch but who concealed their expressions and did not, to a man, doff their hats as their king passed. He realised then that the Parliamentarians had a firm hold on what had been a Royalist island and he had been foolish to consider going there. But then again, did the population realise it was their king riding by with a retinue of guards, did they realise their king was there because of a desperate attempt to regain his throne, did they even care one way or the other? It came to him in a moment of clarity that mostly the men, women and children of his land had no conception of the great struggle which had gone on. They knew perhaps of the claims of the members of Parliament to be independent of his rule, they knew perhaps of the aspirations of those who would depose the king and rule in his stead or use him as a figure head. Did they understand anything of the semantics involved, of the struggle internally before it erupted into violence and bloodshed and death? He doubted it very much.

He wondered about his men, not being able to see them. He wondered what they were thinking and feeling. Did they know, did they understand, that life as he knew it was probably over? He felt that they did, for they were not unintelligent.

His men rode at the back of the group, or so he learned later. He was told this by his equerry who was allowed to stay for a while. They were paid off when the group reached the great gates of the Castle and Charles rode in, having no choice in the matter. He was still surrounded by Hammond's men, riding deliberately close, as if they were making a point. It was foolish of them, he had nowhere to go – before he reached any port they would have recaptured him, for sure. He had no choice but to go along with their wishes – for the time being. There would surely be days ahead when plans could be made and circumstances could be changed. Perhaps. All seemed to be normal, he was greeted, his cloak taken from him, a space by the hearth cleared for him, mead brought to warm him but all the time he had the sense that he would not leave there as a free man, unless something miraculous happened and, after the disasters of the Civil War, he had begun to disbelieve in miracles.

The November weather continued as the summer had been, unbelievably dreary and wet. In the brief intervals when it ceased raining, Charles walked in the grounds of the castle, aware that the thick walls were keeping the worst of the winds from him even as they kept him inside. He climbed the steps to the battlements and stood staring out at the downland, at the clustered villages and tilled fields. Do they know I am here, he asked himself, do the islanders know their king is here, within the castle walls, unable to walk freely among them, even if I wanted to? If they do know, do they care? How much has the war touched them here? Have men been lost from the island? Why don't I know, why didn't anyone think to tell me of the losses – but if they had, would it have made any difference?

The great gates were opening and shutting all the time as men and supplies arrived but he made sure he stayed away from them. There was no point in antagonising anyone by making it look as if he was attempting an escape. If there was a chance, it would not be through something as simple as walking out of the open gate, of a surety.

Letters arrived from Henrietta Maria, plaintive letters that tore at his heart even though they said she was well and safe and the children were fine. The sense of loneliness they brought with them was almost worse than his confinement. Colonel Hammond was a polite and thoughtful person, doing what he could for his royal guest-cum-prisoner but Charles was ever aware that he was in the Colonel's power, that he could not order anything that did not fit with the Governor's orders from the leaders of the New Model Army. Once again he told himself the name was foolish, as if they were playing some kind of game, but if they were, it was deadly serious and extremely dangerous.

November rolled on, somehow. Food was requisitioned, politely, by hints and requests, as the household was short on supplies to keep a king fed, not to mention his entourage, which included the Governor's uncle, by coincidence chaplain to the king, someone Charles relied on heavily at this sad and empty time.

At last items Charles had requested arrived, plate and bedding, furniture and other items, which made life a little more pleasant. He planned to order new clothes for himself too. Moving from place to place, being held in this 'prison' and that his clothes were no longer suitable for a king, no matter which way anyone looked at it.

The days and weeks dragged on, Christmas celebrations were muted, there were no revels as such, just some merrymaking by the guards and a visit from the Governor to tell him that no agreement was being reached with the Army and that there would be people coming to discuss the situation with him.

He was polite, he said 'thank you.' For what, he had no idea. He was Hammond's king, his superior in every way, but Hammond came to deliver messages as if the king was nothing more than a miscreant being held for an indefinite period. Most prisoners knew how long their imprisonment was to endure. When Charles asked, no one had any idea. Or that is what they told him, anyway.

The blackness enveloped him, held him in its close embrace, refused to let him go. He despaired of ever being a free man again.

One of the letters brought to him detailed an escape plan. He was to be given a rope which he would tie round the bars, climb down to the courtyard and there be met by sympathisers who would take him away from the island. He was filled with relief, not only that there was a chance to escape but that people still cared enough to arrange such a thing for him. Relief that bolstered his mood for some days, gave him a belief that he would survive after all, regain all that he had lost. If only...

A servant brought him the rope, concealed in parcel of new clothes. He hid it in his closet and touched it often, it was his way out. His only way out.

Another letter arrived, telling him which night it was to be. The days were counted down, he paced the bowling green, the walls, the steps to the keep with ill-concealed energy but at all times keeping his face totally blank. He lived in fear of the plan being discovered and scuppered. He had to hold on to something, anything!

On the chosen night, full of anticipation and barely concealed excitement – he knotted the rope round the bars and allowed it to hang down. Then he tried to climb through.

Tragedy struck. He became caught in the bars and could not climb out. They had not thought of the possibility that the bars were not wide enough apart to allow his slender body to slide through. He was truly well protected, imprisoned, trapped. The guard was summoned, he was pulled away from the window, the rope thrown out and harsh words were uttered. It was as if his kingship had been taken from him, he was berated as any prisoner would be who attempted escape.

Disappointment and humiliation ate at him, brought the darkness to his mind once more. He refused to eat, to drink, to speak, for some days. A physician was called, but he had no cure for the despondency in which the king found himself. If he could have brought a letter, or better still, the key to the castle gates so Charles could walk free, find a horse and ride for London, all the despondency would have left him in the fraction of time it would take for him to absorb the fact he was free. Because he could not do this, no potions or pills could alleviate that which he suffered. They knew it, those who guarded me knew it, but could not name it as anything but a malady, for fear of causing upset with those who supported him still.

In March, acid was smuggled in for him to burn through the metal of the bars and attempt another escape. Once again he was filled with the desire to return to full life. Once again it failed, as Hammond was either informed of - or discovered - the plot. His hopes were totally dashed and in that, there came the immediate return of the ever-present melancholy which had pursued him for so long.

This time it was worse than before. He had no news of his wife, his children who he knew were held by the rebels, or of his friends, his loyal servants and courtiers. He worried himself to the point of serious illness about them all.

When he admitted, during one of his tedious conversations with the Governor, that he was going slowly mad with boredom, Robert Hammond came up with the idea of converting the bailey into a bowling green for his use and entertainment. It was a good diversion, he watched it being created and, once done, used it to play regularly. He was effusively grateful for that. Why should he have been grateful to his gaoler, one might ask? After a time, even the worst gaoler becomes someone you can be grateful to if they give you concessions or gifts. The bowling green was a gift, of a kind. It was space to walk and breathe for a time.

His room was confining, he found no joy in being there. It had little to offer in the way of comforts, simply because it denied freedom. The most exotic of cages remains a cage if the door stays barred.

Testimony of Colonel Robert Hammond.

I would be exceedingly surprised if any person living at this time had any understanding of the way I feel right now. I was a devoted royalist. This was in my very early days, when the divine right of the King was everything. It was given to me through church, school, and family that this was so. But I grew to disagree with this thinking and I became a parliamentarian.

If I state this at the beginning of my testimony, I trust that people will understand how I felt when I was informed that the King was coming to the Isle of Wight. My first thought was that he was a fool to come to a place which was more parliamentarian than Royal, a place which was not to be suited for him if he was actually trying to escape. My information was that he had escaped from Hampton Court, but in my heart I knew that this was not really so. I had visited Hampton Court, I knew how easy it was to guard that place, and for a king to be able to arrange a so-called escape meant that it was planned that he should do so. What I did not understand was why such a deception should have been put in place.

Not that it was any place of mine to query such a thing. I had my orders. I was governor of Carisbrooke Castle, a role I liked very much indeed, and if the King was coming there, I would greet him with all deference and respect.

He rather took me by surprise in asking me to go to Portsmouth so that we could discuss his plans and mine before he came to the island. On second thoughts it made perfect sense of course that he should do so and I said that I would treat him with all courtesy and consideration. Why not? It was the very least I could do, he was still a sovereign King after all.

And so he came to the island, he rode to Carisbrooke Castle, we made him welcome, we gave him rooms for himself and his entourage, he asked to see Sir John Oglander and we agreed, and I followed my orders and wrote to London to ask what I was to do with the King.

It was couched in diplomatic language, the reply which came post-haste, but beneath the fancy words was a single message, the King is your captive.

I believed I was a parliamentarian. When I saw this letter, no, this order, from the New Model Army, I knew I had not left all my royalist sympathies behind. I sat for some time holding the letter, thinking about the implications of my order, the fact I would be the King's gaoler and I felt physical pain.

The King was a slender, handsome, almost retiring man. He had a calm composed look which never varied. I had him in my charge for over a year and I never saw a change of expression during that entire time, no matter what strains, unhappiness, even illness, came over him. Even when he walked in the ground each week with Sir John, I saw no change in his look, although I saw a change in his demeanour. I could tell by the slump of his shoulders when he was unhappy, I knew by the tilt of his head when he had one of his bad headaches, and I would send a potion to him. He asked me once how I knew and I said; "I'm good like that." I did not tell him I noticed the way he walked or stood, because of the concealment of his almost bland look. He thought he was concealing all his feelings, all his emotions, and I did not wish to disabuse him of that thought. I would not take from my prisoner any of his hopes and aspirations of continuing to be a King, even in captivity.

Apart from his extremely natural efforts to escape, I really had no problems with the King during his time at Carisbrooke. It was my suggestion that we made a bowling green him, it gave him something to concentrate on the while, and he enjoyed his games. There was nothing else I could do. The grooms and others mentioned to me that he would sometimes be associating with the donkeys in a way that was not 'natural' and asked if I would stop it, but I refused. I know how men can be, his wife was abroad, he would have scorned the use of a whore, what else was he to do? It must be remembered he was a young man, in good health, with all the natural desires of a young man. And so I left him alone in this, and until this day have not spoken about it with any person outside the castle. It was just something I had to say if I am giving a true testimony of my time as keeper of Carisbrooke Castle with its most famous resident, King Charles.

I developed a considerable respect for him during his time there, the hours that we spoke on subjects that were far ranging taught me that he had an active, intelligent mind. His 'closed' prejudices were put there by his father King James, and by that person that we consider to this day could be the arch villain, George Villiers, Duke of Buckingham. Between them these two people performed Charles Stuart's character, they turned him from the biddable, seemingly docile boy to a King who wore the mantle of the divine right of kings and never took off. As such he was incapable of accepting parliamentary rule, parliamentary advice, or assistance. He could only see things his own way. It was because of this that the three civil wars were all disasters for the Royalists as all attacks were ill-conceived, ill planned, and uncoordinated. The great sadness is that many good loyal men died for this ill-fated cause.

I felt a tremendous weight of sadness descend on me when the order came that the King was to be removed to Hurst Castle. Seeing him on a daily basis, having his welfare as my chief concern, has become a way of life. To have him moved away took that out of my life. Had anyone told me a year earlier that I would feel that way I would have laughed. At first I found it an imposition, I kept wishing he had not come to my Castle, but he had and I had to make the most of it. It was over time that I realised just what an exceptional person he was, in so many ways. I knew there was only one end to this sad existence, quite simply the parliamentarians could not let him live. And he knew it. And yet he spoke not of it, he gave no hint that he was even contemplating his own execution. Not to me anyway. I am not sure even now with I should reveal the way I know these things, but who is there now to be upset, to take exception to, to upbraid me for my deception? There is none. All who mattered either have no power, or are no longer alive.

And so I will admit now in this testimony about King Charles, that his chapel was built in such a way that his prayers, when said aloud, could be heard outside. At times I stood and listened to the heartbreak of a young man knowing he was going to endure the ordeal of execution, a young man who happened to wear the crown of England, a young man who sought to have no more than a happy family life.

I am not ashamed to admit now that this staunch parliamentarian would stand outside the chapel, hidden, and be aware of the tears that would course down my face as I heard the King at his prayers. If there is truly life after death, I pray that I have his forgiveness for this deception. It began because I sought to ensure there were no further attempts to escape. It continued because I found in his piety a tremendous depth and love for the Lord God and his established church in this country. The King's prayers were meaningful, devout, knowledgeable, scripturally accurate, and were a revelation to me. I already had an appreciation of the depth, the width and the extent of his intellect, I had no idea until I overheard the prayers of the depth, that would, and the extent of his piety and knowledge of God's Word.

I freely admit now too that my own piety left a good deal to be desired up to that time. I learned a good deal from the King without him knowing it, and I became a much more devout and understanding Christian man after that. One man, one year, such changes!

It has to be remembered that Charles Stuart was just 49 years old when he died. He could have given so much more, if only his background had been different, more lenient, more giving, less emphasis on the divine right of kings, and if he had come up against a more giving parliament, not one overwhelmed by Puritanism.

There have been many executions throughout history, many fine knowledgeable men have been put to death for a variety of reasons. I think of Sir Thomas More at this time, and there were others of equal intellect and piety, and of determination of mind and spirit too. In many ways they were all martyrs to their own cause. There is one difference between them and Charles Stuart, they were not consecrated Kings.

England did not realise what it had done unto it was done.

As with all executions, at that point it was too late.

Charles had been aware of a presence in the room throughout all his thoughts, a strong presence. Someone who no longer lived, someone who once lived. He thought, Charles, you are even more foolish than I thought to consider such a thing, but surely angels, saints and others once lived? Saints did, of a surety they did, they were once men and if they lived and are now saints to whom one can pray and get answers, then there is life after death and it is possible that one of these persons, whoever they are, is in this room with me, listening to my rambling recital of a life about to be thrown away. I know it, I say it clear. I do not think it is my father, I do not believe it to be Villiers. I would like to think it is my brother, but having no sight, no thought, no word, I cannot say.

He returned to his topic, of necessity he had to do so, for fear of not mentioning that person who meant so much to him

Sir John Oglander visited every week during that confinement. Every single week, come what may, weather, festivals, demands of him by his family, his house and his farmlands, he went, sometimes for a short while, sometimes for as much as an hour. Then they would walk and talk together. They spoke of nothing contentious; he knew naught of the escape plans, he knew only that if he spoke with Charles of that which was normal to him, the planting, the ploughing, the harvesting, the marketing of livestock and sale of grain, of dinners with friends, of news from London when he had any, it would help his king to remember there was a world outside the castle walls. They spoke of normal things and pretended as best they could that this was a normal relationship, that they were free to come and go as they pleased and spoke of what they wished, whilst knowing it was not so. But it was a fact that if a person thought hard enough that something is, then it can become that thing. For the time Sir John was with him, Charles could believe his life was normal. For that he had his everlasting gratitude for he did his king such a great service such as no one had ever done for him before that time. No friendship was so great; no friend so relied upon, as he. If Charles had ventured to say as much to him, he would have looked away, smiled a little and said: "Your Majesty, 'tis nothing but a pleasure for me to be here."

He came through the brightness and promise of Spring, when they admired the new growth on the trees and bushes and the plants in the walled garden, through the shining days of Summer, when they played bowls or sat under a great tree to drink ale and chat of nothing much, through the sadness of Autumn as the tree shed its leaves and the countryside beyond the walls changed from green to brown as the harvests were taken in and the land ploughed for the winter frosts, things Charles knew nothing of in detail until Sir John spoke of them and then he looked for them, and into the Winter, when the coldness of the air bespoke of bad days to come and they huddled before the fire in the king's room and spoke of nothing very important. It was as if they both knew their time together was winding down, that the king's time in this life was winding down.

He came and he encouraged and he cheered and he made Charles see another side to the aristocracy of England, those who farmed their land and paid their taxes and did their best for their king and country, those who did not seek positions of power and play their part in the politics of the country. A solid man. A true friend.

In between his visits Charles was taken to Newport and there argued with those who wanted this concession and that. What became clear was that no one was prepared to make concessions and so there could be no agreement between any of them.

It was during these visits that he heard of the sadness of the civil war starting up again, of death and destruction and of various mutinies being put down with great cruelty and certitude. He knew too that there were those calling for his blood and so he began the counting down of the last days of his life. There was no harm in being realistic; it was better than being wildly optimistic and having those hopes and dreams crash around him like so many falling boulders in an earth slide.

For a while he thought on his life in terms of possessions: the homes, the gardens, the people who worked for him in so many ways, John Tradescant, the devoted gardener was one who came to mind immediately. Had he not created wonders for them out of nothing, brought them what seemed like exotic plants and created a miracle of a landscape for Henrietta Maria

216

and Charles at Oatlands Palace? Ah, what would happen to the places they loved when he was not there? He recalled his many clothes, robes, boots, jewels, horses – the list was endless.

Then he thought of less material things: his wife, his children, his friends, his loyal courtiers and advisors and wondered again what would happen to them all when he was not here.

And in the thinking he grew despondent and melancholic and none could rouse him from it. Even Sir John Oglander's visits began to feel more like a duty than a pleasure and that was one event he delighted in, but such were the depths into which he was sliding.

They came, those armed men, at the beginning of December on a cold wet day that felt more like the depths of winter. He had instructions to tell his staff – such as he was allowed – to pack his possessions – such as he had – as he was to be removed to Hurst Castle.

It sounded grand but in fact the 'castle' was a cold damp miserable sea pounded place on the coast. When he saw it, his already depleted spirits plummeted even further. He thought his life would be over ere long if he had to spend much time in that place which God truly forgot.

He shivered endlessly whilst there, despite great fires and as many fur robes as he could muster. The 'move' was, in truth, no more than a slight interruption in the melancholic thoughts to which he had surrendered.

He was there but a few days when he was inexplicably told he was on the move again. New instructions arrived, to pack and be ready to depart at a certain hour. He knew not where he was going and he knew not what this was about for some considerable time. Later it was explained that Parliament had declared he had been moved without its consent - he was unaware that Parliament should decree where a king should be, prisoner or not but such were the times in which he lived.

They left the island, travelling over rough seas in ships buffeted by a high wind, with the men on deck clinging to the rail and those below decks holding on to the bunks for dear life. But he was leaving the island and in that was a sense of something moving at last. For the first time in over a year, when his ship docked, he set foot once more on what he thought of as England.

After a long cold wet and unpleasant ride they arrived in Winchester, somewhere he liked very much, where he was met by the mayor and aldermen and for the first time in a long, long time, was treated like a monarch. They did not stay there overlong, unfortunately, they moved on through the cold and the wet and arrived at Windsor Castle where Charles hoped to be comfortable but quickly discovered the meaning of true confinement.

He had long admired Windsor Castle but it became clear that this time it was no more than a place to lodge - and a reduced lodging at that. There were no royal servers for his meals, no public allowed in to see him eating should they so wish. He was granted just a few servants and had a guard with him at all times. Meals were served as they would be to any ordinary person, in privacy and in closed quarters. He felt as if they – those who had his existence in their hands – were stripping his royal life away from him section by section. Remove this, remove that, do everything but stop calling him Majesty, in effect.

He stayed at Windsor throughout the remainder of December, through a miserable and lonely Christmas and into January, a bitter cold and unhappy month at the best of times – and this was far from being the best of times for him. Then he was transported, no other word for it, to St James' Palace. Were they afraid of his arousing popular support? He was dressed in sombre clothes, a dark cloak, a nondescript hat with no plumes and told, actually ordered, to be silent throughout the journey. He had no reason to speak with any of them; he had nothing to say to any of them anyway, so that instruction was not difficult to follow. He refused, even at the end, to use the word 'obey.' A king does not obey, a king agrees to do something of his own volition. Whilst they may have been afeared of a popular uprising to restore the rightful king to his rightful throne, he remained afeared of those in the populace who held a grievance against him for the war and who might seek revenge. It was good that they had sought to cover him against being seen and saw in it his own security, rather than theirs. But he also saw this was the true beginning of the end and his dark mood became even darker and deeper. He was totally lost in his own melancholic thoughts throughout the seemingly endless journey, suffering cold that bit at his fingers and toes and at times threatened to stop the very breath in his mouth. He rode in silence and in a closed world of misery, darkness and utter despair. It was as if all other emotions had been driven out of him by the cold. No matter how he held the thick cloak around him, the icy wind found a space to surge through and place its mark on his body. The terrible thing was, he did not care if he survived the journey or not. He rode as if already dead, seeing nothing, feeling nothing but his intense misery and the cold. The fire that had kept him going for so long had all but gone out. His wife, his children, his palaces, his beautiful grounds, horses, dogs and possessions no longer existed, they were part of another life, another time, one when he was in control of his own destiny. Now he was at the bidding of others who cared not whether he survived the journey either, given the speed at which they pushed on, given the inconsiderate way he was hustled from room to horse and back again during the changes of beast. They were changed to protect them from the cold, nothing was given to him to protect him from anything. He rode, whispering "Lord God, let this be the end!" but no one answered his prayer.

St James' Palace was as close to home as any place was possible to be. There may have been guards at the doors and in the corridors, men patrolling the grounds, ever present, ever annoying but at least there was comfort and warmth and servants to tend to his needs. And, best of all, a bed to sleep in that was not a gift of someone else. He could spend his time in prayer and thought and attempt to work out what was to happen to him, what they had planned, what they foresaw as his 'future', if indeed he had one. He held his memories of his beloved wife and children close to him during the long empty days, for no one spoke unless they had to and the silence was at times quite overwhelming. Here, in a palace, he could once again resume the mantle of monarch, assert himself to some degree, provided he ignored the guards and the silence. He did his best to ignore those who came with proposals for this and that, for nothing accorded with what he wanted: his throne restored to him, his wife and children brought back into England, the army dismissed, all troublemakers banned from London and recompense paid to those who had lost their livelihoods or their husbands in the fighting. He had these thoughts but none asked for them, so they were never spoken aloud.

And so the days trailed past and there was an air of busyness about everyone but him. He could not begin to tell anyone how sad that was.

Chapter Twenty One

They came on the morning of the 20th, those who tended to him, to bring him fresh clothes, hot water to shave, brushes for his hair and beard, food – as if he could eat anything! His stomach roiled at the very thought of food and that which he was to face, his prosecutors, baying for blood.

They stood back, respectful still, as he gazed at his image in a small mirror, seeing the tired eyes, the drawn face, the complete lack of enthusiasm for life. This would not do, he told himself, this would not do for the men out there – and the women too, he had no doubt – wanted to see a monarch, not a crawling prisoner with no dignity left.

He was still the king, he thought.

If he said it often enough he might even begin believe it.

To placate those who fussed around him, he tried a little of the food they brought, enough to satisfy them anyway, if he himself was not satisfied. He wished he could eat, he felt the need to fill himself with something. He felt hollow, empty, dislocated, as if standing apart from himself and wishing himself back together again.

Foolish thoughts, but in truth, what else was there to do as he awaited his escort to take him to Westminster Hall? He had been told of his destination. He knew what he wanted to say, he knew what they would say and he knew too they would clash.

'They.' Always 'they'. The faceless ones, usually.

This time they were not faceless, this time they were his enemies, disloyal traitorous enemies. This time he knew his prosecutors. In the past it has been 'they' who had denigrated his efforts to govern this misbegotten country which was left to him to rule. Apart from Mr. Pym and others, of course. He knew their faces well. He also knew God had taken some of them home. What He would do with them was anyone's guess, for he considered them treacherous in the extreme. Would He forgive them? He wished he could.

And so they came, the guards. Who were they guarding? The same question he had on his journey to St James' Palace. Who were they guarding? The prisoner for fear of his escape or the prisoner for fear of his being attacked? They had stone cold faces. He could not ask them that question.

The day was cold, the water bitter and grey, grey and bitter as his thoughts. They boarded the slightly rocking craft which was shrouded in thick coverings. The men stood shoulder to shoulder on the gangplank to ensure no one saw him and he was escorted on board and into the cabin. The light was almost non-existent. He found a bench by touch and sat down. They set off down the Thames for Westminster Hall, one barge among many, perhaps the only one with shrouded windows but then again, on a bitter cold winter's day, would it really be the only one with shrouded windows? But then again, would anyone believe the King of England would be travelling in such a way, incognito, as if afraid of his own people?

Was he not afraid of his own people?

Charles pushed himself up in his chair, wishing he understood why he was reciting a commentary of the events of that day. He thought, once he had time to think, it was to distance himself from them, as he tried to distance himself from the people throughout his time as king.

And there, in those words, he admitted his time as king had ended.

On board the barge his thoughts ran wild, almost hysterical. It was all he could do to keep what Villiers had called his 'king' face in place for fear of anyone catching a sight of his inner turmoil.

'Oh my dear wife, I am so very grateful you cannot see me now! I would not have you see me like this, guarded or protected, one or the other, travelling to a trial at which my very life is at stake. Believe this if you will, none had told me of this fact. I knew it, though, I knew it the way I know my love for you will survive that of my physical death and stay with you for the remainder of your life. I would not have you worry, for I know well that you would do so and probably you would come with me and cause all sorts of mayhem in your inimitable way, too! It will not help, my beloved wife, it will not help. This is my destiny now, to give my life, if I must, to preserve that which we have right now, a kind of peace in this land. I do not feel it will last and I do not feel this country will go long without a monarch. Our son, our special son Charles, will one day be crowned king of England. I prophesy this and none but my thoughts are aware of it. I was so busy with my thoughts of you, my beloved wife and queen, and what you would do and say if you were there I did not realise we had arrived. So soon I am to confront them. So soon...'

Westminster Hall was a beautiful building, usually. That day, that cold January Saturday, it was not so beautiful. It was a place of ugly heightened emotions. He sensed the anxiety of those who were presiding – there was no other word for it – over a court of people of all names, faces and shades of thought. When Charles surveyed them, he had one thought; none of them were of the peasantry. All were of the ruling class. He wondered how many were there by duress and how many wanted to attend the 'great' occasion. He wished he had been given the time and space to think on who was not there, for those who were not were the true men for his cause. He almost caught the sound of a name as he thought on it but, ethereal as a bubble, it had gone.

The Hall had been altered, making a space for the prisoner, which he realised with a start of apprehension, was him, and a place for the commissioners to stand. The public were allowed in but kept far away. He doubted they heard a word of what was said, in truth, for the shuffling, moving, muttering noises were like an ocean swell against the words which were being uttered, those which condemned him before he could speak for himself.

He knew then it was truly over. How many times had he told himself his life was ended but ever was there a spark of hope, that which everyone retain as long as there is breath in their body and blood in their veins. With the sight of the 'courtroom' that spark was extinguished.

He went cold.

Guards there were, seemingly by the hundred, guards for the king, guards for the commissioners. Had they all been given the same instruction, he wondered? Blank your face, show no one how you feel? They all wore identical expressions – nothing.

The coldness became ice.

There seemed to be a miasma hanging over the court, smoke and body odour, stuffiness of damp clothes slowly drying. The noise was persistent, shuffling, murmuring, rustling, grating, every sound imaginable and some he could not identify. He wished for a moment all would be silent so he could think. It didn't happen. He felt lost, uncertain, out of touch with reality, not knowing who to turn to, not knowing who he could trust, not even knowing that he could speak to and receive a civil answer. A loneliness swept over him, devastating in its intensity. It almost produced to tears. With a determined effort he clamped down on the feeling, pushing it into the depths of his heart so that it would not interfere with what was going to happen that day. He worked in keeping his 'King' face in place, not wishing anyone to know his innermost thoughts.

Somebody approached him and he was given a chair, suitably cushioned for a monarch, in which he sat, and then stood and looked about him, before sitting again to await the words of the court. This was all new to him - as far as they were concerned; nothing had been discussed officially. Unofficially he knew well what they had planned for he had informants in every place it was possible to have informants and he wondered, somewhat idly, whether they knew that. He even knew that Bradshaw, may he rot, had a protective lining in his hat. Fool. Utter fool. If someone wished to assassinate him, they would thrust a dagger into his back or his chest, not aim for the head. Everyone knew that was the hardest part of the body. But of such vanity was hope made.

Finally the court came to some kind of order and a degree of silence was imposed.

But nothing could silence the air of determination mingled with hatred and contempt. There were no faces there which showed sympathy, all were implacably set against him. He could see that without even having to think on it. No one person smiled, no one person nodded or bowed their head to show deference to their king. He was as any other criminal would be, treated with an element of respect as the charade of the trial took place. It was a feeling as intense as the noise had been and he hated it. Hated the sense of it, the creeping tendrils of it, reaching out for him, trying to strangle him.

Who was to read the charge? Oh, the Solicitor General, Mr John Cooke, may he rot in hell. What impudence, what slander! To think the king had 'limited power to govern by'! Was he not king by right of birth and by the sacred oil and crown placed on his head? Was he not the supreme ruler of this land? Limited power! It was all he could do not to rant at them for their foolishness but somehow, how he would never know, he remained quiet and let him read the charges that he had 'traitorously and maliciously levied war against the present Parliament and the people therein represented.' Then he decided he had heard enough. He ordered the Solicitor General to 'hold!' but he was ignored. He poked the Solicitor General with his silver topped stick and said it again. Cooke ignored him once more. He did it again. Cooke continued to ignore him.

Anger began to build, a tiny flame, so tiny it was hardly there, but Cooke's indifference to his command to stop and ignoring the stick banging on his shoulder blew on the flame and pushed it into life. He hit Cooke hard, so hard that the tip of the stick fell off and rolled on the courtroom floor. There was a gasp, quickly smothered. It could have been construed as assault on an officer of the court. Everyone waited to see what would happen next.

There was a long, silent moment. The silver top rolled to a halt. The two men stared at one another in open defiance. Charles nodded to Cooke to pick it up, it being nearer him than anyone. The man did not move. Even more annoyed by now, Charles got up and retrieved it himself, knowing the moment he did it that it was a mistake. The coldness which swept over him almost put the fire out once more, almost sent him back into the dark well of his melancholy, or it would have done, if Cooke had not persisted in reading out the indictment in a tone which suggested Charles had been guilty of the most heinous murder imaginable.

Lawyer that he was to his bones, the Solicitor General had it all written out carefully, every word of the charge to be brought against Charles.

The king sat still, head to one side, listening apparently respectfully until it was said that he was a tyrant, traitor and murderer, and a public and implacable enemy to the commonwealth of England. Then he did something unexpected and outrageous. He couldn't help himself, it just burst out of him.

He laughed.

The shocked faces were sufficient reward for his breakdown of composure. He found the words so ludicrous, the charge so outrageous that he could not help himself. His first thought was, really, was this all they could come up with, after all his lengthy tedious confinement? His second thought was, God help me, I doubt I can answer this satisfactorily, for their minds are fair set already on the verdict.

Having been given some idea of what they would say, but not the words themselves, he had his answer prepared. For once his stammer deserted him and he spoke with all the authority of a king before his humble subjects.

'I would know by what power I am called hither.'

Called? Do I jest with them? Brought under armed guard is not called! 'I would know by what authority – I mean lawful. There are many unlawful authorities in the world, thieves and robbers by the highway.'

And do I not consider every last one of you a thief and a robber, for have you not stolen my liberty and my peace of mind, not to mention stealing from me my wife and my family. I have lost the growing up time of my children, I have lost the consolation of my wife's presence and her love. I have lost those who care about me and who I care about in turn. Stolen, not lost! Stolen by orders of a Parliament whose sole task should have been to support their king in his efforts to rule. Robbers, every last one of you, robbers!

The anger flared, burned, gave him stature, gave him confidence. His voice rang out around the hall.

'Remember I am your king, your lawful king and what sins you bring upon your heads and the judgement of God on this land.'

It caused the outcry he knew it would. It caused the bitter arguments he knew it would but it had to be said. He was, after all, their king. No more, no less than their God sent monarch. One they had the temerity to put on trial.

His feelings were mixed. He felt the righteous burning anger and the ice coldness of fear. He knew he was fighting a battle that had but one end, his failure, for they were set fair to find him guilty no matter what. It was clear in their attitude, their looks at one another, their very presence in the hall which was set out like a court. There was no defence for Charles, no person leaping forward to put the Sovereign's side of the case. Nothing but their words and his, God help him.

The room had gone from chill to cold to bitter cold and still he could not rouse himself to call for a fire or a robe or something hot to drink. As a condemned man, which was the parlous state in which he found himself right then, he was entitled to anything he wished, surely. What he wished for, though, could not be granted to him. He wished for a guarantee of the continuation of his life and the restoration of his monarchy and the closeness of his family. Right then his heart, broken as it was, had no feeling at all. He was a mere statue, albeit a walking talking one.

But then, oh then he had many emotions! He felt a sense of elation that he had an argument which they could ill refute, that his speech had been clear and precise and carried authority, he did not sound weak or vacillating in any way, that he had stated his claim and stated it with clarity. He knew well it was recorded, he saw the scribes writing down his words. And so they would live on - even as he wouldn't. He also felt a sense of denial that this was happening to him, that a king should be answerable to a court staffed by lesser mortals than himself. And finally, sorrow. Deep burning sorrow that his life had come to this pass.

They had one answer to his statement and they used it – they dismissed the court for the interim, to be reconvened on Monday following. Charles was taken back to his rooms, under guard, sorrowing but outwardly calm and very much in control of himself and his world. No one spoke to him as they went back to St. James Palace.

No one spoke to him about anything other than what he cared to eat and drink that entire endless dreary lonely Sunday. He spent a good deal of it in private prayer, if they came when he was praying he ignored them. They quickly went away again and came back when he was sitting before his fire once more. Boundaries had been laid and were respected, without a word said on either side. It was a tiny victory but an important one.

They knew not that anger burned clean through him, taking out all his sorrow and bitterness and replacing it with a cleansing flame of righteousness.

And if they knew, he doubted they would care. They thought they ruled his country now and could do as they wished with his laws, his parliament and his people. Maybe they could, for a while, but the Lord God would take His revenge in His own time and they would not be happy with the consequences of their actions.

The court reconvened on the Monday, with the king being asked how he pleaded. He ignored that and again questioned the legitimacy of the court, asking how it could be legal to try a consecrated king in this manner.

The argument went on for what seemed like hours. The court could not defend its actions, Charles could not persuade them to agree their actions were illegal. Total deadlock seized the court, they could go no further and so once again the hearing was adjourned. Charles was again taken away and held in confinement. But he went proudly, knowing he had taken a stand they found hard to fight against, knowing he had raised doubts in the minds of some of the people there. He went knowing that the sense of menace and hatred he had felt before had changed to a grudging respect for someone who knew their law and had taken a stance on which they were not prepared to move. It was in many ways too little, too late. He wondered why he had not been this confident, this assertive, throughout his life. The many wasted opportunities came back to haunt him as he sat alone, wondering how many more days of his life would be consumed by this nonsense.

The whole of the Wednesday was 'lost' to Charles. No one came to take him to court, no one told him what was happening, no one said a word other than to ask if he wished to eat and drink. He did and they brought food and mead to him. Other than that, he was alone with his thoughts, his prayers and his many apprehensions. It was, he thought, one of the longest days he had endured in his lifetime. He was afraid that being away from Them, as he thought of his opponents, would allow the flame of anger to die down and the melancholia to come in again. If it did, he would not have the desire to argue so vehemently.

He need not have worried. Court reconvened on the Thursday.

Testimony of John Cooke, Solicitor General.

It is right and proper to say that we, the court, were confounded and confused by His Majesty's knowledge of law and the defiant stance he took when brought before us. Not a one of us expected such a thing to happen: we thought we would hear his plea, that he would plead guilty for surely he had brought the country to conflict by his own actions and he knew it, and that we would then proceed to whether or not he should die.

I wonder now how we could have been so foolish. I wonder now how we ever thought that trying a crowned king for such a crime would be legal, would be permitted, would be carried through to its ultimate conclusion.

At the time I know well that we believed in what we were doing, but then I know now what I did not know then, that we had not thought deep enough or long enough about the consequences of what we had undertaken.

The conflict had seemed clear cut to all of us who were there. The king had started a war, we said, we had raised an army and fought back, we said. He would not compromise and had dismissed his parliaments time and again, we said. He chose a Catholic wife, we said, as if that made a difference to the conflict. It did not, but somehow it came into the equation and stayed there.

No one said, how did the king feel about this, how did this come about, could we not have avoided it somehow, some way? No one said, let us look at it again before we do something we will eternally regret.

We were caught up in the determination, the implacable opposition, that the New Model Army had in place against the king. We saw no further than that. And I, who should have known better and now admit it, was part of that.

I was impressed with His Majesty's demeanour when brought into the Hall. He showed defiance but not in a way anyone could at first place. It was just there, in his stance, his face which displayed nothing, his way of raking the ranks of people with a look that dismissed us all as so much rabble and rubble beneath his feet. I knew that even those most vehemently set against him were quietly impressed by his attitude. He showed no fear. Most people, confronted by a court full of officials and onlookers who were there for one reason, to find a way to legally end his life, would have shown some indication of trepidation. He did not. When asked for his plea, he spoke with anger but with clarity and his arguments were such that we had to adjourn the court on two days in succession. We could not overcome his logic.

On the Wednesday, those who were determined to do away with the king produced one person after another, depositions were read to the court, showing the part the royalists had played in the strife. It was only later that I realised that no one had read depositions from the royalists on the parts played by the New Model Army in the strife. It was as if the court had to do something, even this act of desperation, to ensure they got the verdict they wanted, even if it meant this underhand way of doing things. Ah, but there will be those who will argue that what we did was legal and right. And I would say to them, you were not the Solicitor General at the time and I say now, clear and true as I am here saying these words in this testimony, what we did was wrong. The court was illegally convened. It had no legal standing. The king was right. The only way we got our words out was to talk over him, to demand he be silent and listen, we did not account to him for ourselves or our actions at any time.

God knows how many times I have revisited that dreadful period and wished I could relive it and do it differently!

In the end, sixty seven people were sitting in judgement on His Majesty. Thirty seven people signed the death warrant.

May God forgive them – and me – for that which we did.

History will never forgive us. History will be right.

They told him later that some twenty nine depositions were taken and read to the members of the court, reports of the various skirmishes and battles in the Civil Wars which had torn the country apart.

Without hearing any evidence for the defence of the king, the court resolved upon the whole matter, making the statement:

That this Court will proceed to Sentence of condemnation against Charles Stuart King of England.'

'Resolved that the condemnation of the King shall be for a Tyrant, Traitor and Murderer.'

'Resolved that the condemnation of the King, shall be likewise for being a public enemy to the commonwealth of England.'

There was argument but it was ineffectual. No one wanted to listen. With a sinking heart, Charles allowed himself to be led away past soldiers who puffed tobacco at him, something he detested. He did not even turn to look at them, but walked with all the dignity he could muster away from the court, away from all that had been said and done. It was over, as far as he was concerned.

Testimony of Queen Henrietta Maria, wife to Charles Stuart, King of England.

When they brought me the news I broke down in front of everyone as if I were a child told of the loss of a parent. I could not help myself. I found I was full of hatred for the people of England that they could put a crowned king on trial for his life – for doing what he thought right, defending his right to be king. I did not understand, I still do not understand.

They told me he was proud and dignified, that his arguments confounded the court. This was pleasing, a tiny ray of sunshine in the darkness that surrounded me when I read the terrible letter. I knew he would not give in without a fight.

They told me he was allowed to see our son Henry and our daughter Elizabeth the night before they executed him. It was a cruel thing to do. Think on it for a moment! Our children had been held by the rebels throughout the fighting, then on the night before he is to die, he is allowed to see them, talk with them, hold them for a moment, to arouse all his paternal instincts and then to take them away, knowing they will never see their father again and he will never see his children again! Cruel, I say and I say it loud and clear! So cruel, unbelievably cruel, those people in charge of England! I pray God will forgive them, I never will.

And then they took my husband and severed his head from his body. Do they not know what they did? Do they not understand the crime they committed? In the name of heaven, I pray none of them will rest easy when their time comes. They took from this world a fine educated loving man who did no more than live his life according to the way he had been brought up, to believe in the divine right of kings.

My heart is broken. My children are devastated. England will be lost to the powers of darkness for years to come. They do not understand what they have done, what they have lost.

May God be with them.

enrHenry

There was no sleep. No gift of unconsciousness for the hours that were needed to settle his mind. He slept not once. He heard every sound, every night bird, every cough, every shuffle of every person around him in the palace. He slept not and his mind was as sharp and as tormented as ever, whilst his body was totally weary.

The day was ice cold. The room was ice cold where he slept, how did he sleep those other nights? Ah but the

Lord God knows how many prayers he had sent to Him during these days, these days of waiting, of living with the tiniest glimmer of hope that the verdict will be overturned even as he knew well it will not be. It could not be. No man wishes to lose face and how many there would be to lose face if it were to be overturned? No, his time was limited now, to the last time he would get up from this bed, the last time this room would hold his secret thoughts, the last time he would dress himself and prepare to face the greater world than he had here.

His hands did not shake. He was grateful for that small mercy. He decided he would wear another layer, he said he would not have them think he shivered in fear when in truth he might shiver from the cold, for he was not yet separated from his soul and the body would react. The servant who stood there with him was ashen faced, silent and – he believed – afraid. The gentlemen of the bedchamber, each was silent and sad and wishing not to be there. It was clear, so clear to him that they did not wish to be there and that they knew they had to be, for a duty is a duty even on the last day of a monarch's life. He chose a white shirt and black waistcoat, which he thought was formal enough for the occasion. Colour would not do, colour was out of place for such a solemn event. His cloak and hat were black, too. It seemed appropriate. He could not see himself wearing blue or any other light colour. Black was right for a funeral and as he would not see his own, he could anticipate it and dress accordingly.

Charles decided to take no food but drank a little ale. There was no need of food; there was no reason to keep his body going any longer.

They brought him the Sacrament. They brought him the promise of everlasting life. With this within him, absorbed into his body and soul, he felt he could go on.

He sent out his heartfelt silent prayer:

'Oh my beloved Henrietta Maria, at this time does not my heart go out to you, for you will be the one to live on in sorrow. My children, my beloved children, I pray they will be good to you, be kind to you, be not harsh with you for what your father is said to have done. The sins of the father should not be visited upon the child. Oh my heart aches this day with sadness for you all. Oh if only one person would speak with me, to lift this aching, lift this pall that rests on us but none know what to say. So none will. I walk this last walk holding in my heart my love for you, my beloved wife. Let it guide me and give me strength. I need naught else. The Lord God, I know, is with me.'

He told them he was ready to leave St James's Palace, if that was their wish. He loved the palace; he wanted to say goodbye in his own way as he walked through it to leave. He knew the plan; it had been given to him. He was to go to Whitehall and await the word to step out to the scaffold. He would make his speech. He would speak to those who braved the cold to come and see him die, whilst wondering why they had come to see him die. Did they hate him so much? Was there so much enmity in their hearts they must watch a man die? That was the plan. For once, it seemed as if that which was planned would be carried through, unlike his many plans during the war. Had they so been, he would have been victorious and this day his wife and queen would be at his side as they went into a new era of English politics. But it was not to be. He had sinned against his God and the people of my country and he must pay the price.

He realised he had been standing for some time staring at the wall opposite him without seeing the hangings or the person within his line of sight. They in turn stood and patiently awaited his signal that he was ready to leave. It was if they were afraid of him, afraid to speak, afraid to touch, those who had kissed his hand, had knelt at his feet, had handed him his items of clothes, stood back as if he was already a spectre at their feast. Of a surety, not a one would be able to remove from his heart the memory of the day. Of a surety that was a foolish thought, but still one he held dear. He would not remember it on this side of the Great Divide but he would when he stood before the Lord God and confessed his many sins. He felt totally empty. Any fear he had of tears spoiling his dignity was banished. He could not have cried if he wanted to. He was nothing but an empty shell that somehow continued to function. All anger, all melancholia, all longing had gone. He was nothing.

When they stood in the hall of the Palace, he realised some of his gentlemen and some ladies were openly weeping and sorrowful. It brought the tiniest hint of emotion, he wished he could cry with them, but nothing, nothing disturbed the emptiness that was the king of England walking to his death.

The hour of ten was struck, the doors opened and the group, guards and gentlemen, walked out into the winter sunshine, that which, after an interval that day, he would not see again. It was foolish of him but as he walked, he thought, 'I will not take this step again. I will not see that tree again, that grass, that vista of my beautiful park. I will not see how Whitehall looms up toward me, I will not see the wildlife that flitters around the sky and the empty branches, as empty as my life has become. The drums, muffled, I realise, help me keep pace, help me walk, help me be firm in my resolve not to give way. But oh God, oh Jesus Christ, oh blessed saints, I do not want to die! I want to see that bright clear winter sky again, to see the clouds that speckle it, to see the movement of the empty branches as they sway to a wind I cannot see but I can feel on my skin which still lives, dear God at this moment it still lives. The drums hurt my ears, they resonate with the beat of my heart, the heart that will soon be stilled forever.' It was a dangerous moment, he came close to giving way but he pulled an image of Henrietta Maria from his memory, put it before his eyes and walked toward his destination with her name on his lips.

There was silence. It was strange but there was silence. The birds call, they did not understand or appreciate the momentous moment which was to occur so soon, too soon. He heard the footsteps of the guards, he heard the sound of their arms and the drums; he heard that, of a surety he did. What he do not hear was the sound of London. It was stilled. Its great heart was stilled. There were no carriages, no horses, no people it would seem, for London was stilled for the day. He walked in a kind of vacuum, his people were with him but elsewhere was nothing.

Cold. Bitter, bitter cold. He was afeared of holding his cloak around him against the chill; he would not have even his gentlemen say he was cold and afeared.

They were there. Whitehall at last. Warmth and a degree of protection – they gathered, those who were to officiate and their anguish was stamped clear on their faces. They struggled to speak. He would wish them silent but that was not the time to ask them to desist from speaking. They would have no other chance to speak with him.

They followed Charles' instructions to allow him the use of his cabinet chamber. Here for a time he could mayhap put from his mind that which was to come. Alas, he was wrong in thinking this.

He was offered and took a glass of claret and a crust of bread. Why, he did not know, unless it was an inbuilt compulsion to act as if life was not about to be ended. His sorrow was such he all but choked on the bread, for the grief within him, which had welled up and overtaken his mind when he called up the image of his Queen, was like a block and stopped everything reaching his internal organs. It was a physical pain and he could not allow anyone to see it. He could not … would not be seen to be weak. There was an ordeal to get through yet, the speech, the final moments, all must be with dignity and pride and majesty as befits one who even at that moment wore the crown of England.

Oh, God, Lord God, keep my Henrietta Maria safe! I would not have wished this upon her lovely head! For this alone I should atone!

They indicated to him, with almost reluctant gestures, it was time to go. His escort walked proud, how often did they get to do such a thing, escort a king to his death? They walked with pride, or was it that they were determined, as he was, not to allow themselves to give way to whatever emotions were consuming their being at that moment?

The Banqueting Hall was silent. It was shabby and damaged and needed restoration. He saw it, wished to comment on it and realised again he had no say in anything that happened any more. It was over. From the moment the verdict was given, life was over. This was nothing more than a masque, albeit a final one.

He saw it.

Everything shouted in him STOP! But he could not. He simply could not. This was the final act of the masque and must be played to its end. It was no more than a masque. No more than a masque, believe it, say it and believe it. But it was there. Death waited. For a long, awful moment he was on the verge of being violently sick, such was the fear which slammed into his stomach. It took a supreme effort to stand erect and keep the bland, stony expression in place so none knew of his inner anguish. It was too soon, there was too much to live for, there was too much to regain, there was too much to lose!

The scaffold was covered in something black and the floor covered black too and there, which caught at his throat and stopped me breathing for a moment, was the axe and the block.

It was not high enough.

How stupid was that thought?

There were soldiers everywhere, bright armour, pikes, battle axes. There were horses, their harness jingling, snorting into the cold air, wearing wreaths of steam. Did they think even at that moment he could escape, that someone could rescue him and destroy the final act of the masque? Of course not. They were there for the occasion, the majesty of it. He said it, he did not believe it.

Oh. God. In. Heaven.

The people. He had not seen the people. He saw those who were there for the final act, he saw that which would remove his head, he did not see the people straight away. When he did, he was shocked. How many? Hundreds? So many that they filled the roads, they filled the space, they – were silent. How could so many be silent? Where was the sound of voices as they shuffled for position, the noises as they moved their feet, the murmur of a thousand bodies breathing? There was nothing but silence. Did they come to mourn, to celebrate, to mock, to cry?

Silence said they come to mourn. Celebration would have meant cheering or mocking cries. He saw no tears but he was too far away from them to see anything but the crush of people come to watch.

In God's name, he knew he always had been too far away from them. He knew nothing of their lives, their hopes, their dreams. He knew nothing of their desires for their country. He took them and their men and he killed them in pursuit of his dream, to rule alone.

He could see nothing for his eyes were filled with tears.

He turned to the person at his right.

"Colonel, cannot the block be made higher?"

"It seems not, Your Majesty. I trust it will not-" he broke off his words, realising he was about to say something foolish.

Charles turned and spoke to Colonel Thomlinson, standing on his left, stone faced and taciturn. He had thought long on his speech. It was his last chance to impress those around him with the truth of what he had felt throughout this time.

"I shall be very little heard of anybody here, I shall therefore speak a word unto you here. Indeed I could hold my peace very well, if I did not think that holding my peace would make some men think that I did submit to the guilt as well as to the punishment. But I think it is my duty to God first and to my country for to clear myself both as an honest man and a good King, and a good Christian. I shall begin first with my innocence. In troth I think it not very needful for me to insist long upon this, for all the world knows that I never did begin a war with the two Houses of Parliament. And I call God to witness, to whom I must shortly make an account, that I never did intend for to encroach upon their privileges. They began upon me, it is the Militia they began upon, they confessed that the Militia was mine, but they thought it fit for to have it from me. And, to be short, if anybody will look to the dates of Commissions, of their commissions and mine, and likewise to the Declarations, will see clearly that they began these unhappy troubles, not I. So that as the guilt of these enormous crimes that are laid against me I hope in God that God will clear me of it, I will not, I am in charity. God forbid that I should lay it upon the two Houses of Parliament; there is no necessity of either, I hope that they are free of this guilt. For I do believe that ill instruments between them and me has been the chief cause of all this bloodshed. So that, by way of speaking, as I find myself clear of this, I

241

hope - and pray God - that they may too. Yet, for all this, God forbid that I should be so ill a Christian as not to say God's judgements are just upon me. Many times he does pay justice by an unjust sentence, that is ordinary. I will only say this, that an unjust sentence that I suffered for to take effect, is punished now by an unjust sentence upon me. That is, so far as I have said; to show you that I am an innocent man."

He noticed a scribe writing down his words as fast as he spoke them. This gave him confidence to go on, his words would be remembered, would be read when he was no longer there. His children might be able to read them, to understand their father's motives for doing what he had done, for their future as well as for his own. It was a tiny ray of light in the darkness of the sickness which consumed him. He fought it, as he fought the desire to rant and scream and yell his defiance to those who would end his life.

"Now for to show you that I am a good Christian. I hope there is a good man that will bear me witness that I have forgiven all the world, and even those in particular that have been the chief causes of my death. Who they are, God knows, I do not desire to know, God forgive them. But this is not all, my charity must go further. I wish that they may repent, for indeed they have committed a great sin in that particular. I pray God, with St. Stephen, that this be not laid to their charge. Nay, not only so, but that they may take the right way to the peace of the kingdom, for my charity commands me not only to forgive particular men, but my charity commands me to endeavour to the last gasp the Peace of the Kingdom. So, Sirs, I do wish with all my soul, and I do hope there is some here that will carry it further, that they may endeavour the peace of the Kingdom."

Peace in the country was all he desired, after so many bitter conflicts. They had to know that he was sincere in this.

"Now, Sirs, I must show you both how you are out of the way and will put you in a way. First, you are out of the way, for certainly all the way you have ever had yet, as I could find by anything, is by way of conquest. Certainly this is an ill way, for conquest, Sir, in my opinion, is never just, except that there be a good just cause, either for matter of wrong or just title. And then if you go beyond it, the first quarrel that you have to it, that makes it unjust at the end that was just at the first. But if it be only matter of conquest, there is a great robbery; as a Pirate said to Alexander that he was the great robber, he was but a petty robber: and so, Sir, I do think the way that you are in is much out of the way. Now, Sir, for to put you in the way. Believe it you will never do right, nor God will never prosper you, until you five God his due, the King his due, that is, my successors, and the People their due, I am as much for them as any of you. You must give God his due by regulating rightly His Church according to the Scripture which now out of order. For to set you in a way particularly now I cannot, but only this. A national synod freely called, freely debating among themselves, must settle this, when that every opinion is freely and clearly heard.

"For the King, indeed I will not."

He saw one of his men touching the axe as if he was touching a relic of a saint. It amused and bothered him at the same time.

"Hurt not the axe that may hurt me for the King, the laws of the land will clearly instruct you for that. Therefore because it concerns my own particular, I only give you a touch of it. For the people. And truly I desire their liberty and freedom as much as anybody whomsoever. But I must tell you that their liberty and freedom consists in having of government; those laws by which their life and their goods may be most their own. It is not for having share in government, Sir, that is nothing pertaining to them. A subject and a sovereign are clean different things, and therefore until they do that, I mean, that you do put the people in that liberty as I say, certainly they will never enjoy themselves."

He wondered if he was going on too long but this was his last chance, his only chance, to be heard. They did not allow him the time to speak at his fiasco of a trial. Now they had no choice but to listen. The sickness had abated, his thoughts were directed to what he wanted to say and the best way to say it.

"Sirs. It was for this that now I am come here. If I would have given way to an arbitrary way, for to have all laws changed according to the power of the sword I needed not to have come here. And, therefore, I tell you, and I pray God it be not laid to your charge, that I am the martyr of the people. In troth, Sirs, I shall not hold you much longer, for I will only say thus to you. That in truth I could have desired some little time longer, because I would have put then that I have said in a little more order, and a little better digested than I have done. And, therefore, I hope that you will excuse me. I have delivered my conscience. I pray GOD that you do take those courses that are best for the good of the Kingdom and your own salvations."

It is done. It is said. But no, that fool Juxon speaks, asking him to speak on his affection to religion. In the name of Heaven …

With a huge sigh he hoped no one would notice or mention, he began again.

"I thank you very heartily, my lord, for that I had almost forgotten it. In troth, Sirs, my conscience in religion I think is very well known to all the world: and, therefore, I declare before you all that I die a Christian, according to the profession of the Church of England, as I found it left me by my father. And this honest man I think will witness it."

Enough. This had to end. The pain was too great. "Sirs, excuse me for this same, I have a good cause and I have a gracious God. I will say no more."

The man with his blank mask was waiting. "I shall say but very short prayers, and when I thrust out my hands-" He had his instructions. Charles prayed he held good to them. There was one final prayer he had to make. His cap was there, his hair put under it.

"I have a good cause, and a gracious God on my side. I go from a corruptible to an incorruptible crown; where no disturbance can be, no disturbance in the world."

Standing there cold, wishing it was over, not wanting it to be over. The air was fresh in his throat, in his mouth; he sensed his blood rushing endlessly around his body. The speech making was over. The trivialities were done. He would have wished the block to be higher but was he in any position to demand? They said again it was as high as it could go. He thought they were wrong but it was too late to argue.

He removed his cloak and jacket and handed them to an aide. Then he knelt down, looking up for a moment into the clarity of the winter sky as if seeking the touch of the sun on his skin. His sickness was back, it had to be over soon before he disgraced himself. The dignity of the monarchy was his to uphold and he would.

The executioner knew Charles would give the signal when he was ready. He would put out his hands. He had his instructions and at this moment, this final moment, he was still king. He could still command.

He rested his head on the block and began his final secret prayer.

Then he put out his hands.

He almost heard the sound of the axe falling.

In that brief second before eternity claimed him, he had one thought.

'I am a fool who was a king.'

Testimony of Oliver Cromwell, later Lord Protector of England

In the bible it is said the Lord Jesus said, at His crucifixion, 'forgive them, Father, for they know not what they do.'

I would wish, with all my heart, that those of us who signed that death warrant could think the same, but it would be untrue. We knew well what we did and we have to live with the consequences.

I sat through the trial. I sat through it and marvelled at his composure, his logic, his fine speeches, his ability to out talk us and confound us. On this I know I share my thoughts with the Solicitor General, for was he not as equally confounded as I? We thought not to find such a fine mind. Why, I do not know. Perhaps because he made such a disaster of the wars he fought, his indecision, which we knew well of, his inability to listen to one and another and take the best of advice and use it according to his own instincts and mind, but rather would be swayed by the one who had the strongest personality. For this was the root cause of the King's problem, he listened to many who were stronger than he but who knew less than he. Would that he had not listened to that fool Villiers, or that slip of a wife who knew less than anyone but who would have her say and her way no matter what.

I believed we were right.

I believed we had the right way for the country.

I believed all this until the 30th January and the bitter cold day when I stood and watched a young, brave, dignified man, who must have been torn apart inside, walk to his death with pride and defiance. I heard the speech, I saw the wait before the axe fell, I wanted at that moment to shout "Hold!" as he had done during the trial. But I knew, even as I thought it, that I would be ignored even as he was.

The axe fell, the blood spouted, the head rolled and a huge collective sigh went up from the gathered populace who had braved the cold and the horror of the sight to witness the death of a king.

I felt a sickness to my very bowels for I knew we had done an evil deed and that none, especially myself, could ever admit to it. The country was ours to govern, to restore from the horror of the conflicts, to put the money back into the coffers to pay our way, a thousand thoughts went through my head of what had to be done.

The one thing which could not be done was the restoration of a man to his head.

'Forgive them, Father, for they know not what they do.'

We did. And there will be no forgiveness for us. History will see us for what we are, murderers. I know it, I confess it and in that moment I wonder how much of a fool I was – and am.

Author's note:

Charles I is one of those enigmatic monarchs whose life story never fails to fascinate historians and readers alike. But, like so many historical figures, mention his name to most people and they will remember so few things about him: in this case, that he caused a Civil War; was held prisoner in Carisbrooke Castle, was tried as a traitor and beheaded.

Charles came to me in January 2006. When he made himself known, I realised that for the previous ten years, mediums had been saying 'can you take a Charles?' and getting my standard answer, 'no, but I will hold the name for now.' There had been no Charles in my life as far as I was aware. When I finally got to speak to this quiet, gentle, loving, yet autocratic man, I asked if it was he who had tried to reach me during the preceding years and he confirmed it was. But, like so many spirits, he had to wait until I was ready to accept his coming into my life. Once he was there, I found myself full of questions about his life.

I asked Charles what drove an intelligent, cultivated man to abandon Parliament and rule alone? What compulsion led him to the execution block at such a young age, when he had so much still to live for? What were his feelings throughout the meticulously recorded trial? Living as I do on the Isle of Wight where he was held prisoner made the story even more vivid. I walked the walls of Carisbrooke Castle with him one summer afternoon, growing more and more distressed as I did so. He told me to go down a flight of steps and through a gateway. I did and there was the bowling green which had been laid out for him. When we entered, there were tourists everywhere. In what felt like a fraction of a moment they had all left the green and I was able to break down in tears without anyone seeing me. They were his tears. It was the first time he had been back to the Castle since his death. I look at the same landscape he did, parts of the Island are still as he saw them: the downs, the cliffs, the ever-changing, but endlessly the same, sea. This island is very much part of his history and he is very much a part of English history, this complex, fascinating, charismatic character who was much more than just a monarch who brought the country into Civil War and who was executed by his own people for treason.

He died as a martyr to the Church, and is venerated today by the Charles I Society as a man who stood by his principles, even though they tore him apart. I have to say, in all honesty, that writing of his execution tore me apart. I was a complete emotional wreck for the rest of the day.

Charles is a diffident, quiet, regal yet self-effacing man when he comes to me. From the start he refused the title of Majesty, saying he was a former king and seeking his role in the spirit realms. He found it difficult to write of some things, so, on the advice of Ann-Jacqueline, I went outside my author and spoke to those who came with their own stories of this enigmatic king. With them I had to explore some very dark pathways to get the true nature of the man into this book, some of which was shocking and startling, but which he needed to have talked of to release himself from the ties were holding him back. It has been an honour and a pleasure to work with him and it is my fervent hope that by writing this, he may be released from all that has troubled him for so many years.

His book was incredibly painful to write, but rewarding. His friendship and affection is ongoing and worth all the sorrow the book caused me. I hope you will find in his words a clearer understanding of a potentially great king who took the wrong pathway for what he thought were the right reasons.

Thank you for buying this book and for reading it to the end. If nothing else, you should have a different opinion on the man known as Charles Stuart, which is what we set out to achieve.

You may well decide not to believe that this is a channelled book direct from spirit, that I am a good author and wrote an interesting work of fiction, in which case I hope you enjoyed your read. If you choose to believe that I channelled the work, then you will have had an insight into a period of history usually only seen through the distorted eyes of historians. There are more such insights to come from a great variety of people who have approached me with the same request, to tell their story and put the truth in front of the world. Watch out for them!

Dorothy Davies
Isle of Wight,
In the year of Our Lord 2010

ACKNOWLEDGMENT

My grateful thanks go to:

Charles Stuart for entrusting me to write his story,

Mary Holliday, devoted friend, could anyone ask for more in the way of friendship than that which I have with her?

Lynne Mulrooney, who knows how much help she has been;

Terry Wakelin because he is Terry Wakelin, my rock and my anchor as always;

My Inner Circle for support, love, laughter, guidance and for always being there.

My thanks go also to:

George Villiers, duke of Buckingham, for all the help he gave me during the many rewrites of this book, together with Isaiah Scratton, Jeffrey Hudson, John Tradescant, Sir John Oglander, Hannah Wybrand, Charles' physician, John Pym, Robert Hammond, John Cooke, Oliver Cromwell and Queen Henrietta Maria for their energy and – in some instances – great love they brought to their testimonies for the book. Without them, it would be much the poorer.

I also wish to mention Mr and Mrs Aylmer of Nunwell House, Brading, Isle of Wight, who kindly permitted me a private visit to see the room where Charles stayed in what transpired to be his last night of freedom and who are working to keep His Majesty's memory alive in their beautiful home. My grateful thanks are sent for their kindness.

Note: a percentage of the royalties from this book is to be donated to The Churches Conservation Trust which works at preserving redundant parish churches. It is an appropriate charity for King Charles I.